To Lorrie G. and Jack

The Suicide
By Mark SaFranko
Honest Publishing

Manufactured in the United Kingdom
by Lightning Source UK Limited

Cover: Slava Nesterov

The Suicide

Mark SaFranko

H

Honest Publishing

Tuesday, March 16, 2002

Victim: Gail Kenmore, female, Caucasian, age 29. Jumped or fell from eleventh-floor window at 209 Hudson Street at approximately 11:10 a.m.

Detective Brian Vincenti had passed the horseshoe-shaped high-rise called the Hudson Arms on the northeast corner of Second and Hudson Streets a few thousand times en route to headquarters, but he'd never paid the massive hulk of ocher-hued brick much attention one way or another, since it belonged to the new version of Hoboken, and he always thought of himself as part of the old – as in Ol' Blue Eyes, baseball, and Guild guitars. But this afternoon, before entering the courtyard, he counted eleven floors up to a long row of black windows and winced at the notion that a human body had come hurtling out of one only a few hours earlier.

What a way to go. He shook his head and grabbed unconsciously at his coat collar as he pushed against the juggernaut of icy late-winter wind shrieking like a battalion of spooks off the Hudson. *What a goddamn horrible way to go.*

The courtyard was a wasteland; the saplings stripped of their leaves and the flowerbeds devoid of color, except for the crusty dung-brown soil where in just another month or so the tulips would shoot up, show themselves off like gaudy streetwalkers, and transform the entire landscape. A blind man in a herringbone overcoat and a Stetson hat was walking towards him. With a scythe-like motion he brandished one of those rarely seen long, white-tipped canes. Vincenti tried to cut the guy a wide swath – blind people creeped him out – but like a kid skipping rope, he had to jump over the damned thing. Out on the wide gray water, across River Street and beyond the turned-up earth of the waterfront, a quaint, fire-engine-red tugboat straight off a picture postcard was towing a barge, probably full of the shittiest New York refuse, toward the sea while the stoic skyline of Manhattan posed as an indifferent backdrop. At that moment, Vincenti caught a whiff of dank, raw sewage, a common smell in Hoboken. If he had the energy to think about it, the scene would have depressed him.

But he didn't. It had been a typically frenzied day on the job and he was weary as hell. What made it worse was that last night he'd had that dream that he had now and then – that he'd killed someone by accident and was afraid the body would be discovered. The information about the incident at the Hudson Arms, in the form of a report from Patrolman Gregory Franks, had been dropped into his IN box, and he worked it into his schedule so that he'd drop by on his way home. With a suicide, there wasn't much you could do after the fact anyway. The dead were just that – dead. Nothing could bring them back. So there was no real urgency.

DOA at Saint Mary's Hospital at approximately 11:30 a.m. Probable cause of death is suicide or accident.

There were a few other incidental bits, like what the victim had been wearing at the time (a sweatshirt and jeans). Around noon, Chief Hampton himself had summoned Vincenti into his office and asked him to take a quick look into it.

"I'm sure it's nothing, but why don't you just swing on by if you got a few minutes. You know the drill – do what you have to do to make 'em feel like we showed up."

Vincenti knew what the words "make 'em feel like we showed up" implied. *Don't waste any precious time on it* was the most precise translation. These days as a cop in Hoboken, you swam in the ugly crosscurrents of modern life – from terrorism to drug-dealing to mob hits – the last thing you could afford was to fritter away hours on something likely to be of absolutely no consequence to anyone but the victim and her family.

Vincenti struggled against that bitch of a wind to pull open the outer door. The vestibule doors were locked, accessible by key to residents only. The words "No Soliciting" were printed on a gold placard. Through the glass, he could see that the lobby desk was vacant.

Before leaning on the buzzer, the detective took in the ambience. He'd never been inside 209 Hudson before, which, now that he thought about it, was surprising given that one crime or another had taken him into damned near every building in this city over the years. Against his will he was impressed by the glittering surfaces, including the lush chandelier suspended from the ceiling between the elevator banks. That ornate piece, as well as the baroque wallpaper, lent the interior the veneer of being more a luxury hotel than a place where people actually lived. The building was relatively new, dating from the mid-nineties (he could remember when the frame was going up, and the old-timers who lived on nearby streets grumbling that their perennially unblocked view of New York City was being heisted), and the only folks who could afford to live here were professionals and kids with hot-shot Wall Street or dotcom jobs – or wealthy parents. Or all of the above. Vincenti both envied and resented them, especially the spoiled twentysomethings, who thought they had it all coming to them as their birthright. That was because he hailed from blue-collar parents as well as the west end of Hoboken, where most folks were never going to get anywhere near the river and its stunning vistas. But he recognized likewise that there was no use in fighting the tide of the future: Hoboken had changed enormously since he was growing up in the fifties and sixties, when it was nothing more than a dead-end shithole of a seaport known for the birth of baseball, one classic American film, a famous clam bar, countless barroom brawls, and had long since seen its best days pass into the history books. Back then you couldn't give away the decaying brownstones that lined Bloomfield and Garden Streets, and now they were routinely flying off the overheated housing market at upwards of a million apiece – and that was on the cheap end. Vincenti thought he'd never see the day.

But by far the worst part of being a cop in this town was that you had no clue who anybody was, not anymore. The turnover of human beings on a daily basis could be nothing short of staggering, and what that meant was you could never count on a contact. Already today he'd passed three or four moving vans on Hudson Street alone, and it was only the middle of the month. That added up to a whole crowd of new faces. The newcomers could be anyone, from wannabe actors to members of a terrorist cell to serial killers. Yeah, the days when a man could say he knew his neighbors in Hoboken were long gone, too ...

A lanky, black fellow, late twenties, thirties, with tightly cropped hair and a uniform consisting of navy blue necktie, pressed white shirt, charcoal trousers and plastic nameplate suddenly materialized on the other side of the door. He was in the process of placing something small and white onto his tongue. Vincenti made a rolling motion with his hand and the guy reached down and opened up.

"No solicitors," said the doorman mechanically, his eyes traveling up and down Vincenti's torso.

He flashed his badge, which was hooked as always to the inside of his London Fog. "Detective Vincenti. Hoboken Police."

The doorman pushed the door open wide while regarding him with what Vincenti knew was the reflexive suspicion of most African-Americans upon confronting the authorities, especially the ones with white skin. But maybe that wasn't it at all. Maybe, like lots of other people in the world nowadays, the doorman's flinty expression reflected the fact that Vincenti's being a cop meant about as much to him as a pile of dog shit.

"Here about that dead girl, I suppose."

Vincenti reached for his tie and loosened it. "Were you here when it happened?"

"Yeah, I was."

"And you're – Lenny Jenkins" he said, checking the nameplate.

"I got the eight-to-six most days."

Jenkins retreated behind the wraparound desk, dropped into the swivel chair and glanced at the four-inch monitor that was broadcasting a static view of the underground parking garage. There was no movement anywhere in the frame, nothing except for a few rows of mostly glossy, high-end vehicles – Saabs, BMWs, Audis, SUVs. Must be boring as hell, keeping an eye on that thing all day long, thought Vincenti.

"So what happened, exactly?" he prodded. Looked like if he didn't ask, the doorman wasn't giving.

Jenkins' head twitched with uncertainty.

"Course I didn't *see* anything, you understand. I was right here at the desk studying for my securities exam when Freddie Opallo from the deli around the corner comes running in."

Vincenti stole a glance at the open textbook on the desk. The page was covered with several long columns of numbers separated by decimal points. Impressive.

"Poor son of a gun could hardly get a word out of his mouth, he was so freaked. Seems the young lady dropped to the sidewalk right in front of Freddie – I mean like within a couple of feet or so." Jenkins chuckled. "Never seen a guy so white – he was like a bed sheet. 'Girl fell out of one of your windows!' he finally spits out. At first I didn't know what the hell he was jabbering about. It took a few seconds to sink in, understand what I'm saying, because it didn't make any sense. It would have been funny if it wasn't so, you know – so tragic."

Funny – now that was something. The notion of a

human being dying like shattered cantaloupe was the last thing that would tickle his funnybone. This dude had a unique sense of humor.

Jenkins' walkie-talkie went off, blasting a squawking message that the doorman was somehow able to decipher.

"In a minute, okay? I got Detective – sorry, what is it again?"

"Vincenti."

"I got Detective Vincenti here."

Another squawk.

"About the Kenmore thing, right."

Vincenti watched Jenkins speak into the mouthpiece. The man was articulate. A cut above your typical desk jockey. And studying to be a securities broker, no less, or whatever it was. Camelot Housing, the parent company – and the tenants of the Hudson Arms – could afford the best, evidently.

"So anyway, the guy you really wanna talk to is Freddie Opallo," said Jenkins when he gave the over and out. "Far as I know, he's the only actual eyewitness to what happened."

Vincenti took the information down in his notebook.

"Freddie –"

"O-p-a-l-l-o."

"Thanks. She live alone, this Gail Kenmore?"

"Two roommates, young ladies. Both at work, neither back yet. Probably they got no idea what happened."

"So she was alone when this happened, you figure?"

Jenkins shrugged. "Far as I know. But that's just a guess."

Didn't you even give it a thought, pal? wondered Vincenti. On the face of it, Jenkins couldn't care less.

"Everything up there left the way it was when it happened?"

"I went up as soon as your guy arrived – what was his name?"

"Officer Franks."

"Franks ... He said 'Don't touch anything,' and that's exactly what I did. Said somebody would probably be by later to investigate."

"Nobody was up there when you went in?"

"You got it."

"See anybody walking around that floor?"

Jenkins shook his head. "And I didn't go knocking on doors. They want me down here when I'm on duty. Besides, that time of day there's usually nobody around anyway."

What else was there to ask? "Okay – mind if I head on up?"

Jenkins stood and rattled the loaded keyring that dangled from his belt. He veered around the desk and pressed the button between elevator shafts on the east bank.

On the ride up he pulled out a rectangular tin and rattled it.

"Breath mint?"

"No, thanks," said Vincenti.

Jenkins slipped a pellet into his mouth and returned the container to his pants pocket.

At six, the car stopped. When the doors parted, a dusky-skinned workman, Dominican or Guatemalan or whatever, was leaning on the grip of a flatbed cart packed tight with paint cans, plaster pails, brushes and brooms. He looked at Vincenti and Jenkins, then shook his head no – he wasn't going up. The detective made a mental note to try and talk to the guy later if possible.

"By the way – any workers up on eleven this morning?" Vincenti inquired when the doors closed and they'd resumed their ascent.

"Not according to the logbook. I already checked. You can look at it yourself, but we're pretty strict around here when it comes to knowing where people are in the building at any given time. Except for the tenants, of course. It'd be impossible to keep track of them. But you can never be completely sure on anything."

"Right," nodded Vincenti. Didn't he know it.

After stepping out of the car on eleven, Vincenti was confronted with a floor-to-ceiling rectangle of clear glass that gave out on a breathtaking panorama of the island of Manhattan, from the George Washington Bridge all the way down to the Empire State Building. How placid it all seemed from this distance – no crowds, no sirens, no madness.

"So, this way," said Jenkins, pointing in the opposite direction.

1108 was on the inside wing, on the Hoboken side of the building. Which made sense – Gail Kenmore had kissed the sidewalk on Hudson Street.

"How long she live up here, Gail Kenmore?" Vincenti asked as they trundled over the thick carpet.

"Uh ... don't know. They'd have that information over at the office. A year or so, maybe ... at least a good few months, but I can't say for sure. It's musical chairs in this place; they come and go like nobody's business. What you have mostly is folks picking up a roommate when somebody moves out. At these rents, most of 'em can't afford to live here by themselves."

Vincenti made a second mental note: to contact the business office in the event it was necessary.

It was as silent as a tomb on the eleventh floor until the dull thud of a pile-driver commenced in the construction zone across River Street. Jersey was forever trying to lure businesses out of the big city for a silver platter full of juicy tax incentives and cheaper rents. These days the state was succeeding in its campaign, and development was heavy down on the waterfront, creating traffic snarls the likes of which the town had never seen. There would come a day, and in the not-too-distant future, reflected Vincenti, when you wouldn't even be able to squeeze a car through the streets of Hoboken.

"Not even gonna knock," murmured Jenkins, fitting his key into the lock of 1108, "which is company policy. Unusual circumstances today." He propped the door open with his foot, then shimmied aside to let the cop go in first.

"Just like she was when we left it," the doorman whispered. In his voice was a hint of reverence for the closeness of death.

Vincenti didn't know what he'd expected to find – he had no preconceptions, actually – but the gaping maw of a window at the other end of the living room wasn't part of it. The Venetian blind was bunched evenly near the top of the frame and the long sash twisted and snapped like a cranky serpent in the invading March winds. They'd made the room as frosty as an icebox.

At a sweep Vincenti took the rest in. White walls.

Standard-issue beige carpeting. A royal blue ottoman along the north wall. A coffee table splashed with magazines, *Travel*, *People Weekly* and *Vanity Fair*, a paperback by someone he'd never heard of – not that he was the greatest reader – a tiny basket filled with a tangle of dried sprigs, the TV remote. The set was a few feet away, in a cabinet against the south wall. There were a few frames on the walls, bland illustrations from photo and art exhibitions and the like. In other words, nothing out of the ordinary. Nothing that told him anything.

What was interesting was the portable telephone tautly drawn to the end of its cord beneath the windowsill. As if the victim had been talking to someone just before she took off on her death flight. Inches from the phone was a glass ashtray with a few stubbed-out butts and an open pack of Marlboro Lights next to it on the carpet. The answering system was approximately four feet away.

"You're sure nobody disturbed anything in this room, Lenny?"

"Not far as I know. But again, I couldn't be a hundred percent on that, know what I mean."

It was a peculiarly tense moment, as if something had been missed or overlooked. But what?

Vincenti edged across the room to the window. A fresh blast of frigid air seared his eyeballs as he poked his head out the window and looked down to the street. The random bodies passing on the pavement below were like miniature soldiers – ants.

Christ. Eleven long stories, feet first, according to Franks' report – nasty. Very, very nasty. For a vertiginous, scary instant, Vincenti was in the dead girl's skin, and he felt the excruciating, unbearable pain of impact. Pulling back inside, a film of cold sweat coating his body, he immediately forced the vicarious experience out of his mind. As a cop you weren't supposed to get personally involved. You couldn't, really, if you expected to do your job. And it certainly helped matters if you didn't.

Without touching them, he studied the frame and sill – no blood spots, nothing to indicate that an event requiring the use of force had occurred. The pane appeared to be scuffed from normal wear, but without solid evidence of a crime there was no point in dusting for fingerprints.

The detective heard Jenkins' hand-held crackle behind him. The doorman gave it a terse answer.

"Mind letting yourself out?" he said to Vincenti. "They want me down in the garage for a move-in."

"Not at all." Vincenti turned and indicated. "One thing before you go – was that door locked when you came up here with Franks?"

Jenkins shook his head. "Nope."

"Sure about that?"

Jenkins hesitated. "Mm ... Sure as I can be."

It didn't signify anything one way or the other, but you never knew when something you picked up early on would bear fruit down the line. Most times it didn't.

"Okay. Hey – thanks for your time. If I need to talk to you again –"

"Eight to six, Monday through Friday, mostly, but sometimes weekends, and I get days off here and there. If I'm not at the front desk, I'm somewhere in the building."

The doorman disappeared, leaving Vincenti alone with his thoughts. If that door was open, then it was possible – though not necessarily likely – that Gail Kenmore wasn't alone in the apartment before she went out the window. He made one more mental note to himself: remember to ask Lenny Jenkins if he noticed any strangers – someone he didn't recognize and who wasn't a worker – in the building before the fatality. Though he was fairly sure Jenkins would have said something if he had.

But so far there was absolutely no indication whatsoever that any kind of hanky-panky had occurred inside this unit. Vincenti did a slow lap around the big room: no blood spatters visible to the naked eye on the walls or furniture, no signs of a struggle, no evidence of ransacking or burglary. He made up his mind then and there that he wasn't going to delve too deeply into this thing.

He went around the corner. The kitchen was as clean as a whistle and as neat as a pin; there wasn't so much as a dirty coffee cup in the sink. As he started down the hall toward the interior of the apartment, it crossed his mind that Jenkins had probably just flouted Camelot Housing policy by leaving him alone on the premises. As Vincenti well knew from long experience, lots of rules and regulations were conveniently forgotten in the exigency of the moment.

Without laying a finger on anything, he eyeballed the bathroom, all done up in white, including the oval rug. Then, through the open door, the bedroom directly across from it. There were framed photographs of formal affairs, families, even dogs and cats, on the walls and bureau. Not the room of a suicide – probably.

He stopped at the closed door of the next room. Out of sheer habit he knocked before reaching out and twisting the handle. The bed in there was narrow, ascetic almost, tightly made, covered by a brassy yellow comforter adorned with the outsized prints of sunflowers. Very cheery. Too cheery. A pair of stuffed toys, a white bear with a collar and a mottled boxer pup, sat up against the pillows as if they were waiting for their keeper to come home.

Vincenti moved in. This room intrigued him. On a circular wicker table near the hallway wall was a nine-by-twelve, amateurish, oil-on-canvas portrait of a young woman with dirty blond hair in a faux wood frame. The detective knew at once that it was the likeness of Gail Kenmore – he didn't know how, but he did.

He pulled out his handkerchief, flapped it open and lifted the frame off the table. There was something vaguely familiar about the image, something he recognized in the sloping eyelids, the melancholy cast of the cartoonish blue eyes, the flare of the nostrils. Was it supposed to be a movie actress? Reese Witherspoon? Laura Linney? He tried to think of celebrity names. No. But how would he know this person? The name, Gail Kenmore, didn't ring a bell, for sure. Had he seen her in passing around town? That was likely it. But maybe not. It was possible that he recognized her from elsewhere – or at least thought he did.

Nah. Ridiculous. The same person – presumably – appeared in a snapshot that was lying flat on the wicker table, her arm around a middle-aged woman with a lion-like mane of black hair. The picture, which had been taken with one of those instamatic contraptions, was fuzzy and faded, the background indistinct. On second thought, maybe it wasn't a photo of the girl in the portrait after all.

Unlike the first bedroom he'd stuck his head in, there were no other photographs anywhere in the room. For some reason, that struck him as odd. The only other object that caught Vincenti's eye was the garish daub – of a clown, maybe, in the crude style of one of Picasso's (at least he thought it might be him) sad mountebanks – on the wall over the bed. He moved closer for a look. No, it wasn't Picasso, it was some Frenchman he was thinking of, or trying to, a painter who did clowns exclusively. The artist's name began with the letter R, but he couldn't recall the whole thing. Roo-something. That guy he remembered from a high school art class. The colors were deployed in bold slashes, royal blue for the shirt, crimson for the mouth, purple, of all things, for the eyes. A little demented. Was it supposed to be a man? A woman? Who the fuck could tell? Maybe it wasn't supposed to be either. It was pretentious crap. But the oddity appeared to have been produced by the same hack who'd produced the weird portrait on the table.

Then Vincenti's memory lurched, chucking something up. The subject of the painting looked like a kid he once knew. Not *knew*, but had an encounter with. *A kid who didn't have to die.* Years ago, this was. Funny how that kid kept coming back to him at the damnedest times. Having to witness death was the price you sometimes had to pay as a cop.

He pushed it out of his mind. He was probably just imagining things anyway.

He made a quick swing through the second bathroom

and the last of the three bedrooms, which was situated at the end of the unit and was pretty much a clone of the first. Not a thing out of order, no disarray whatsoever. Typical yuppie quarters, except for bedroom number two.

In the living room he revisited what he'd already been over. Why would a young woman with all of life ahead of her want to take her own in such a gruesome fashion? It was a stupidly simplistic question, he knew, if you were looking for the reason or reasons for a suicide. There were a hundred million reasons why (like there were hundreds of millions of motives for the vast array of brutal human misdeeds that occurred in the world every single day), ranging from a broken love affair to an incurable illness to a complete loss of faith in life itself. What they all had in common was some sort of irreversible despair. And, as some experts theorized, anger, or a desire for revenge on those left living. But simplistic or not, it was a question that had to pose itself.

He checked his watch: she'd been dead for hours now. That was another odd thing – if she'd killed herself, and she probably had, she'd done it in the morning, the time of day when the sun was high, the day was still young, and most people felt relatively good about being alive. Or was it not so out of the ordinary? He wasn't up on the latest statistics on hari-kari, so maybe he was off-base here.

From the periphery of his vision Vincenti noticed that the answering device was blinking. Since the control panel was facing the wall, he'd missed the tiny red flash when he first entered the unit. He squatted beside the machine, turned it toward himself, and pressed the "Play" button.

The first two messages were nothing that he could hang anything on: a call for Heather (whoever she was) from a woman named Pat, announcing that the time for an art department meeting that morning had been changed from nine-thirty to ten. Next was one of those piped-in pitches from a telecom company explaining how much better off the household would be if they switched providers for their long-distance service.

It was the third call that stopped him cold.

"Gail! Call me back! Gail! Please call me back!"

The caller was a male, older. By the end of the loop he'd pleaded his voice into raspiness. There was an interval of maybe ten seconds when there was nothing, nothing but some muffled, unidentifiable, background commotion – bumps or thuds. Then, again, *"Gail! Gail! Please – talk to me!"* Another gap, briefer this time, then a click and a buzz.

The fourth call was pretty much a repeat of the preceding message, only more frantic. The man didn't leave his name, which meant that he had to be known to the deceased, that they had to be on familiar terms. That much was obvious, wasn't it? The question of course was who the hell he was. Boyfriend? Brother? Father? There was nothing to go on.

The calls seemed to imply that the man understood that Gail was in some kind of distress or trouble. But what? Did it mean that he'd been trying to talk her out of it just before she jumped? Or did it mean that she was in some other kind of difficulty – that, for instance, at the time of the call she was being *forced* to jump, or being *pushed* out the window? But if that were the case, how had she managed to carry on a conversation at all? Good questions – all very good questions.

Vincenti pressed the "Repeat" button, bypassed the first two messages, and played numbers three and four again. They were the only lead he had, but it was a lead that went nowhere, since there was no caller ID and he didn't have a clue who the caller was.

He closed the front door. Before heading back down to the lobby, he walked to the end of the corridor and tugged open the door beneath the red "Exit" sign. Nothing out there but fractured flights of battleship-gray stairs leading up and down. Stubbed-out cigarette butts on the landing. Harsh light cascading from the ceiling fixtures.

He listened, but heard nothing except for the earthshaking beat of that pile-driver, which was beginning to give him a dull headache. View or no view, how could anyone stand living here and having to listen to that infernal racket all day long? There was a price to be paid for everything.

He let the door fall shut and retraced his steps to the elevator.

———

Vincenti stopped off on six, but the grunt he'd caught a glimpse of on the way up was nowhere to be found. And no, Lenny Jenkins hadn't seen anyone unusual prowling around the building before Gail Kenmore died.

Exiting the building, Vincenti checked his watch. Five-thirty. Normally he would have liked to be home by now, but being at home wasn't appetizing anymore. In fact, he'd rather *not* be at home. Which was why, he supposed, he rarely was. He shook his head, tried to shrug off the thought.

"You Freddie Opallo?"

The man Vincenti addressed was leaning on the outside wall of the Riverside Deli in a ketchup-smudged apron and jeans, half-smoked cigarette in hand.

"That's me ..."

The detective recognized Freddie from the rare occasions when he stopped into the little store for a newspaper or pack of chewing gum on his way to headquarters, but until now he hadn't known his name.

"Vincenti, Hoboken PD ..."

Actually, Freddie Opallo was one of those odd figures you see on the streets who you couldn't miss if you tried. He was grossly overweight, with his corpulence concentrated in his enormous belly, and he had stringy, peroxide hair that fell to his shoulders, and the pink, deep-eyed, bulbous features of a pig. He looked, Vincenti concluded, like a gnome from Hell. He noticed that the gnome's hands were trembling.

"Christ – I mean – I didn't know what the fuck she *was*!" Freddie whined, after Vincenti explained why he was there. He kept glancing nervously up to the high floors of 209 Hudson Street. "Ever see a body drop out of the sky? I mean, I coulda been *killed*. She landed, like, two feet away!" He positioned the cigarette between his thin bloodless lips and stuck out his hands, which were tiny for someone of his girth. "Look at me – I'm still shakin'! Been like this since it happened. Can't get it outta my head. Think *you* ever had a nightmare? *This* was a nightmare! Except it was *real*. I keep waitin' for another frickin' body to come rainin' down, know what I mean?"

"Mind showing me exactly what happened? Where you were standing, where she came to rest ... what you heard?"

Without a word, as if he'd been waiting all day to do just that, the fat man led the detective with unflinching assurance to a spot on the wide sidewalk just south of the deli, at the entrance to a multi-tiered parking garage that sat between the store and the Hudson Arms. Like lots of overweight people, Freddie Opallo could move with surprising swiftness.

Just like a scared pig, thought Vincenti.

"Right here," he said, pointing with his stubby forefinger at the concrete. It was as if the exact point of impact had been seared into Freddie Opallo's memory. Vincenti squatted for a closer look. There was nothing to see, not even a single fleck of blood. A few inches away there was a smear of dog feces.

"So I'm just moseyin' along, right, about eleven this morning, on my way back from the bank over there on Second, when all of sudden, out of the corner of my eye – *bam!* – I catch a blur, this big blue blur, right? Then I hear this ... this odd noise, like a thunk or somethin'. I musta jumped about ten fuckin' feet in the air, no lie – pardon my French, Detective. Now you gotta realize I can't jump even an inch off the ground, normally, so you *know* I was shook. I mean, I didn't even know which way to *turn*. It took a coupla seconds before I realized what in the hell was goin' on. By now I was like, starin' right at her – at the body. I'm like, *where the hell'd she come from*, y'know? I looked up to see if maybe there was more on the way. Like maybe we were being bombed or somethin'. Then it hits me – that's where she came from."

Freddie's gaze scaled the high rise again. He was worked up now, all of his strident panic having found its way into his rapid-fire, high-pitched voice.

"What'd you do then?"

"I just – I ran. Bolted. A few feet, that way, past the door of the deli, but ..."

Suddenly Freddie was sheepish. His face grew redder. Embarrassed, figured Vincenti, by his skittish reaction.

"Then I kinda went back and ... and *looked*, but ... I didn't know what the hell to do. She wasn't movin' or nothin', wasn't makin' no sounds. Later, when I found out exactly where she fell from, it made sense."

Still dazed, he wagged his head.

"By that time Jorge from the parking garage already dialed 911. The two of us stood near his booth and waited for somebody to come. Like I said, neither one of us knew what the hell to do – I mean, we didn't even know if we should like ... *touch* her or nothin'. I don't know first aid or CPR, or nothin' like that, so ... I mean, I felt bad I couldn't help her, but what the hell are you s'posed to do when somethin' like that happens? Never saw nothin' like it in my life, I swear to God! Wow. Man, I'm just – I still can't seem to get it out of my mind. And I'm supposed to be in there takin' care of customers."

Freddie jerked his thumb over his shoulder, then lit another cigarette with his vibrating digits.

Vincenti informed him that he was welcome to psychological counseling at Saint Mary's Hospital under the auspices of the Hoboken Police Department. The offer seemed to leave the deli man unfazed, and with the same shell-shocked expression on his puffy features. It was the detective's hunch that Opallo was the type who would never dream of seeking out professional help – he'd rather talk his head off about what happened to anyone willing to listen. Which was pretty much the same difference when you got to the bottom of the matter.

Not that Vincenti was any more enlightened. Hell, he didn't talk to *anybody* about what bothered him. And there was plenty. Mostly it was that thing with the kid – that's what started it all. Crazy. You go out to meet a friend on a summer evening, and your life is never the same again …

Freddie went on to explain how he and Jorge heard the victim moan from their post at the toll booth, which was maybe ten or fifteen feet inside the garage, just beyond the moving arm. They then approached her and tried to communicate with her, but she was floating in and out of consciousness. The worst part for him, explained Freddie, was that by now he recognized the girl, or what was left of her – Gail was her first name, he knew her from when she stopped into the deli now and then for a bottle of spring water or quart of milk. She might have been a nurse at a hospital somewhere – he thought he remembered her once saying that. No one else appeared on the scene to help, though pedestrians stared and passing drivers rubbernecked. Within a minute or two there was a siren. In another few seconds the ambulance pulled up. Freddie was surprised that no police showed, since this neighborhood was usually crawling with them as they went back and forth to headquarters on the very next block. He told EMS what happened, and the medics rolled the woman onto a stretcher, popped her inside the back hatch, and the vehicle took off like a bat out of hell. An hour later, just after noon, Jenkins came around during his lunch break and informed him that she was dead. Which of course was what he'd expected.

"Lousy way to go, huh?" Freddie whistled to no one in particular, looking up yet again in disbelief at the high rise. "Man, I don't even want to *think* about what it must have felt like."

Exactly, thought Vincenti. And that's exactly what we're both doing. But instead he said, "Look on the positive side – maybe she was already unconscious when she hit the pavement."

Opallo blinked. "Y'think ...?"

The detective didn't answer. He never liked to get familiar with the witnesses on the street unless he had to, unless there was information to be had from it.

"All right, Freddie, thanks. You remember anything else, get in touch."

"Say – you got any idea why she did it?"

———

Vonda Ramfar already had her coat on and was gathering her things – gloves, handbag, hat – to leave when Vincenti came through the door of the brownstone at 328 Eighth Street.

"How'd everything go today, Von?" he asked, unbuttoning his coat, more out of a desire to be polite than a real desire to know.

"Very good," Vonda answered in her distinctive South American lilt. "Nicky be very good today. Teacher say he was behaved like an angel."

"That's great, Vonda, just great."

And it was, given that the past few weeks of his four-year-old son's pre-school attendance had been marred by "incidents" – scratching, punching, and biting of classmates – which had Vincenti concerned that his little boy was about to gain the dubious distinction of getting himself expelled from All Saints'. What a joke that would be! Kicked out of preschool! Most of the street trash he picked up couldn't even boast of something like that on their rap sheets. Not that Nicky's behavior wasn't broadly within the range of normalcy, as Miss Rothstein, his teacher, explained. But Vincenti suspected there was something more, something connected directly to his own domestic problems, to this sudden surge of feistiness.

"Where are they?" he said next. The question was a daily habit.

Vonda nodded toward the rear of the apartment.

"Thanks, Vonda. You have a good one, hear? And see you tomorrow."

The nanny smiled, a speckle of gold flashing in her mouth, as she waddled toward the door. Despite the fact that the Guyanese national had worked for him for well over three years now, he never felt completely at ease in her presence. It seemed to him – and it could just be his funky imagination playing tricks on him – as if she were sitting in some kind of silent judgment of him, and he was in the dark as to why. Well – maybe he did know, or at least have some idea. Maybe it went something like this: whenever Vonda encountered him she thought *Big, tough cop. Big tough cop can't even keep his own home in order.* It was particularly disconcerting since he was the one who was used to taking the measure of people. He had the nagging feeling that no matter what, she'd always have the upper hand.

But there was something else to it. It had to do with Vincenti himself. Of late he was distracted, agitated, on edge. He wasn't himself, and he was sure that Vonda, like any good domestic, picked up on it. And maybe, when all was said and done, it was simply the fact that as the product of a blue-collar upbringing, having someone do his bidding was enough in itself to make him uneasy.

Vincenti tiptoed around the messy sea of toys scattered over the living room floor between the TV and the sofa – one more chore Vonda had begun neglecting over the months since Nicky had grown bigger and more unruly. There was a time, early on, when he'd come home and find the place as neat as a pin, but those days were a distant memory.

The instant his son set eyes on him, he leaped off the floor where he was pushing a toy steam engine and dashed head-first into his knees.

"Daddy! Daddy!"

The father-son greeting ritual lasted all of a few seconds, during which Vincenti briefly locked eyes with his wife. Reggie was still in her real-estate sales uniform – black suit and scarlet scarf – and as usual she was delectable. Vincenti's arrival was her cue to get up from the floor, where she'd been playing choo-choo with their son, and dash into her private bathroom, which was just off the master bedroom in the small west end of the flat. Without a word to him, of course. Little Nicky never seemed to consciously pick up on the cold shoulder routine, but how could he not, really? The detective would have liked to believe that his deteriorating relationship with his spouse wasn't having an effect on the kid, but he knew otherwise. Nicky just didn't know how to articulate his distress, and that's why he was beating up on his little classmates. Psych 101.

Moments later, when the boy was absorbed in the cartoon dinosaurs in his *Land Before Time* video, he pushed open the door of the bathroom, where Reggie was touching up her makeup.

"Are you here tonight?"

Whenever he addressed his wife nowadays, he tried his best to keep even the slightest hint of an inflection out of his voice if he could help it. Sometimes he couldn't.

Reggie's oversized, unearthly turquoise eyes bounced off him icily. Ice was the temperature he'd come to expect.

"Nope. Appointments 'til late."

Vincenti knew what that meant. Work, sure. But other stuff too … stuff that if he let himself get carried away with –

He gritted his teeth, hating the steely flippancy in her voice. Her attitude was a far cry from the soft, even deferential way she treated him in the early days of their relationship, but there was no way, and he knew it, that anything of the like could ever be recaptured. Once a certain rubicon has been crossed in any marriage, there's no turning back. Now their life together was a matter of pathetic attrition, and the hovering, unspoken question of what was going to become of them. Had it not been for the kid, the ship would already have gone to pieces on the rocks.

"By the way," she added as he was turning away, "he's already had his dinner. All he needs is a snack after his bath. Graham crackers and milk. And don't forget to get him to brush his teeth."

Vincenti was tired. Suddenly he noticed the pulse of a dull pain, set off by that goddamned pile-driver, inside his skull, behind the bony ridge of his eyebrows, and microscopic blind spots wherever he tried to focus his vision. He pictured that place in his head as a desolate no-man's land of gray cells, and wondered irritably why pain had to choose that area to settle in. He was having headaches a lot lately; it occurred to him more than once that maybe he had a brain tumor and didn't realize it. But he'd done nothing about them, hadn't seen a doctor. In some ways it would be a good thing to go out fast, before you even knew what hit you – except for the boy, of course, who would no doubt be rocked forever by his passing.

He listened to the rapid to-and-fro tapping of his wife's heels at the other end of the flat as he stood at the kitchen counter shoveling cold leftover pasta from a plastic container into his mouth. When was the last time he and Reggie had eaten a meal in each other's presence? Had to be months. Probably the time they tried in vain to talk out their differences over dinner at that new Brazilian bistro across from the hospital. A disaster – they hadn't finished their meals and went home separately. That was way back in November, before the holidays. Now there was nothing between them except for those infuriating passive-aggressive stares and strained two-word exchanges that never bloomed into real conversation. It couldn't go on this way forever. It just couldn't.

He heard Reggie's voice sweetly intoning goodbye and goodnight to little Nicky before the front door bumped shut. A wild fury flared in Vincenti's gut. He tried to ignore it. He tossed the container and fork into the sink with a clang and went to join his son in the living room.

"Hey there, big guy."

The towhead was still absorbed in the antics of his animated prehistoric creatures. He didn't even look up.

Vincenti dropped onto the sofa and spread out his large frame. Occasionally he reached down and mussed the boy's incredibly thick hair. Sitting idly with Nicky was normally a nice, relaxing counterpoint to the day; this evening he would rather have crawled straight into bed.

Because for some reason he was thinking about Gail Kenmore. Her vague familiarity. That weird painting. And yeah, his hunch had been on the money: that second bedroom had been hers. At least Lenny Jenkins said he thought so, when he'd gone back down to the lobby. Vincenti didn't want to let the dead woman in, but there she was anyway, a vaguely ominous presence fluttering around the edges of his consciousness.

But what the hell. The case of Gail Kenmore wasn't even a real case. She was nothing but a suicide, one of hundreds, maybe thousands, that happened every day all over the planet.

For a long time Vincenti stared at the loony images on the screen while Nick sat on the floor, cross-legged and transfixed, and talking back to the screen in a language all his own. "Again! I wanna watch it again!" the boy demanded when the credits rolled.

Vincenti checked his watch. "No, it's too late. Time for a bath, big guy."

After weakly protesting, Nick gave in. He was just about to fall asleep in his little bed when he asked, as if reading his old man's mind: "Daddy, why do the peoples have to die?"

Vincenti had fielded lots of similar questions from his son in the past few days. It was uncanny how the boy seemed to pick up what was streaming through his father's brain, as if he netted his thoughts by osmosis. Some of the other things he asked (once he wanted to know "Why didn't Mommy stay in Japan and marry me instead of you, Daddy?") led Vincenti to wonder whether there was indeed some kind of spirit life before birth, especially since neither he, his wife or Nick had ever set foot in the Land of the Rising Sun in this life.

"Why do you want to know, Nicky?"

"I dunno."

"Who talks to you about that – about death, Nick?"

"I dunno."

"Your mommy?"

"No."

"Your teacher?"

"No."

"Vonda? Does Vonda talk to you about people dying?"

"No."

"Then who?"

"I dunno ..."

"Well, that's just the way things are, Nicky. Things are born, they grow, then they die." Not a great answer, but then it was a tough question. He'd learned to stay on his toes and always come up with answers, which were invariably followed by more questions.

"What's a 'soul,' Daddy?"

"It's like – like a spirit. It's like the engine that runs the car. Know what I mean?"

"What's inside a soul, Daddy?"

"What's inside? Oh, something ... something like gold dust. Yeah. That's it – gold dust."

"Do the peoples come back again after they die?"

"Sure they do, Nick."

"Why?"

"That's just the way things are, too."

Nicky's brow darkened. He wasn't completely satisfied with something.

"But why, Daddy? Why do the peoples have to die?"

And again, for that question, Vincenti had no good answer.

Wednesday, March 17

March seventeenth. The single day of the year Vincenti truly detested, especially when he was on duty. Saint Patrick's Day in Hoboken was nothing but an excuse for hordes of punks to pour in from the suburbs as far away as Westchester and Rockland counties, to get bombed, piss on the shrubbery, puke on the sidewalks, and make more annoying racket than Manhattan heard on a bad day. Vincenti usually tried to avoid being around on March seventeenth, including taking a vacation or sick day, packing up his wife and son, and leaving town.

This year, though, Vincenti didn't mind so much that he was on Hampton's schedule. Along with the reality of his corroded relationship with Reggie – meaning the Vincenti family wasn't going anywhere anyway – being in town afforded him the opportunity to have another look into the Kenmore matter, provided there was something to look into.

He couldn't deny it – he *was* curious. Curious as hell.

Gregory Franks was just about to hit the street for his patrol when Vincenti was coming through the front door. They talked for a minute or two, but the officer who responded to the call for help from the Hudson Arms could give him nothing more than he already knew from his own investigation.

At about nine-thirty the detective and Hampton crossed paths in the men's room.

"By the way – get anywhere on that thing where the girl jumped out the window?"

The cold-bloodedness of the question was pure Hampton.

"Not yet," Vincenti answered, gazing down at the yellow stream he was shooting into the porcelain.

The chief tilted his head toward the ceiling and let out a cow-like grunt. In the merciless glare of the restroom his waxy skin appeared even unhealthier than it normally did. That the guy was overweight by forty or fifty pounds, smoked cigarettes, and had lost most of his hair didn't help. It wouldn't be the least surprising to Vincenti if his boss dropped dead of a heart attack or stroke one day in the not-too-distant future. But sometimes guys like Hampton fooled you – they ended up living forever.

"Well, like I told you yesterday, don't go wasting time on it. Rivera and Westover are out on vacation this week. I need every last body on call."

Hampton was referring to the rowdy crowds that would begin roaming the streets in two or three hours. Minutes after leaving the lavatory Vincenti found himself roped into crap he wouldn't normally go near as a senior officer in robbery/homicide – checking out the toy-gun knockover of a liquor store on Newark Street, even putting the clamps on a couple of winos for public urination at Elysian Park.

In the early afternoon he managed to shoehorn a call into the business office of Camelot Housing and was informed that Gail Kenmore's roommates, after being told the news of her death at the front desk, didn't return to their apartment last night. "Totally freaked out" by what happened, was how the lady put it. Of course she'd gotten the news second-hand, from the night doorman who in turn told the building superintendent, but it stood to reason. And no, she couldn't give out their work phone numbers, not even to the police. As far as Gail Kenmore went, there was no "in case of emergency" contact listed.

Vincenti would have to remember to talk to those girls whenever they finally did go back up to unit 1108.

Saint Paddy's Day proved to be a long, draining, pain-in-the-ass ordeal. What else was new? The icy drizzle that fell from time to time didn't seem to faze the mindless revelers in the least, and only made navigating around the city that much tougher. In addition to the petty street incidents, a drunken brawl broke out at a billiards parlor on Willow Street, and a pedestrian was killed around the corner on Washington Street when an epileptic in the throes of a fit drove his vehicle up onto the crowded sidewalk. It was seven-thirty in the evening before Vincenti had a chance to grab a sandwich and put in a call to home.

Vonda answered, with her mournful, woe-is-me voice. He didn't hear it that often, but when he did it set his teeth on edge.

He was surprised that the nanny was still on the premises. "Is my wife home yet?"

"Reggie call at around six. She have a late appointment, she say, and she won't be home 'til later."

Shit. Since Vincenti and his wife no longer communicated – let alone coordinated – their movements when it came to coverage for Nicky, he never knew anymore what was happening at home. As far as Vonda went, was there some hidden message in her words? Vincenti always suspected that she was privy to far more about his marital troubles than she let on, and that the knowledge was the source of her air of omniscience, which in turn allowed her to wield her subtle power in the Vincenti household.

"Do you have to leave? Can you hang on a while longer?" he asked, injecting saccharine into the question and tensing against the answer.

"No, I'm all right. I can stay as long as you need me."

"Thanks, Vonda – thanks a lot."

Vincenti knew that extra hours for the sitter meant more dough out of his pocket, but at moments like these Vonda was worth every penny of her time-and-a-half.

"I'll be there soon as I can," he assured her.

"Very well."

Very well. She always used those words. But it wasn't very well, nothing was very well, not by a long shot. Anyhow, now he had at least a little wiggle room to head back over to the Hudson Arms and try to talk to some of Gail Kenmore's neighbors.

Behind the desk tonight was a chubby guy with darting eyes, a friar-like fringe of steel-gray hair on three sides of his balding skull, and old-fashioned tortoiseshell glasses. When he spotted Vincenti on the outside of the glass, he jumped up and let him in.

"I'm looking into what happened up on the eleventh floor yesterday."

"Oh yeah, sure, Lenny told me you were around." The doorman shook his large head. "Sad. Very, very sad."

"You knew Gail Kenmore, did you?"

The guy's head bobbed. "Oh yeah, sure, I knew her.

Talked to her every day when she was on her way out the door to work."

"Which was where?"

"A hospital in New York. I think it was Saint Vincent's in the Village."

Vincenti asked for his name.

"John Rebecki. Call me Johnny."

Johnny. The last thing in the world this man looked like was a Johnny.

"What was she like, Gail Kenmore?"

"Sweet as honey. Sweetest person in the world."

Spoken with emphasis, Vincenti noted. He wondered how Rebecki could be so sure.

Interesting. This was practically the first insight Vincenti'd gotten into the victim's living personality.

"Why do you say that?"

"All you had to do was look at her. There was always a smile on her face. She was never in anything but a cheerful, sunnyside-up mood. At least to me. A real sweetheart, like I said."

"When was the last time you saw her?"

"The night before it happened – Monday. That's what makes it tough. We talked a little before she went to work. It was quick-like. The weather, how are you, good, how are you – the usual banter."

"Notice anything different about her that night?"

Rebecki shook his head. "Nah. She was the same as she was all the other times I ever saw her. Which is why it's such a shock." He pursed his lips. "So what do you figure happened to her, Detective?"

"I plan to talk to a few more people, try and put the pieces together. Probably, at the end of the day, she jumped – for whatever reason."

Rebecki stared out at the dark courtyard and shook his head again. "No way Gail Kenmore jumped out that window."

Vincenti was struck again by the doorman's adamant certainty. "What makes you say that?"

"Just ... from the little I knew her. She just wasn't the type. You'd know if you met her, if you talked with her for even five minutes. Nicest, friendliest person in the world. That's how I know. And I'd bet the house on it."

"Was she the happiest?"

"Well, *that* I don't know about, but ..."

The detective's curiosity was even more strongly piqued now.

"Let me reverse the question. What do *you* think happened, Johnny?"

"Not a clue. But like I said, I can tell you this – there's no way that poor girl did herself in."

Vincenti had seen enough in his time as a cop to know that a human being's perceptions about a given situation – or person – could be influenced by any number of stimuli. But Johnny Rebecki was standing firm.

"Then something else had to have happened up there, right?"

Rebecki gave a frustrated shrug. "Who the hell knows? All I can tell you is what *didn't* happen – in my humble opinion."

"Well, what else does that leave us with, then?" asked

Vincenti, almost rhetorically, in his most laid-back manner.

"God only knows." Rebecki was back in his chair behind the desk now, eyeballing the monitor that Lenny Jenkins had been watching yesterday.

Vincenti rested his elbows on the desk top. "Think maybe she fell?"

"Maybe. But how? I mean it was frigid yesterday morning. From what I heard, that window was raised up as far as it could go. Why would Gail do that on a freezing cold day?"

Vincenti remembered the Marlboro Lights and the tray full of stubbed-out butts. "There were cigarettes not far from the window. Maybe she was smoking in the open window and she took a tumble."

"Once in a while I did see her puffing out in the courtyard. Probably her roommates didn't want her stinking up the apartment ... But if she was having a smoke up there, why open the window all the way?"

"All right, then – she was going to jump, and she needed enough room to squeeze her whole body out," challenged Vincenti.

"Nah – I don't buy it," Rebecki shot back, rocking back and forth in his chair.

"Okay – she was helped along. Pushed. Let's say that for argument's sake."

Rebecki shook his head again, a little less avidly this time. He seemed to be considering the possibility.

"Know of anyone who would have been interested in doing Gail Kenmore in?"

"See, the thing is," said the doorman earnestly, "we

didn't talk on that level – personal. So no, I wouldn't have any idea. And I can't think that anybody would actually want to – like I say, she was a very sweet girl. But then again, it's a crazy, effed-up world, isn't it? You don't know who's out there anymore. You never know what's gonna happen."

He gave an almost imperceptible nod through the glass doors at the hole in the skyline where the World Trade Center once stood.

Vincenti couldn't disagree. He'd seen enough in his day to know that what the doorman said was true.

"Heck, there are enough weirdos walking around this building, you know?"

"Oh, yeah? Like who?"

Just then the phone rang. Rebecki picked up and held a terse confab.

"She have a boyfriend?" Vincenti asked when he hung up.

Rebecki shrugged. "They all have men hanging around, don't they?"

Vincenti could have sworn he picked up a fleck of bitterness – jealousy – in the doorman's voice. He wondered where it came from. For some reason, and maybe it was just the milksop figure he cut, he got the impression that Rebecki's bitterness stemmed from wanting Gail Kenmore for himself.

"Ever meet anybody like that – a boyfriend?"

"Can't say I did."

Vincenti wasn't sure whether or not he should believe the guy.

"Seen anything of her roommates?"

"Not a hair. I wasn't on last night when they showed up – Joe Zirkilian had the desk. But they were nice kids, too, same as her. Not the kind to – you know what I'm saying."

"But how do you know for sure?"

"Aw, you just know ... I mean, I don't know how they got along or anything like that, but they were at work when it happened, so draw your own conclusions."

"How about someone else in this building who knew her? Has anybody said anything about what happened up there? Maybe one of the 'weirdos' you mentioned?"

Negative again. "If they did, I don't know who they are. Know how many people live in this building? You probably got in excess of three hundred. There's so many tenants, it's just about impossible to get to know who's who, even so much as last names. 'Cos the register changes almost by the hour, see. The building supervisor is out there in the entrance switching names on the directory every day. And that's no exaggeration – every single day. Then you got the freeloaders bunking with their sister or their cousin, the friends visiting from California or Europe, the maintenance workers, the messengers, and so on and so forth."

"But you *knew* Gail Kenmore. She was an exception to the rule."

Rebecki nodded. "There's a few. She was one of them."

The impromptu interview was going nowhere. "Hey, I appreciate your time," said Vincenti, pushing himself away from the desk. "Think of anything I should know, you give me a ring."

"Will do."

"Guess I'll go up and knock on some doors."

"Good luck." Returning to his *New York Post*, Rebecki chortled. "How 'bout those Knicks, eh?"

Before the elevator arrived, the detective and the doorman exchanged a few words about the hapless local pro basketball team, which was supposed to have had a much better season with its new, high-octane cast of players and championship coach, but who were going to end up laying another egg.

Vincenti shared the car with two young, crisp Wall Street suits; both debarked before the eleventh floor. On eleven there wasn't a soul to be seen. Down in the street the raucous Saint Paddy's Day party was really cranking up with the onset of night, and Vincenti could hear the din all the way up here. He rounded the corner, stopped at 1108, and pressed his ear to the door. Nothing.

He moved on and knocked at 1110, but got no answer. Same with 1109 across the hall. He banged on a few others too on his way back to the elevator, but it was soon obvious that the residents of this floor were either not home from work yet, not about to answer, or were taking part in the semi-riot down below. For an instant the void caused Vincenti to feel a little strange, as if the floor was haunted.

Lost in a daydream, he waited for the elevator to take him back down to the street. The sound of light footfalls roused him out of it. Passing in front of the nocturnal panorama of the city outside the big window was a familiar figure – Lenny Jenkins.

"Double duty, huh?" called Vincenti. Didn't Jenkins have the day shift?

"Sort of," answered the doorman, who kept walking without looking back.

The detective took two steps to his right and watched Jenkins disappear out the exit to the stairs.

Lenny Jenkins had to be the only person aside from himself on the eleventh floor tonight. He had to wonder why.

Back downstairs, there was no one around, not even Rebecki. He had no other choice but to toss in the towel, at least for today. Trudging home past the knots of drunks milling around outside the pubs, Vincenti felt frustrated. He wasn't getting anywhere with this thing. Even with the talkative Rebecki, he hadn't been able to pry much loose except for a vague testimonial about Gail Kenmore's character. All of which added up to nothing, really. It was like Gail Kenmore's death had occurred inside some sort of a vacuum. Maybe it had.

Her purse, coat and gloves beside her, Vonda was on the sofa reading her South American newspaper. No Nicky in sight.

"Got our boy down, did you?"

Vonda grinned with satisfaction. Coaxing Nicky to bed was indeed a remarkable feat, especially when neither the detective nor his wife was around. The kid seemed to need one of his real parents on hand for security before relinquishing his hold on the waking world.

"How'd you manage that, Vonda?" teased Vincenti with a tired smile.

"Nicky very tired ... play hard today."

Vincenti thanked her again for bailing him out. He drew out his wallet and handed over a few bills, adding a hefty tip for good measure. Without looking at them – she never did in his presence – Vonda folded the green sheets and slipped them into her purse.

After she left, Vincenti tiptoed to the narrow bedroom at the rear of the apartment, gingerly turned the door handle, and looked in on his son. The boy was lying on his side, hands clasped together prayerfully under his ear, lips slightly parted, eyes shut. Dreaming of something, no doubt. What?

He shut the door softly, moved down the hall and ducked into the powder room, which had become by default his private bathroom in the wake of his estrangement from Reggie.

He peered at his reflection in the mirror. It was a face that didn't belong to a cop. Too soft, too smooth, too unmarked. His mug belonged on an accountant, maybe an appliance store salesman.

Tonight there were puffy pouches beneath his pale blue eyes and deep creases in his skin that he hadn't noticed before. He was solidly into middle age now, and that of course was the problem, especially as it impacted what was left of his relationship with his wife. It was so fucking incredibly stupid to have married someone fifteen years younger! What the hell had he been thinking?

On the other hand, it was way too late for beating up on himself. The damage, as another cliche went, had already been done. So it had to be repaired or lived with – if he could do either, which was highly doubtful. Of course he'd known what he'd wanted with Reggie in the first place – she was beautiful and classy – but what had she wanted with him? It was a question he often asked himself, and one that he'd never been able to answer, despite the obvious reasons that could be proffered: that he was handsome, at least according to some people, smart, ambitious, and a damned good cop. Still, in the equation with Reggie, he saw himself as lacking something, as being at a disadvantage, and somewhere in his mind he always suspected that it was those fifteen years.

Vincenti wandered into the kitchen and cursed at the sight of the pell-mell stacks of dirty dishes sitting in the sink. "Light cleaning," even though it had been written into her contract by Reggie, was definitely not Vonda's forte.

It was irritating to come home after a long day in the streets and have to load the dishwasher and scrub pots and pans. But he popped a beer, rolled up his sleeves, and did it all anyway, because he loathed disorder. If only he could straighten out the mess his life had become as easily as he could the kitchen.

When he was through, he cranked open a can of Rubinstein's fancy blueback red salmon and flopped on the living room sofa. For a while he looked at the TV – a late-season college basketball game, a few segments of a celebrated mob movie, a frighteningly unfunny sitcom. Then, at eleven, rather than watch the news, he stepped to the front window and looked out at Eighth Street. The street lamp threw a yellowish glare against the sidewalk, where a stray party boy who'd finally had enough of the never-ending bash up on Washington Street happened to be staggering by.

But no sign of Reggie, and he knew what that meant. His wife's professional obligations for the evening had long since been wrapped up and now she was elsewhere – with another man. She would finally come home when he was already asleep, or at least trying to, on the futon in the den that had been converted into his not-so-temporary bedroom.

Like acid in his gullet, an old resentment rose up in Vincenti but he was too weary tonight to give it full rein. And the realization that he fought so desperately to block from the light of day shot through his brain with the velocity of an exploding bullet: *I still love her.*

If it had been a lousy way for Gail Kenmore to die, then this was one hell of a lousy way to live.

"... and a house is not a home when there's no one there," with its tear-jerking melody revved up on Vincenti's internal stereo. He wasn't one to walk around feeling sorry for himself, but there it was anyway, sobs, sentiment and schmaltz. Not to mention an ugly reminder of his age. Embarrassing as shit, even if no one but him could hear the song.

He turned away from the window. His feet hurt, his knees ached, and his temples throbbed. The days he hated most were the days when nothing much got accomplished. He had the craving for a drink to help him sleep, but he'd been drinking too much lately.

He retraced his steps to the powder room, opened the medicine cabinet and shook an oblong tablet out of a plastic vial. He placed the Ambien on his tongue and washed it down with water from his cupped palm. Then, like a prisoner readying himself for lights out, he padded into his tiny cell.

Within seconds he was in that no-man's land of reality distortion between wakefulness and sleep. Lying there in the darkness listening to the occasional remnants of the expiring revel, he kept irrationally hoping the phone would ring with a lead he could follow in the Gail Kenmore death, but it didn't.

Thursday, March 18

The next morning had a fuzzy, unreal feel to it. It wasn't just the after-effects of the sleeping pill; he'd had that dream again. This time the body was right there under his bed. Whenever someone came in, he was in a panic that it wouldn't be seen.

The world itself was a gigantic daguerreotype that was melting around the edges. Walking south on Hudson Street toward headquarters, Vincenti could feel the first hint of spring in the air. From behind a pearly mist that resembled the inside of an oyster shell, the sun was struggling to break through. Scattered around the gates of the brownstones were shards of green and sepia glass that were once whole beer bottles, shreds of fast-food wrapping, and stray leaves of newspaper. The Saint Paddy's Day blast was history for another year.

Vincenti had managed to slip out of the house this morning before Reggie and Nicky even opened their eyes. Just as well: he wasn't in the mood for butting heads with his wife, and he'd discovered that sometimes it was better to be absent altogether than to be less than one-hundred-percent "all there" for the boy.

After phoning the hospital and being diverted a few times, he discovered that an autopsy had been performed at the behest of the coroner's office – routine for a suicide in this jurisdiction – and that Gail Kenmore's remains had been claimed by her family. The preliminary in-hospital report stated that she'd succumbed from massive internal injuries as the result of a fall from a high place. The final report would take a few more days to complete, but no doubt the conclusion would be the same.

Did the hospital have the names of Gail Kenmore's parents? He kept getting bounced back to the front desk, and someone named Kendra. Confusion at the other end. They should be here somewhere, swore Kendra, but she couldn't locate them. Vincenti swore under his breath. Phones jangled. Doctors were being summoned over the intercom – could he possibly call back later?

"Sure ..." What choice did he have?

The day quickly shaped up as another unproductive number, which Vincenti couldn't abide. For some reason, not much was getting done: people he needed to talk to weren't in, telephone calls went unreturned, even the two temp secretaries brought in to help with the logjam were so backed up with incident and arrest reports from yesterday's insanity that most of his own paperwork was failing to get processed.

Vincenti found himself growing more and more restive throughout the morning, anticipating the moment when he'd be sprung free to get back to the high rise at Second and Hudson. The Kenmore thing was still jabbing at him.

Besides the painting on the bedroom wall, he could still hear Rebecki's voice echoing in his head: *"No way she jumped out of that window ..."*

A little after noon, when he was working on a veal parmigiana sandwich from Caruso's Deli on First Street (the likes of which he'd tried swearing off, without success, after a recent elevated cholesterol reading), the telephone on his desk sounded.

"Vonda can't stay tonight."

It was Reggie, without so much as a hello, making her announcement in a chilly, business-like voice. Vincenti could hear the jabbering of her office-mates in the background as they worked the phones of Uptown Realtors on the other side of Hoboken.

"So what do you want me to do?"

"Can I count on you to be at home tonight?"

"Gonna be late again? Showing another house?" He did his level best to ask questions without being cynical, but the bite showed through anyway.

"As a matter of fact, I am," Reggie shot back defensively.

"Come on, Reg. I wasn't born yesterday. Nobody shows properties until midnight."

"The market's hotter than ever. You know that. Sometimes things run late."

"The only thing that's hot is –"

As soon as he allowed the words to escape his lips, Vincenti regretted them, even though he felt at least partially entitled to his rage. Before he had the chance to finish the accusation, however, his wife had hung up, leaving him in the absurd position of squeezing an instrument that was transmitting nothing but a yowling dial tone into his ear.

He was about to ring her back, with the intention of escalating their row into something really ugly, something worthy of the quantity of venom between them, when the phone rang again. It was Boccardo at the front desk, ordering him over to the Chesterfield Gardens at Jefferson and Seventh on the double – a woman had been raped in a parking garage there.

———————

By evening an icy rain was falling outside Vincenti's smudged office window. Even though the days were growing longer, a sludgy haze hung low in the sky. This was the season that he and everyone else who lived in the East abhorred, the ass-end of a ceaseless stretch of dreary nothingness that commenced when the Christmas holidays were over. And as each year passed, he found himself scheming to pull up roots and stake a place in the sun for himself and his boy – if Nicky wasn't ultimately lost in a custody war. Florida or Arizona or California – those were the places, man. Take Santa Barbara – if there was a more exquisite city in America, then he didn't know it. But the Keys were his favorite. How could anyone bitch about living with the turquoise Gulf of Mexico on your right, and the blue Atlantic on your left? Vincenti had visited or vacationed in all those places, and he knew he could easily slide into a more than tolerable existence in any one of them. Hell, he could apply for work as a private operative in a city like Tucson, or Miami, where his experience on the mean streets would have to count for something, right?

But he never got far in the fantasy. The problem was that to get anywhere near a full pension from the police force, he couldn't retire for a few more years. Nicky was going to have to be supported – sent to school all the way up through college – and so he needed the money from a decent salary.

It would probably be better if he stayed in one place once the kid started elementary school. Until then, the weather, Hoboken, his life, would have to be endured.

The rape investigation – always one of his more unpleasant duties to say the least – had taken up the better part of the afternoon. The victim, a thirty-something florist's assistant by the name of Maria Fuentes, was in a state of near-catatonic hysteria when he arrived on the scene and could hardly provide any solid, usable information about the attack. Which was to be expected. What Vincenti was able to piece together in a brief interview at her apartment was that she'd been just about to get into her car in the underground lot at about 11 a.m. – she was scheduled to start a half-hour later than usual at the Jersey City concession where she worked – when she was grabbed from behind, thrown to the cement between her vehicle and another, and viciously assaulted. The ordeal had lasted all of three or four minutes, she estimated, and she hadn't really seen a thing. Since her assailant was unbelievably strong – "like a gorilla," she kept repeating – once she was subdued there wasn't a thing she could do to break free. Did she try to fight back? She couldn't actually remember. Did she inflict any damage on her attacker? Ditto was the answer. It was the most horrible experience of her entire life; nothing else came close. Even the medication she was prescribed at the hospital after providing her rape kit didn't help subdue her overwrought emotions. She was in fear for her life. If this demon could brutally violate her, what would stop him from killing her?

Vincenti had forced himself to put on a compassionate

face, but it was the kind of crime, he knew, there was slim hope of solving. And even if the Neanderthal was caught and successfully prosecuted, Maria Fuentes would never be the same.

If nothing else, interviewing the victim and scoping out the garage with a crime scene tech had forced the detective to forget, for the first time in the past couple of days, all about his domestic problems and Gail Kenmore.

At a few minutes past six he hit the speed-dial button and was surprised, even astonished, to hear his wife pick up at home.

He'd meant to try and persuade Vonda to hang on and watch Nicky a little longer; Reggie's "hello" threw him. These days he had to be mentally prepared to talk, let alone wrangle, with his wife.

"Ah – you're there?" Inane. Clumsy.

When she coolly answered "Who did you expect?" he said, "Just wanted to make sure Nicky was covered," and depressed the cradle button without saying goodbye.

So – she'd changed her plans after all and gone home after work. It meant that he could continue his snooping into the Kenmore thing like he wanted to. Before his wife had the chance to phone back and botch his plans, he grabbed his coat and bolted.

Rebecki was at the desk again. No, the roommates still hadn't shown, and no, according to the log, no one had been in apartment 1108 since the last time the detective himself had been up there. Vincenti said thanks and rode the elevator to eleven. This evening he got a swift answer to his very first knock.

The twentysomething in 1110 was very attractive and dressed in a navy suit with matching leather pumps. She looked like she'd just pulled in from work. Her skin was the shade of a pale Spanish olive, and Vincenti computed that her blood was Mediterranean or Middle Eastern – or she spent lots of time in the tanning salon or vacationing in the Caribbean. The preoccupied, even slightly annoyed look on her face was all-American, though – she had absolutely no interest in being distracted from whatever it was she'd been involved in, whether it was making dinner reservations or checking her mutual funds online.

"Yes? Can I help you?"

Trying not to be obvious about it, Vincenti peered over her shoulder into the apartment – with the switch of a piece of furniture here or there it might be a replica of Gail Kenmore's place.

He showed his ID. "Detective Brian Vincenti, Hoboken Police. I'd like to ask you a couple of questions."

Was she about to roll her eyes? Jesus. He nearly apologized for intruding.

"I don't know whether or not you're aware of what happened up here on Tuesday morning –"

"No." Her response was framed as an irritated question.

The detective went on to explain how Gail Kenmore had fallen, or jumped – or was pushed – out of her window in the very next apartment two days earlier.

She didn't blink. "Sorry. I don't know a thing about it."

She didn't seem in the least fazed, shocked or horrified. For her, the news had all the impact of a coup in Ethiopia or an earthquake in Japan.

Just then a telephone chimed, and she made a move to close the door. Vincenti stuck out his foot to stop it.

"Did you know Gail Kenmore?"

"No."

"Sure? You never even *saw* her?"

"I haven't lived here all that long. I'm out all day, and I don't pay attention to the neighbors."

"Live here by yourself, do you?"

Suspicion replaced irritation on her swarthy features.

"I have two roommates."

"Could I talk to them?"

"I'm sure you could, but they're not in."

Wow – helpful.

She gave Vincenti a quick up and down, as if suddenly she wasn't convinced that he was who he claimed he was, that maybe he was a con man out to gain entrance to her apartment for some slimy reason.

"So is there a better time?"

"They should be in later," she said with deliberate skepticism. She stole a rapid glance of her own into the hall; was she looking for some sort of help in the event Vincenti tried to jump her or force his way in? "They usually get in a little later than I do ... but I have to tell you honestly, I don't think you'll find out anything more from them than I already told you, since neither of them mentioned this – this thing you're talking about. Actually, they're here even less than I am most of the time. I mean, we really don't know anyone or see anything around here ..."

Like deaf and dumb monkeys. Vincenti chuckled. Ah, yes, the new Hoboken. Okay. He'd play along. "This is kind of like just a place to sleep – that it?"

"That's exactly it."

She didn't crack a smile at his little joke. Because she was probably telling the truth.

Vincenti might be back to check in with the absent roommates, but he didn't say when. One last thing. Could he have her name, just for his records?

"Rena Demas."

"Thanks. Sorry to disturb you, Ms. Demas."

There. He'd apologized. At 1109, the tenant was a bit more accommodating. From the instant she opened up, Vincenti could see that Ann Harrison was cut out of the same mold as her across-the-hall counterpart, but with a subtle difference. There was something, for lack of a better word, *sad* about Ann Harrison. While she was about the same age as Rena Demas, and dressed in a nearly identical suit, she wasn't nearly as easy on the eye. But she did seem a little softer around the edges.

"How long have you lived here?"

Even as the detective asked questions, he was in the process of sizing Ann Harrison up. It was unavoidable, a reflex, something his groin did automatically whenever a female was involved, whether the case was breaking and entering, rape or murder. And it wasn't something he was proud of.

No, he decided, he wouldn't be interested in Ann Harrison, even if he was on the prowl. Slightly overweight – broad in the beam, as they say – was a turn-off.

Guys. Wired altogether differently. Most of them, anyway. Always thinking with their "little heads." What assholes.

"Oh – since when the building went up," Ann Harrison was saying. "Seven years or so, I guess. It's been so long now I've forgotten." Her laugh was genuine, even slightly infectious.

"Live here by yourself?"

"I do."

Suddenly she seemed hesitant. And just like across the hall, Vincenti was not invited in. Ann Harrison kept the door pulled half-shut behind her so that he couldn't get an unobstructed look inside. Nobody trusted anyone around here, it seemed, least of all a cop.

When Vincenti explained why he'd come, she nodded.

"I heard." A shudder seemed to ripple through Ann Harrison's body. "It sounds awful. Absolutely awful."

Vincenti stood holding his notebook, his London Fog draped over his left forearm. Did she see much of Gail?

"Uh-uh. I work all day, take courses for my masters degree at NYU four nights out of five, and I'm gone most weekends, to my sister's house up at Greenwood Lake. Once or twice I bumped into her dumping trash, actually. That's about it."

"So you knew her?"

"I knew who she was. I didn't really know her. There's a big difference."

"Could you describe her?"

"Blondish hair. Medium height, slender build, I guess you'd say. Um, I don't know what else to add, really ..."

That was her, all right, the young woman in the photo in bedroom number two. No way to know for sure if it was her in those crappy paintings, though.

"Ever notice anything out of the ordinary about Gail Kenmore?"

Ann Harrison's fine chestnut brow crinkled. "Out of the ordinary? How do you mean?"

"Did she seem depressed, or act strange ... did she ever say anything that caught your attention? Did you ever see anybody with her – men? Boyfriends? Ever see her arguing with anyone? Stuff like that."

"First of all, she didn't seem to me the type to jump. Not at all. I know you can't judge a book by its cover, but –"

"Why do you say that?"

"Whenever I saw her, said hello to her, she seemed ... fine, you know? Happy. Content. Whatever word you'd want to use."

"So what about the men?"

"Guys stopped by her apartment – occasionally I'd see them knocking on the door – but I wouldn't be able to tell you a thing about any one of them, even if they were there to see *her*. They all looked like nice guys, if you know what I mean." She shook her head. "Sorry. I really am. I wish I could help you, but –"

She shrugged helplessly.

"Sure? Give yourself a few seconds. Think back."

Vincenti knew he was grasping at straws, but in the past, sticking it out just a little longer had sometimes produced a sudden windfall.

"Well – they weren't the guys I worried about."

"No?"

Ann Harrison looked up and down the hall, a little apprehensively, judged Vincenti, as if she wanted to be certain nobody else was around.

"This may appear to be a safe building, Detective, but sometimes I have my doubts. Actually, I've been thinking of looking for someplace else to live. The problem – as I'm sure you know – is that housing in Hoboken is tight. Plus the hassle of it all ..."

"Sure ..."

"... but there are some odd people running around here."

"How do you mean?"

"They look like they don't exactly *belong* here, if you know what I mean."

"Would you happen to have any names?"

Ann Harrison's lips tightened. "One of them happens to work right *in* this building, in my opinion. But I would never say a word to management."

"Why? Because you're afraid?"

Ann Harrison gave a noncommittal twitch of her head.

"Well – it could be a little uncomfortable."

"Has anything ever happened?"

"I hope I'm not saying too much, be-"

"Whatever you tell me doesn't ever get past right here." Vincenti pointed at the floor for emphasis.

"This doesn't prove anything, but ... I once asked Lenny Jenkins to –"

"Lenny Jenkins, the doorman?"

Ann Harrison nodded.

"Not too long ago I asked him to bring a UPS package up to my door because I didn't want it sitting in the lobby. Which he did ... but afterwards something unusual happened."

She flushed and shook her head, as if she didn't know whether she should go further. Or as if she couldn't quite believe what she was about to divulge.

"Yes?"

"The next day, I happened to notice that several pairs of my ... my underthings were missing from my bureau. I checked and re-checked, and I never did find them. The thing is that I know Lenny has keys to all the units, and I've seen him ... well ..."

"Yes," Vincenti said again.

"*Lurking*. Just ... at odd times, when I don't expect to see him all the way up on this floor. I mean, why would he be up here when he belongs at the front desk, right? Anyway, in my mind that's what I call him – 'the lurker.' And I'm not the only one."

Vincenti remembered his last visit up here, when Jenkins passed him like a wraith.

"But I'd never say anything to anyone, for the reason you mentioned. And maybe I just misplaced my clothes. Accusations are – they're dangerous. They can destroy someone's life. I'd never do that if I wasn't one-hundred-percent sure beyond the shadow of a doubt."

"That's admirable of you," said Vincenti.

"So, really, I guess, there's nothing I can tell you."

"You've been very helpful," lied Vincenti.

As per routine, he asked her to call him in the event she remembered anything, but he knew it wasn't likely. Once the initial connection was lost, you couldn't generally expect much.

Ann Harrison's door shut with a rude bang. Vincenti looked up and down the corridor. Was there a point in going on? His own life was a wreck – why the hell should he give a good goddamn about someone else's? He was still among the living. As far as Gail Kenmore was concerned, it didn't matter anymore, did it?

If he had any sense, he'd head home, put it to sleep. But his bloodhound's instincts won out, as they always did.

The last unit on the south end was number 1111. Vincenti was still in the process of rapping when the door swung open.

"Hi, there."

The guy was around six-four, six-five, in his early forties, in dire need of a shave. Watery eyes – very watery eyes. There were flecks of gray in his lank, greasy hair. He wore a frayed red and black checkerboard flannel shirt, jeans torn at the knees, and flaccid sweat socks. There was, thought Vincenti, even a whiff of body odor coming off him. Different from his neighbors, all right. Maybe this was another one of the creepos Ann Harrison was referring to. And he was right next door, which would be why she wouldn't want to identify him by name.

Inside 1111 was a mess, Vincenti could see. There were heaps of toys on the floor. The maplewood dining room table was littered with plates, cups, glasses, silverware. The aroma of a recently consumed meal – a not very appetizing one at that – hovered in the air. This place looked a lot worse than his own, even on one of its most chaotic days.

"Who is it, hon?"

The voice came from deeper in the apartment and it belonged to an invisible woman. It was accompanied by the chirping of a small child's voice.

"Hoboken Police."

"It's the police, Lisa!"

"The *police*, did you say?"

"Sorry. It's bath-time for our little princess," the man explained with a dash of irony.

"Got one of my own," said the detective.

"God bless you," laughed the man.

"Sorry to barge in, but I'm following up on the death of your neighbor down the hall here, Gail Kenmore."

"Right. Come on in."

A rare gesture. The detective crossed the threshold.

"Alex Danko," said the fellow, extending his hand. It was clammy and hard, like a chunk of wet leather. "Don't mind the mess. Have a seat."

Vincenti laid his coat over the back of the only chair devoid of clutter. Outside the brace of three windows was a stunning view of the Big Apple, all black, ash gray and sand-coloured outlines, speckled with thousands of yellow and white dots of light. Vincenti calculated from the latitude of the old federal building on the other side of the water that he was directly across from Christopher Street, an association that always darkened his mood. Because that's where the incident with that kid, the incident that changed everything in his life, went down. Where he went to meet a friend one hot summer night and his world crashed and burned and to this day hadn't been resurrected. Whenever it crossed his mind, it still freaked him out.

After bumping a stuffed Elmo to the carpet, Danko took a seat across the kitchen table.

"So she jumped, isn't that right? That's what I'm hearing around here."

"Well – I'm not exactly sure. That's what I'm trying to determine."

"Ah." This seemed, oddly, to enthuse Danko.

Vincenti put on his disarming smile. "So you're hearing that Gail Kenmore jumped – who's been saying it?"

"Lenny, the daytime doorman. And maybe I heard somebody else mention it when I was in the elevator. Very sad."

"Very," agreed Vincenti, trying to appear nonchalant.

Lenny again. Lenny certainly got around.

Something about this guy Danko was interesting. It wasn't that Vincenti harbored any immediate suspicions about him; it was simply that like most better-than-average cops, he had a fundamental inquisitiveness about human beings, especially unusual ones. Danko was out of the mold for the Hudson Arms. A little squirrelly.

"Did you know her, Gail Kenmore?"

Danko shook his head. "Y'know, I'm not sure that I did. My wife apparently knew who she was, but I can't quite picture her in my mind's eye, know what I mean?"

"Ever pick up anything about her?"

"Pick up anything? How do you mean?"

"You know," Vincenti continued, "about her boyfriends, her habits, anything like that?"

"Nah," laughed Danko, who was twisting a teaspoon into the ketchup-crusted place mat in front of him. "I'm not hooked into the social network around here at all. Between my little girl and work – well, I don't have to tell you, I'm sure."

"What is it you do for a living, Alex?"

Danko loosened his neck muscles. "Writer." He said the word without inflection. It probably meant that he wasn't all that well-known. Or that he wasn't known at all. Maybe it meant that he hated being a writer. Or maybe it didn't mean anything at all.

"Who do you write for?"

"Everybody. Nobody. Mostly myself."

"That's quite an audience."

Danko made a face. "Freelance. Mostly magazines. Had a few articles picked up by the *Times*. Actually, I'm trying to write mystery, suspense. That's where I spend most of my time."

"Tough row to hoe, I would think."

Vincenti had bumped into scores of writers over the years. They ran all over New York, like cockroaches; the less successful species were crawling over Hoboken, too. Everyone and her brother was a would-be writer with something – a screenplay, a novel, the next Pulitzer Prize-winning play – they were "showing around."

"Tough? Try damned-near impossible. How about you – you write?"

Vincenti snorted. "Sure – case reports."

"It's a start. But you gotta work twenty-four-seven to even have a remote chance of making a go of it. Competition's fierce. Myself, I've already knocked out five, six novels and can't get myself arrested. Aside from a handful of short stories in the small literary journals, that is. With all the rejection, sometimes I lose my motivation. I get lazy. Why should I kill myself, I figure ..."

Arrested. Interesting word choice. Again, not that it

signified anything. But was this guy Danko trying to tell him something? That was another thing a cop always had to be on the lookout for: the subtle cue, the Freudian slip that might lead him somewhere.

"You say you work seven days a week ..."

"Yeah."

"You work right here, in your apartment?"

"Most of the time. It's hard, with a toddler underfoot. The only time I get a breather is when the babysitter shows up, which means not all that often. But I got my ways of relaxing ... We can't afford to have someone full time, so a lot of the care falls to me since I'm at home. The rent in this building's a killer, it sucks out everything we bring in and then some. Don't ever live in a place that isn't rent-controlled, that's my advice."

"I hear you," said the detective.

"Wanna see my office?"

"Sure," said Vincenti.

Now this was *highly* unusual. Maybe Danko had nobody to talk to. Maybe he was lonely. Which had to be the case if you sat scribbling by yourself all day.

His ungainly host led him down a short hallway and into the first door. Vincenti could hear the playful splashing of a child in its bath through a closed door a few feet further on.

Danko's cave was crammed with books, magazines, newspapers, CDs. Along one wall was a scarred, three-leaf antique table serving as a desk for a computer terminal and stacks of junk. There was hardly room to turn around.

Danko sat at his desk, picked up a small glass ashtray, and dumped its contents into the wastebasket. Vincenti was half-tempted to ask what they were, but he didn't want to get sidetracked.

Vincenti picked up that stale-sweat smell again, mixed with the unmistakable scent of weed – marijuana. Maybe that was how Danko "relaxed."

The single window offered another dazzling view of Manhattan. How could a struggling writer, his wife and child afford to live in this place, especially if Danko wasn't all that gainfully employed?

"Were you here the day Gail Kenmore went out the window?"

"Let me think ..." Danko's forehead furrowed.

"It was Tuesday," prompted the detective.

"Tuesday ... Well, I guess I was here, now that I think about it ..."

"Working?"

"That's right – on an article on beating the odds in Atlantic City for the *Star-Ledger*."

"Uh-huh. Didn't hear anything, any commotion, three doors away? Didn't see anything?"

Danko rubbed his stubbly chin, pondering. Vincenti had to wonder why: Gail Kenmore's death would be an event that would stand out in anyone's mind, wouldn't it? Especially the mind of a would-be mystery writer.

"No. Nothing. Sorry. The thing is, I wouldn't have been paying attention anyhow. When I'm absorbed in something, I'm oblivious to the world around me."

Curious. When he came in, Danko was completely fascinated by the tragedy. Maybe the whacky weed had short-circuited his brain.

"Now let me think ... That day the sitter had taken the baby out for the morning. So without the distraction, I was *really* absorbed."

Vincenti decided to cast his line out.

"See, I'm thinking that maybe Gail Kenmore didn't jump out her window at all."

"No?"

"No, what I'm thinking is that maybe she was pushed."

"No kidding? What would make you think that?" Danko blinked his dewy eyes.

"My job is to consider all possibilities. More than that, I can't really say."

Vincenti kept close watch on Danko's face, to see if he rose to the bait. But it was cloudy and bleary, an impression underscored by the dark pouches under his eyes.

Just then he heard a door open, and Danko's wife appeared in the study doorway clutching a writhing, pink-faced, wide-eyed kid cocooned in a bath towel.

"My wife, Lisa. Lisa, Detective Vincenti. And that's little Jacqueline." He pronounced it "Jock-eh-leen."

Precious, thought Vincenti. The child was cute, but not quite the sparkler his Nicky was. But then every parent thought the same thing about his kid.

Vincenti repeated his apology for barging in on the Danko family, and the purpose of his visit.

"Oh, that poor girl!" exclaimed Lisa, who looked about the same age as her husband, and even more haggard. She'd been attractive once upon a time, figured Vincenti, but he couldn't make up his mind about whether she had anything left. "I can't stop thinking about her. Thank God we're about to move out – living here now will give me the shudders forever."

Like most people who found themselves parents in Hoboken, the Dankos' next stop was likely to be somewhere out in the suburbs where there would be more room, better schools, cleaner air, and so on. More than once it had occurred to Vincenti that had he moved his family out, they might not be in the impasse they were in. But he also knew that his troubles were far more complicated.

Danko took the child out of his wife's arms when the conversation shifted to her.

"You didn't happen to be here on Tuesday when it happened, I take it?"

"I was at work all day – thank God."

Her occupation? Personnel manager for a Manhattan think-tank, some fancy-ass company he'd never heard of. No doubt she was the breadwinner. Now it made sense how her spouse could afford to sit at home all day, bang on his computer keyboard and smoke dope. The question, of course, was what she saw in him. But when it came to women, that was a perennial mystery.

"Anyway, that sort of thing totally freaks me out. Alex is the one into blood and guts."

"Not really," her husband objected, rocking the cooing little girl back and forth. "She's exaggerating. What she means is my work – that I've written about murder, crime. You know, the mystery stuff I mentioned. It's all vicarious, second-hand stuff. Never been near the real thing."

"Did you know Gail Kenmore?" the detective asked

Lisa. By now he'd posed the question a million times – or so it seemed. He was tired of hearing himself ask it.

"Oh, yes. Not well, but I knew her. She was very, very nice. Always pleasant to Jacqueline. She always stopped to say hello, treated her like a grown-up person."

"So you never saw her depressed, angry, emotional, anything like that?"

Lisa Danko shook her head vigorously. "Not me, absolutely not. Never. Maybe a little tired once or twice, but who isn't?"

"Doesn't it strike you as odd, then, that she would leap out a window?"

"Oh, absolutely, it does. Who knows what happened over there?"

Danko cut in. "The detective thinks she may have been forced, hon."

Lisa's eyes widened. "Really? By who?"

"That's a bit premature," admitted Vincenti. "But it's one theory." He declined to add that it was *his* exclusive theory.

"Gosh – now *that's* scary," Lisa shivered. "*Murder*, in this building?" She took her child back from her husband in an unconsciously protective gesture. "Time for bed, darling. Nice meeting you, Detective. And good luck. I hope it all turns out to be nothing but an unfortunate accident."

Alex Danko shrugged. "Jeez – I wish we could help you somehow ..."

He led the way back to the living room.

Before leaving, Vincenti was determined to try one last tack. "Were you ever inside that apartment, number 1108?"

"Me? No. No reason to."

"I mean, since there must be at least a handful of folks around during the day who get a little bored and want to shoot the breeze. Heck, there are probably even a few afternoon affairs going on in this building, right? Not that I'm suggesting you'd be involved in one of those, but ..."

Danko struck the detective as the kind of guy who required a bit of needling to snap out of his haze. It was a shot he had to take.

"I'm a married man, Detective. I don't go around looking for extracurricular activity."

Gee, no sense of humor about it whatsoever, even for a pothead.

"Mm-hm. Ever see anything unusual when you were passing by? Any strange people hanging around – a man, maybe? Somebody you didn't recognize?" Again, he was just playing his line, hoping for a strike.

"Mm-mm. Nope ... Well, check that. Once – no, a few times – I saw a guy out there knocking on the door."

"Tell me about it."

"The reason I remember is 'cause the guy was older. Like in his sixties or something, if I'm any judge of age. Silver hair. Slim and good-looking and dressed fine. I remember he was wearing a real high-end coat – shearling, something like that. He stood out, kind of. I just assumed it was one of the girls' fathers. But for all I know, it was nobody but the plumber."

It might be something, but then again ... In the end Vincenti had to conclude that he'd probably been barking up the wrong tree. Danko was a half-assed voyeur, a vulture scavenging around for material, and that's all there was to him.

It was going on ten-thirty – too late to call on any more of Gail Kenmore's neighbors. Passing 1108, he noted that the space beneath the door was black – still no sign of the roommates. Hell, they might never come back.

Before calling it a night, he decided to head back first to headquarters. He nodded at Stilden, who was manning the front desk, then went to his tiny office and flicked the computer to life. He ran an Info-Cop check on Alex Danko, but came up with zilch. Other search engines coughed up nothing except for the titles of a few of his articles in local rags, and contents tables for a handful of obscure literary quarterlies which had published his short stories. Since he was still wide awake and wired, he tried the same thing for Lenny Jenkins and Gail Kenmore, but there wasn't a single match to be found.

Nothing. *Nada.* Just one dead end after another.

Friday, March 19

The follow-up interview with Maria Fuentes was not going well. Out of habit, Vincenti had run a check of known sex offenders living on the so-called Gold Coast in the morning, but there were so many listed on the database it wasn't even mildly funny. There were at least a dozen alone living within a 25-block radius of the victim. It could be one of several hundred people he was looking for, without taking into consideration the possibility of a perp with a New York City or other out-of-the-area address. Then again, maybe not. Maybe it was someone who'd never raped a woman in his life and decided to start yesterday. He cruised down to Jefferson Street only because he promised he would, but after a few minutes he wished he hadn't come at all.

The victim was still in a state of confused anguish, her emotions out of control. In fact, Maria Fuentes was worse off today than she was yesterday. (This wasn't an unusual phenomenon. Vincenti often found victims in surprisingly fine shape in the immediate aftermath of a crime; when the reality settled in, however, when the shock started to wear off, usually after the first twenty-four hours or so, their condition was likely to deteriorate.)

Maria sat on her lime-green velour sofa, tearing up, honking her nose into a tissue, shaking her head with disgust and disbelief. This was the worst kind of casualty to have to deal with. Vincenti found himself darting glances around the apartment, comparing it to his own and Gail Kenmore's, so as not to get mired in the woman's misery. This place seemed more lived in, somehow, than Gail Kenmore's; maybe it was the profusion of family-and-friend snapshots stuck to the refrigerator door, or maybe it was the fact that the ceiling needed paint. Certainly it was more modest than his place and the high-rise up on Hudson Street, the chintzy and threadbare furniture testifying to another income level. This place had the trace of an odor, too, of stewed tomatoes and fried ochra and onions all mixed together, that neither his nor Gail Kenmore's suffered from.

"I've lived in this city all my life, and I never ... I mean, I could never, ever *imagine* that something like this would happen to me, you know? I've heard about it happening to *other* women, but to *me* ... I just never –"

Her words dissolved into a plaintive yowl that made Vincenti wince. He'd always hated having to listen to a woman's pain. The discomfort came, he supposed, from holding down a gig that required the absolute repression of any dangerously anarchic emotion. He averted his gaze from her blotched, tear-stained face and looked out the window that presented an ugly view of the lower intestine of Hoboken with its tar-paper roofs and rust-coated fire escapes.

"Ms. Fuentes – I have to ask you again, like I did yesterday, is there anything else you can tell me about the attack ... anything you didn't give us before?"

He knew that the timbre of his voice was less than sympathetic, but he had a job to do, an objective to attain. With her right thumb and forefinger Maria pressed on her tear ducts and tucked her chin into her rubbery neck like a tired bird. Today the poor woman was carelessly dumped into jeans and a shapeless purple sweater. A few years ago she may have been pretty, in a heavy sort of way. But she was beyond that; she'd "hit the wall" as they said nowadays. Vincenti knew that he was thinking like a callous dick, but you had to be damned near made of stone to deal with ugliness and tragedy on a regular basis like he did.

Nevertheless, he tried to apply the techniques he'd picked up in the sexual assault seminars the department irregularly conducted. There was, he knew, a hell of a lot more to the process than submitting evidence by way of the rape kit.

"Think hard," he urged. "Anything, anything at all you can come up with will help."

"That's the most frustrating thing," said Maria Fuentes. "It all happened so fast. I never even heard any footsteps, and it was like ... like the animal was on top of me before I had a chance to even react, and –"

Vincenti nodded, waited for more. Maria's eyelids clamped shut against something – a memory.

"What I *do* remember is his breath," she whispered, cringing. "It smelled like ... like dog shit. That's what it smelled like – dog shit."

At that moment Vincenti thought of Lenny Jenkins obsessively popping his breath mints. Where had Lenny been on Wednesday morning? But suspecting the doorman of rape was really stretching it, wasn't it?

"And he was like ... humming to himself all the time he was – when it was going on." Like it was some kind of fun little game he was playing with himself. You know, he seemed amused, satisfied with himself. When he was through, he left me upside down – on my face." She took a deep breath. "You can guess why."

She started to break down again. Vincenti knew that she'd been anally penetrated, because he'd seen it on the rape kit form when it was sent to headquarters. Anyway, these were the kinds of details victims of blind attacks eventually coughed up. Mostly they were as good as intangible – you might not go very far with what they told you. Still, it was always worth the try – you never knew what might bubble up to help bust a case.

He waited until Maria Fuentes was through weeping.

"Before this happened, was there anything out of the ordinary going on in your life? Unusual phone calls ... did you notice anyone following you, anything like that?"

She shook her head. There'd been nothing abnormal, nothing whatsoever she could remember.

"Have any trouble with a male acquaintance – a co-worker, a neighbor, for instance?"

No, nothing like that either. He stopped short of asking whether she'd had trouble with any relatives. But hell, these days you never knew.

"Something I didn't ask you yesterday."

"Yes?"

"I take it you're not married, since you would have mentioned your husband."

"Divorced. A long time ago."

"How long ago?"

"Ten years. Eleven in May."

"You never see one another?"

"He went back to the Dominican Republic right afterward. As far as I know, he never came back."

"Was he your only husband?"

Maria nodded.

"No current boyfriends ... or old boyfriends?"

A cloud – of bitterness, or disappointment, Vincenti couldn't make out which – passed over Maria Fuentes' strained features.

"No. There's been nobody for a long time."

Vincenti didn't press the issue. He got it: when Maria Fuentes was young she'd been able to land a guy, but for whatever reason – who knows how many reasons, including the harsh fact that in the sexual marketplace middle-aged women are consigned to the junk heap – it hadn't worked out, and now all she had was a job. It was the story of untold millions.

In her turn, she didn't press Vincenti for what the cops had been doing to apprehend her attacker, for assurances that she would get satisfactory answers at some point in the future. It was as if her initial daze had given way to pain in its purest form, and she was marooned now in that very private realm. Furthermore, she seemed to realize that both she and the detective were at a dead end. Nevertheless, Vincenti repeated what he told all victims when a crime was unsolved: "Call me any time you have anything new to share." And, of course, that old, hollow promise, "We'll do everything we can to get this guy off the streets."

When he got up to leave, Maria Fuentes was sitting in the exact same position, the exact same spot as when the interview had commenced, tissue balled up in her hand, mouth slightly open, eyes distant. He had the feeling she was going to be sitting like that for a long time.

Back at headquarters, Vincenti found an intriguing message in his voicemail.

"Detective Vincenti – I believe I have the right name – this is Hugh Kenmore. I understand you've been looking into my daughter's death ..."

The call had come in approximately an hour ago, when he was first sitting down with Maria Fuentes. Vincenti recognized the voice at once. It belonged to the caller who left two frantic messages on Gail Kenmore's answering machine on her last morning.

"Gail's funeral is tomorrow, so we'll be in and out all day today taking care of the arrangements. You can reach me at ..." Etc.

Bingo. Now he might just be able to get somewhere with this thing, if there was anywhere to go. He replayed the message and punched the number in. After ten rings there was no answer, not even a machine. He tried again, same result. He hated phone tag, but he wasn't even going to get to play. No choice but to try again later.

Today the detective was supposed to be somewhere for lunch. Just after noon he threw on his coat and walked the block and a half to the PATH station on Hudson Place. The sky was still overcast and threatening, but the edge was off. He hurried down the grimy stairs, slipped his fare card into the metal lips of a turnstile and then headed for a second set of steps that took him down to the platform. The next train bound for Christopher Street was waiting on

Track 1, its doors open, its interior empty. Vincenti picked up a discarded *New York Post*, took a seat, and flipped the pages. Normally sports or the gossip columns would have kept his attention, but today he was thinking about the fact that the Kenmore death hadn't rated a blurb. Not even a local paper like the *Jersey Journal*, which deemed the Fuentes rape a front-page story this morning, so much as mentioned Gail Kenmore's fall from an eleventh-floor window. It was tough to figure. Probably just wasn't sexy enough.

The train screeched to a halt. A damp, foul backdraft pressed against him as he climbed up the steep, twisting stairs to the street. As he moved into the daylight, it had morphed into an icy wind.

He turned left on Christopher Street and darted across Hudson to Bedford. Seventh Avenue was a parking lot, and it was only the middle of the day. Vincenti zigzagged between cars, delivery trucks and honking cabs to the other side. Microscopic flurries of snow swirled in the air, and suddenly the edge was all the way back.

The Hideout was a combination bistro-pool parlor that had been standing on the corner of Leroy Street for as long as Vincenti could remember. The string of Christmas bulbs in the front window were flashing, and as usual the inside was as shadowy as a cave. Vincenti took the last empty stool at the bar. When the bartender came by, he ordered a beer from the tap. Before he had the chance to bring the glass to his lips, his elbow was being jostled.

He looked into the mirror behind the bar. The middle-aged lady standing there was tall and bulky. She was wrapped in a charcoal-gray overcoat and wore black calfskin gloves and a scarlet wide-brimmed felt hat.

"How's tricks on the other side of the river, Detective?"

Her voice was a sandpaper rasp that seemed to have trouble locating its true pitch. She leaned forward until her elbows rested on the bar.

Vincenti stared at the woman's reflection. "Tommy. Hey, Tommy."

He swiveled on his stool and they shook hands. They were old friends – partners once upon a time on the Hoboken Police Department, in what seemed another lifetime. Tommy Flaherty had in fact been one of the finest homicide investigators and toughest sons of a bitch the force had ever numbered among its members. And he'd had it all, too: a direct bead on Hampton's job, a loyal wife, three good kids, a fine home out in the suburbs. Then something went wrong. Horribly wrong. As godawful wrong as anything could go if you were a man – and a cop. The catastrophe in Tommy Flaherty's life hadn't happened all at once. It had been a long, long time in coming. And nobody, including Brian Vincenti, had had a clue.

"When you gonna quit with the 'Tommy' stuff, man?"

"Shit. Sorry. Old habits die hard."

Both Vincenti and the lady laughed, but it was a mirth tinged with melancholy.

"Forget it," she sighed heavily. "Sometimes 'Ellen' sounds fuckin' weird even to me."

Vincenti finished off his beer, and they moved to a booth. Even though it was obvious that Tommy Flaherty –

"Ellen" – was an unusual-looking woman, to say the least, she didn't attract so much as a look.

A few feet away, two young bucks dressed in black from neck to toe were shooting eight ball, a contest frequently interrupted by outbursts of their braying laughter. Vincenti tried to guess what they did for a living. Actors? Graphic designers for a Soho ad agency? NYU grad students? It pissed him off that they could be so carefree during the meat of what was a workday for the rest of the world. But he knew he was just jealous.

A rough-around-the-edges waitress with several nose piercings and a sprawling tattoo of a raptor on the back of her neck dropped menus in front of them. Vincenti went for the fish and chips. He stole a glance across the table. The fiery red enamel on the nails of Tommy Flaherty's big hands, the thinning but permed and henna-dyed hair, the pointed, tortoiseshell reading glasses perched on his wide face, were all still something of a jolt. And yet anatomically and hormonally his friend had been altered forever, into something altogether different from what he once was – a female. A faux female, anyway.

At first they gabbed over doings in Hoboken like a pair of old pros, but there was strain beneath the unenthusiastic exchange. When it got out that Tommy Flaherty had changed his sex, shock waves rippled out from the epicenter of the earthquake all over the city, and those waves hadn't disappeared, right up to this day. It was the biggest – and, it goes without saying, strangest – scandal to ever affect Hoboken government. Tommy, who had, unbeknownst to his fellow officers – including Vincenti – undergone several treatments and operations while still wearing the badge, decided to go public when he reported for duty one day wearing a goddamned *dress*. Simply put, aside from spilling the beans to his shrink, Tommy Flaherty hadn't prepared anyone, except for his wife and kids, and at the eleventh hour, Vincenti, for the firestorm that was about to come down.

Reaction from everyone at the department, from Hampton on down to the janitors, was swift and merciless. Tommy was sneered and guffawed at and immediately suspended. The story hit the papers with the impact of an atomic detonation. The *New York Times*, especially, made a *cause célèbre* out of it – but then that type of story *was* their particular cup of tea. The fallout made going on as a cop all but impossible for Tommy. His marriage wasn't destined to withstand the pressure – how could it, really, in practical terms? – and the new Ellen Smith (eventually Tommy felt compelled to change even his last name) was driven deep into the shadows, not to mention involuntary retirement. That meant a series of closet-sized studio apartments, in Jersey and across the river in Brooklyn and Manhattan, at locations she would divulge only to her best friend and former partner on the force: Brian Vincenti.

"Believe it or not, Vincenti, you happen to hold the dubious distinction of being the only person I still talk to from – what the hell am I supposed to call it? – my old life. And that includes my ex-wife and kids, who have absolutely no interest in knowing me anymore, except when they want to hit me up for more money, though I guess I can't say I blame 'em. Course there's my shrink, but she's *paid* to listen, right? Oh – and there's my attorney. They don't count as human beings most of the time anyway, so if you don't care to count Hal Berlin, no loss. They should include his invoices in that old saw about death and taxes. No matter where I move, somehow the motherfucker keeps finding me."

Vincenti let out a morbid chuckle at the memory of Flaherty's ugly civil suit, which had been settled out of court for an undisclosed sum (presumably what Ellen Smith was living on), against the Hoboken Police Department for discrimination. The bills he was referring to also included, Vincenti knew, demands for alimony and child support, which he himself would be facing sooner or later.

Ellen smiled, displaying two slightly uneven rows of oversized, nicotine-stained teeth. "Yup, it's only you now, Vincenti. Though it would be a lot smarter if we didn't have anything to do with each other. Ain't that right?"

Vincenti had nothing to say to that. For lots of reasons – reasons he tried not to think about – what Ellen was saying was true. Which was why they tried to stay away from each other most of the time. The reasons included the fact that Tommy Flaherty was just plain bad news now that he'd gotten his nuts chopped off and his cock turned outside-in. To the people who used to call him friend, the men who'd worked beside him on the Hoboken Police Department, he was a pariah. Transforming yourself into a female could do that to a guy; it could make everyone you'd ever known feel very, very uneasy in your presence.

But the biggest reason of all was unmentionable. The biggest reason was because of that hot summer night years ago, that one night that dogged him wherever he went, no matter what he was doing, and caught him off guard like a mugger when he least expected it.

When Tommy Flaherty was first in the process of becoming Ellen Smith, he'd wanted to see Vincenti, to talk to him about something, something important. More accurately, he'd asked his partner to meet him where Christopher Street dead-ends at the Hudson. In those days it had to have been very rough on Tommy Flaherty – how can it ever be easy for a grown man to accept that he's really a female under the skin? And it had to be rougher still to try and turn yourself into the opposite of what your body said you were.

But it was tough for Vincenti, too, to come to grips with what would be a cataclysmic revelation, to have to wrestle with the fact that someone he'd worked with on a daily basis, someone he'd relied on and admired, someone he'd confided in, was a freak in the eyes of the world. Because the truth was that he'd never seen it coming from Tommy Flaherty. They'd spent upwards of a dozen years working together at that point, cruising the streets of Hoboken, investigating crimes, making arrests, filing reports, briefing the press, knocking back a few pops in the pubs when their shifts were over before going home. And aside from a shroud of depression that Tommy seemed occasionally wrapped in (a condition he chalked up to the pressures of being a cop, nothing more), Vincenti hadn't picked up a thing.

And so he had to question his own *blindness*. But hell, on the other hand, why would the idea of a close friend's sex-change operation ever register on your radar in the first place, especially when the man in question was a six-two hulk like Detective Flaherty? Hey – all the other cops on the Hoboken force had missed it too.

Anyway, that's where Vincenti stood – completely in the dark – the night Tommy Flaherty asked him to come to the river and talk because he had something to tell him, something that would turn their world upside down. And while Vincenti was baffled, still oblivious to what awaited him, he'd done what any good pal would do under the circumstances.

Why the hell there, on Christopher Street, he'd asked.

"Just be there. You'll see."

It had to have been something to do with a pair of open Hoboken murder cases they were looking into, Vincenti remembered thinking. But why the West Village? He couldn't figure it out.

But he'd been too busy at the time to think about it further. What he hadn't expected to confront when he got there was an unsightly middle-aged transvestite with badly applied makeup. And in fact he didn't even recognize his buddy when he stood at the mouth of the pier looking up and down the asphalt spoor at the joggers, roller-bladers, cyclists, and milling homosexuals on the lookout for a connection ...

Vincenti shook his head. He wasn't down on the Christopher Street Pier anymore. He was in the Hideout, sitting across from someone who used to be Thomas Flaherty. He'd been mugged yet again.

He spent the next fifteen minutes filling Ellen in on the death of Gail Kenmore. In the telling he realized all over again how little he had. Which was why he'd wanted to see his ex-partner in the first place: he'd always considered the former Detective Flaherty a master, as good as a crack profiler, when it came to the workings of the human mind – even if Tommy's own was an impenetrable mystery to himself. That fascination with character was what had drawn them together, made them stay in touch with one another, even when they were no longer side by side on the job.

There was other glue, too. Like that Tommy Flaherty had saved his life when Vincenti's back had been turned during the handling of a routine 240 – simple misdemeanor assault – down in the projects, and some Librium-deprived maniac came charging at him with a butcher knife.

And that he'd introduced him to Reggie.

The glue had long ago come unstuck, but some of it was still congealed around the surfaces.

"So tell me – how – and why – does a twentysomething girl with her whole life ahead of her do a swan dive out an eleventh-floor window?" mused Vincenti after he polished off the last morsel of his spicy batter-fried cod.

Ellen laid down her fork. "Good question. Maybe she was terminal?"

"No indication. But the autopsy's not in yet."

Ellen made an awkwardly dainty swipe at her mouth with her napkin, pushed aside her unfinished Caesar salad and shook her large head. "But let me tell you, at this stage of the game I've learned that good questions never have a simple answer – or a single answer. I only have to think about myself to – shit, you get what I mean. But at the end of the day, the truth of the matter is that it happens all the time. People off themselves.

And I don't give a damn about the notes they leave – nobody really knows why. Kind of like Jesus Christ rising from the dead, you know? Nothing you can do to make sense of it."

"I guess," Vincenti concurred half-heartedly, though he himself didn't believe that anyone had ever come back from the grave, and he couldn't believe that Ellen Smith did either, despite their heavy-handed Catholic upbringings. "But remember – remember when you and I would do a crime scene and know within a matter of minutes what was what? Nothing at this scene makes any sense, Tommy – fuck, sorry – Ellen. Nothing really adds up to anything, except for –"

"She jumped." Ellen gazed at her old partner steadily.

Vincenti thought it over yet again. "Well ... I dunno. I really don't. All I can say is that something doesn't seem right. And, by the way, she *didn't* leave a note."

"Sometimes the explanations are right there, man, they practically smack you in the face. So don't go getting carried away with this thing. And don't be too hard on yourself. I mean, what's the –"

Vincenti pursed his lips. "Hey, normally I wouldn't give it a second look, but it's like there's a lid on it or something. Even though there probably isn't. Problem is, I can't seem to get anywhere at all with the damned thing."

"You mean –"

"Well, nobody really seems to know anything – it's one of those numbers. The guys who work in the building, their opinions cancel each other out. The neighbors are like monkeys – see nothing, hear nothing, know nothing. It's Kitty Genovese all over again. And I know you're old enough to remember *her*, so don't try to deny it."

"That's the fucking asphalt jungle for you."

"And I wouldn't put it past a couple of those characters to have been in her apartment ..."

"Talked to the roommates?" said Ellen, lifting her coffee mug with thumb and forefinger, fat, gnarled pinky extended into space like a duchess's.

"Not yet – looks like they took off for the hills. Totally spooked, no doubt. Eventually I'll get to them, but tell you the truth, I don't expect much, way this thing's going. Plus, Hampton doesn't give a fuck one way or another, so there's no –"

"She got family?"

"Her father – you know, the voice on the answering machine I told you about. Though I haven't talked to him personally. Funeral's tomorrow. I'm hoping to attend."

"Ah. Tricky. Funerals have never been my favorite occasions to conduct interviews. Most times the principals are in no shape to talk."

"Tell me about it. But sometimes you can get a feel for things."

"True. But what you need, my friend, is more solid shit. I mean, hiking out to Long Island for a funeral – hell, that might be nothing but a wild goose chase. And on Saturday morning? Don't you have better things to do?"

'More solid shit' was cop-speak for when an investigation wasn't turning up anything worthwhile.

"So – what else?" said Ellen.

"What else, what?"

"Like what else is eating you about this thing? Like why do you even give a damn in the first place? It's not like this is the first side-sooey you've ever seen."

"You're right about that ..."

"But something's got you, though, right? I can smell it."

"It's crazy."

"Lay it on me."

"Ah – I don't know. It's ... nothing."

"If there was 'nothing,' there would be no 'it.' Right?"

"Well, what it is, is ..."

"Yeah?"

"You're gonna think I'm losin' it here."

"*Me?* Oh, sure – I'm the first person to cast judgment. Me – a guy who turned himself into Janet Reno's twin."

"All right, then ... I saw her picture in the apartment. I don't know – for a second or two there, she kinda looked ... familiar."

"Familiar. How do you mean, familiar?"

Vincenti stopped short of talking about the kid. *That* kid, and that night out on the Christopher Street pier. It was a subject they never touched, never went near.

"Who knows ... Like I said, it's nothing. One of those weird fucking things that just comes into your mind and –"

The corners of Ellen Smith's mouth turned downward in a frown. "Shit's getting to you, is what you're saying."

"I don't know – maybe."

"Sooner or later it happens to all of us – cops, I mean. You been good so far, Vincenti, you gotta keep that in mind."

"Think so? Think I've been good?" asked Vincenti emotionlessly.

"Good as any of us can be. You fucked up here and there, but you been through a lot. For Christ's fucking sake – look at *me*."

What could he say to that?

"Y'know, Brian," said Ellen Smith, lowering the shaky remnants of her baritone to a whisper, "I really appreciate you not jumping ship on me. I mean it. Especially after –"

Her beefy hand made a futile, nearly imperceptible move to go for Vincenti's. Vincenti didn't pull back, but he was relieved that the gesture wasn't completed. Some part of him would never stop believing that Ellen Smith was really still Tommy Flaherty, but that wasn't the whole of it.

"Yeah, well ..."

A blunted fury lurched into life inside of Vincenti. There were things he wanted to say, that he could have said, but he didn't want to, not now. It wasn't the time or place.

"So," continued Ellen in a conscious attempt to change the subject, "should I or should I not ask about your lovely wife?"

"Don't bother. It's ugly. And it's bound to get uglier."

Ellen shook her head with mock reproof. "These goddamn women. They'll always let you down. Especially the beauties. And to think I'm the one responsible."

Vincenti didn't react. The remark was loaded, and both of them knew it. They were remembering how Tommy Flaherty met Reggie McLean when he was investigating a homicide in an apartment that Uptown Realtors was the agent for, how he found out she was single and relatively new to the city, and how he suggested that she get together with a divorced buddy of his – Vincenti – if she was ever looking for something to do and wanted to get the real lay of the land. And how he'd stopped by the agency with Vincenti in tow one afternoon and made the introduction that changed his ex-partner's and Reggie's lives forever.

And they were thinking about that dead kid too, they had to be, and how he'd shown up on that goddamned pier one summer night and contaminated everything.

But Tommy couldn't be blamed for everything.

"It's not so much what's actually going on – though that's bad enough – but the fact that Reggie and I never talk. Not that I was always the best when it came to marital 'communication'. But even a 'Good morning' or 'How was your day?' would be a bonanza these days. It's the Cold War all over again, with no relief in sight, know what I mean?"

Ellen snorted. "Maybe that's part of the problem – that you remember the Cold War."

"If it wasn't me you were busting on, Smith, I'd find that very funny."

"So what are you going to do?"

"Who the fuck knows ... The really messed-up part of it all is that my boy picks up on what's happening."

"They pick up on everything," interrupted Ellen. "I know from when I used to be a –"

Vincenti's eyebrows arched. He was genuinely curious about how his old friend might complete her thought. But she didn't.

"One way or another I gotta get him out of there – or get myself out – before his mind is poisoned forever," Vincenti went on. "He's old enough now where it could happen, for sure."

Ellen nodded, a little guiltily. Vincenti wanted to ask how Tommy Flaherty's own kids – two adolescent boys and a girl – were coping with the fact their father was now a sort of absentee or runaway second mother, but he wasn't in the mood to inflict pain. The only reason to ask in the first place was because the answer would probably make him feel a little less miserable about himself.

"You ever need anything ..."

"What can you do for me?" Vincenti fired back testily.

"Just be careful with this here suicide thing," warned Ellen, letting out a tired stream of air. She tapped the tabletop with the tip of her fingernail. "Don't let it become something about you instead of what it really is. You got enough shit on your plate."

Just then the check arrived. Without looking at it, Vincenti and Ellen tossed twenties onto the plastic tray.

"You and me, man, we got things ... secrets – that make us different," Ellen whispered somberly after the waitress whisked the tray away. "You always gotta keep that in mind. You have to be careful, whatever you do, that what you're carrying doesn't destroy you. Because it's like we have a disease. A deadly disease."

"No thanks to you," said Vincenti.

A demented smile, exacerbated by her less than expert application of lipstick, appeared on Ellen Smith's face as she pushed herself sideways out of the booth.

"What do you want me to say?"

———

Back at headquarters there was a spate of phone messages for Vincenti. One was from Hugh Kenmore, with the details of his daughter's funeral service, which he quickly wrote down.

Then Hampton buzzed to let him know there was a suspect in the Fuentes rape case. The guy was in the building right now and Vincenti should get his ass down there and talk to him ASAP.

"By the way – where the hell have you been?"

"Long lunch."

"On the *job*?"

"A little. Don't worry – I'm not filing a voucher."

"Nice. *Lunch* ... I should do that myself sometime."

The bastard actually sounded cranky. Did Hampton surmise that he still had contact with Tommy Flaherty? It wouldn't shock him if word had gotten around. Despite the size of the city on the other bank of the Hudson, it could still be a small world.

Vincenti grabbed his notebook, a pen, a box of Marlboro regulars and a plastic lighter from the top drawer of his desk and took the rear stairwell to the bowels of the building where suspects were questioned, booked, processed and held; sometimes for an hour, sometimes overnight, sometimes longer; usually until bail was posted, unless the offense was serious enough to warrant immediate transfer to the Hudson County Jail in Jersey City. A quarter of the way down the scarred concrete steps, the stench of sweat and piss wafted into his nostrils. It depressed Vincenti whenever he had to come down here. It wasn't just the putrid odor that bummed him, but what was likely to happen. No matter how good a job he did breaking a suspect down, the likelihood that the scumbag would walk free was increasing by the day on account of any number of scenarios: the street officer might have screwed up when taking the alleged perp down, or evidence wasn't gathered properly, or, further down the line, if the case ever made it through the judicial maze to trial, the jury wouldn't be able to make up its mind whether or not to convict. Ever since O.J. Simpson wriggled off the hook after carving up his ex-wife and her boy toy, it was tough to make a charge stick on damned near anybody, especially if the case got any kind of media exposure. You practically had to have a crime on videotape these days to get anyone to believe it had actually *happened*. In fact, you had to wonder who was actually *doing* all the evil things that happened in the world. It had reached the point where Vincenti hardly cared what happened anymore.

Rodriguez at the processing desk pointed down the hall opposite the holding tanks.

"He's in number three, all by his lonesome. Name's Mohammed Phillips. Here's his log-in and rap sheet."

Rodriguez slid a few eight-and-a-half-by-eleven computer printouts across the gouged surface. Vincenti's eyes moved swiftly through the clusters of words. Phillips was twenty-five. He lived down in the projects and was currently unemployed. His priors were marijuana possession, possession of downers, another pot bust – this time with suspicion of intent to distribute tacked on – and simple assault. All the arrests went down in Hudson County, but shit, they amounted to pretty much nothing. Phillips wasn't even on *probation*. And nothing at all to do with sex. Interesting. Criminals usually stuck to the same class of offense.

The Xerox of a newspaper clipping was attached; it carried the most fascinating fact about Mohammed

Phillips: he'd attended a big-time Midwestern university, Ohio State, on an athletic scholarship. Vincenti vaguely remembered now: the suspect had been touted as one of the most ferocious outside linebackers ever to play college football – another Lawrence Taylor – a dead lock to go in the first round of the NFL draft, until he blew out his knee a few games into his junior year. After which he never played another down.

"Why the hell was this guy brought in?" said Vincenti when he was through reading.

Rodriguez turned his palms over. "Naughton and Villas found him loitering in the area."

"*Loitering?* What the hell does that have to do with –"

Just then Villas exited the locker area cradling his yellow helmet – he was about to head out again on bicycle patrol.

"What's the story with this Phillips dude?" asked Vincenti, walking over.

He was doing his best to keep his pique in check. Herm Villas was very young and very ambitious. And very fucking stupid. A product of Hoboken's large upwardly mobile Hispanic population, he'd come straight out shortly after joining the force and announced to anyone who would listen that he was going to be chief someday – that kind of ambition, that kind of stupidity. The kind that hung a 'TARGET' sign on your back.

Vincenti noticed that every jet-black hair of Villas' head was gelled into place and that his mustache was so perfectly trimmed that it looked pasted on. The hard black marbles that were his eyes were fierce with humorless intensity.

"For the past week or so I've noticed the guy hanging out

on the corner of Jefferson and Sixth near the Contreras fruit stand. Sometimes with his homies, sometimes by himself. Like he owns it. So I kept an eye on him, since I never saw him in that area before." Villas tapped his temple. "Happens to place him in the vicinity of the Fuentes attack in the same general time frame. Since we got nobody else to talk to on that case, I figured why not bring him in so's you two could have a little chit-chat."

And busting Brian Vincenti's case sure would look good on your next departmental write-up, wouldn't it?

"I was gonna do it myself, but I got pulled in on the sixty-five down on Monroe and Fifth."

Code sixty-five. Burglary. By now Villas was smiling, like a kid who'd done his household chores and expected congratulations – or thanks, but was so conscientious about his next assignment that he couldn't hang around to accept them.

"Okay."

Vincenti decided to squelch the urge to reprimand Villas for wasting his time. Besides, departmental protocol dictated that you took your brothers up on a favor. And maybe there was something to Villas's suspicions. He had to admit that he wasn't giving the Fuentes case the attention it deserved. But he stopped short of thanking his fellow officer.

Phillips was slumped in a chair, chin in hand, staring at the floor, when Vincenti opened the door. He didn't appear to be nervous or depressed – maybe he was resigned to yet one more rabbit punch from fate.

"I'm Detective Vincenti."

Scowling, Phillips looked up.

There was nothing else in the room except for an empty chair. The unshaded light fixture hanging from the center of the ceiling gave off a sickening glare.

Phillips said nothing, looked away, shifted in his seat. His hard muscles quivered beneath his outfit – orange sweatshirt and baggy black warmups – whenever he moved. It passed through Vincenti's mind that this boy could be at least a general fit for Maria Fuentes' attacker.

He grabbed the empty chair and shimmied its legs into the floor, then sat face to face with the suspect.

"Know why you're here, Mohammed?" he asked, reaching into his jacket pocket.

He flipped open the box of Marlboros. Phillips hesitated before reaching over and plucking out a cigarette.

"Uh-uh," he grunted.

"Not supposed to do this in here anymore, but what the hell, right?" Vincenti muttered, as if talking to himself. "Sometimes a guy needs a smoke." He produced the lighter from the same pocket and flicked a flame into life. He wanted Mohammed Phillips to know that he was a different kind of policeman – he wasn't above cutting a fellow a break.

Phillips took a deep drag and squinted his eyes.

"Well, here it is. Seems Officer Villas – you know who he is, right? – thinks you might know something about –"

Vincenti paused and brushed the smoke away from his face. As he did, he watched for Phillips' reaction to his broken thought.

The suspect's brow knotted and Vincenti saw his body vibrate ever so slightly. "'Bout what?"

"He didn't tell you?"

"Said somethin' bout some shit went down on Jefferson Street. And I told him I din't know nothin' 'bout nothin' over there. Ain't my turf."

"No? Where is your turf, Mohammed?"

A cryptic smile appeared on Phillips' lips. He wasn't giving anything up.

"Mm-hm. Don't know anything ... So – what you been up to these days, Mohammed?"

Switching subjects on a dime was one of Vincenti's favorite tactics. It could really open up the playing field, so to speak.

Phillips' eyes narrowed. "Like – whatchu mean?"

"Like ... what have you been doing for a living? Like how you making ends meet?"

"Been drawin' on my Swiss bank counts, know what I'm sayin'?" A sneer twisted Phillips' mouth.

Vincenti nodded. "Must be nice."

"Sure is. And when they dip too low, I sell off some a my stocks."

"*Very* nice ... So, in between your adventures in high finance, you work a job or anything?"

"I pick up stuff here and there. 'Counta people like you, I can't get a muthafuckin' steady job."

Vincenti didn't know whether he was being reviled as a white male or a cop, or both. He was genuinely curious to know, but didn't want to disrupt the flow of the conversation to ask.

"How about lately? Who you been working for lately?"

"Lately – nothin'. Been slow – know what I'm sayin'."

"Well, whatcha been doing to kill the time? Especially since you're not playing ball anymore?"

For the first time Phillips seemed mildly interested in the conversation. "You know 'bout me playin' ball? How you know about me playin' ball?"

"Easy enough. You made the local papers. And some information travels with your record."

Vincenti assumed that the suspect was under the influence right now, of something heavy probably, like smack or ludes, but the curtain had parted and an emotion tugged at the corners of the suspect's eyelids and mouth. It had to be tough to have enjoyed your moment in the sun as a raw youth and lose the chance to ever get close again, to be consigned forever to the footnotes, or worse, to the police log of the newspaper.

"So how about it, Mohammed?"

"Aw, man, I dunno. My mama take care of me, know what I'm sayin'? That good enough for you?"

It took a few seconds for Vincenti to decipher what Phillips was saying – his speech was a little slurred.

"That who you live with, your mother?"

Phillips shrugged.

So – the kid was probably lying. Which meant nothing. Or it meant that Phillips was using, and that he didn't have a regular source of income. Like a lot of other lost fuck-ups on the street. Maybe he was trafficking again, but if he was, it had to be strictly small-time, or else he would have shown up on the radar screen before today. Vincenti cleared his throat. "Okay. Let's quit fucking around here. I want you to get real here with me, man. You been hanging around

Jefferson and Sixth the past few days. Mind telling me why?"

"Got some friends down there, man. No other reason." Anger flared in Phillips' coal-colored eyes.

"Ever make any connections round there, Mohammed – you know, dope connections?"

"Nah, man, I'm off 'at shit a long time now. Never touch the stuff."

"Not even a little Dona Juanita? Some Texas Tea once in a while?"

"Nah. No way. Like I say, I'm off 'at shit."

Vincenti leaned forward. "That why you're fucked up now, Mohammed?"

Phillips chuckled. "I ain't fucked up, man. You the one fucked up."

"Then why's your mouth moving in slow motion? And what about those stars in your eyes? What are they from – the sheer joy of being alive?"

Fury, sheepishness and confusion collided in Phillips' gaze. The detective had him exactly where he wanted him. It was amazing that Phillips wasn't screaming for a lawyer. He had to know the drill, having been brought in a half-dozen times before. Every last lowlife on the street knew his rights. Then again, he hadn't been charged with anything; Villas had explained to him that he was just being asked to answer some questions.

"Know where the Chesterfield Gardens are, Mohammed? Ever been inside that place?"

Phillips pumped his shoulders again.

"Wouldn't've happened to be near there yesterday – like, say, about eleven in the morning?"

Phillips shook his head violently and rapidly – too much so, thought Vincenti. The clouds in his brain had suddenly cleared up, and he was fully awake and aware now. Heat from the pigs will do that to you.

"Uh-*uh*. Nuh. I wasn't nowhere near there."

Vincenti leaned back slowly in his chair. He'd know the right moment to pick up the tempo. But now it was time for another detour.

"Got yourself a squeeze these days, Mohammed?"

Mohammed Phillips was a handsome kid. Kind of *looked* a little like O.J., come to think of it. Vincenti couldn't imagine he'd have much trouble scoring pussy, though that ability, he knew, had nothing to do with whether or not a man was a rapist.

"Hunh? Why you wanna know?"

"Because I'm interested in whether you're getting it regular. You know what I'm talking about. Cooze. *Mogambo*. That's what I want to know."

"I get it when I need it."

"Mind giving up her name?"

"Her name?"

"Yeah. Your main squeeze's name. Unless you get so much pussy you can't remember."

Phillips sniffed and appeared to be thinking it over.

"Understand the question? Or do you need me to spell it out for you?"

He took his time answering. "Elisha Wilkins, 113 Varick Street, Jersey City. 989-3777."

"Whoa-whoa-whoa there ... slow down. Slow down." Vincenti reached into his inside breast pocket for his notebook. He asked Phillips to repeat the information.

In the retelling, some of the information got jumbled. Was it the dope, or had Philips been lying through his teeth the first time?

"This girl, Elisha – she good to you, Mohammed?"

"How you mean, she 'good' to me?"

"You know what I mean. She keep you ... satisfied?"

"She do all right by me. Better than your bitch do for you – if you even got one."

As many times as this sort of thing had happened to Vincenti over the years, it could still take him by surprise, ruffle his feathers a little. And as far as Reggie was concerned, Phillips had hit the nail right on the head, he thought bitterly.

He floated the question again.

Phillips' nose flared like a bull's. He was indignant. "*Mutha-fucka*. What the fuck you –"

"See, what I want to know, Mohammed, is whether you ever forced yourself on any woman."

"Get outta here with that shit, man! No way! Uh-uh, no fuckin' way, man! That's whatchu tryin' to stick on me?"

Spittle flew out of the suspect's mouth as he went on vehemently denying the detective's insinuation. Whether or not he was guilty of anything, Vincenti seemed to have touched a sensitive nerve. Maybe this kid was all sensitive nerves.

"All right, let's try again – you ever rape anybody?" Phillips had had the gall to insult him, so he was going to push back a little harder. He was human – it was human nature.

"This shit's what I'm down here for? For this muthafuckin' shit?" Phillips' voice had risen half an octave. It sounded to Vincenti like fear had supplanted his rancor. He was practically yelling now.

"For *rape? Man*, I never touched no goddamn bitch! Never! Tell you what, mutha-fucka – I had me more free white ass than you ever even seen!"

"How do you know she was white, Mohammed?"

"Who else live in that place? Huh? Who else?"

Vincenti paused. The Chesterfield Gardens wasn't one of the spanking new yuppie digs in Hoboken. All kinds of people lived there – white, Hispanic, black, Asian. Maybe Phillips hadn't ever been inside the Chesterfield. Maybe he *was* telling the truth.

"Did you commit a rape yesterday in the parking garage of the Chesterfield Gardens? How about it, Mohammed?"

Phillips squirmed in his chair. His nerves had begun to get the best of him. And why not, thought Vincenti coldly. He was being accused of a major-league offense, something that could send him up the river for a long time, decades. If he wasn't demanding his Miranda rights or an attorney by now, it was only because in his confusion he'd forgotten to.

"So how about it, Phillips?"

"No! No fuckin' way!"

"Where were you on Thursday morning, just before noon?"

Phillips eyes were like twin laser beams gone berserk in the night, darting here and there, bouncing off the walls. "Thursday morning?"

"Thursday morning. Think hard. Think real hard."

"How the fuck do I know! But I wasn't committin' no rape, and you can take that to the bank!"

"Any *ideas* where you might have been? In case I want to check up on it?"

"My momma's place ... Yeah, that's where I was."

"You're lying."

"I ain't fuckin' lyin'."

"Can she verify what you're saying?"

"Aw, man. How the fuck should I know? She wasn't there at the time."

"Come on, Phillips, don't jerk me around."

Vincenti kept his eyes fastened on Phillips as he assessed the situation. Aside from a few flakes of dried semen on Maria Fuentes' underwear, forensics hadn't come up with a shred of evidence so far: no blood, not even pubic hairs. He was wearied by the idea of having to sit here and grill this loser for another hour when he already had the feeling he wasn't getting anywhere anytime soon. Moreover, he had no clue whatsoever that Mohammed Phillips was the person he was really after. In fact, he half-*believed* the kid.

Nevertheless, he led Phillips over the same ground two or three more times, but still came up empty. Not a chink in his armor, aside from that BS about being at his mother's apartment.

"Would you voluntarily submit blood and hair samples for testing?"

No response. Not even a shake of the head.

"Okay, Mohammed. I got other business to tend to. We'll have to talk it all over again later."

"Not without no lawyer, we won't."

Ah. So there it was. Phillips wasn't that out of it after all.

"That's your right."

"You mean I can go?"

There was a speck of disbelief in Phillips' voice. When he was half out of his chair, Vincenti leaped up like a rabid fox, grabbed him by the sweatshirt and yanked his mouth close to his nostrils.

"Wha-what the fuck you doin', man?"

It was a surreal moment. Was Phillips afraid that Vincenti was actually going to lay one on him – *kiss* him?

Too funny. Too fucking funny.

Nevertheless, with those few words, the detective collected some hard evidence – even after a cigarette, Phillips' breath didn't match Maria Fuentes' dog-shit description.

Vincenti was wasted. He decided to pack it in for the day. Hampton was on the phone in his office when he stopped by after coming back upstairs.

"... not our jurisdiction," Hampton was explaining into the mouthpiece. "You know how much I'd like to help you out, Dick, but right now we're a little short-handed. Tell you what. Run it past Blumenthal – that's what I'd do if I were you."

Blumenthal. The DA. Vincenti knew from the names being bandied that it was Jersey City on the phone, asking for help on the suspected arson of an ancient Baptist church near the waterfront two days earlier. After listening for a few more seconds, Hampton rolled his eyes in Vincenti's direction. Jersey City was always begging for something.

"Just wanted to tell you," mouthed Vincenti, "nothing on Mohammed Phillips."

Hampton covered the mouthpiece with his soft hand. That hand was more feminine than Ellen Smith's hand, which made no sense, the way most things in life didn't. "That the guy Villas brought in?"

"Yup."

"Nothing at all?"

"Not so far."

"Stay on him?"

Vincenti made a supplicating motion with his palms, which could have been interpreted as a yes. He didn't know what he was going to do. He wasn't interested in Mohammed Phillips, wasn't really all that interested in Maria Fuentes, despite the terrible thing that had happened to her. And that was odd, too, because he was the kind of cop who once upon a time had been conscientious to the point of zeal when it came to his duties and the people they impacted. He couldn't say that he cared that way anymore ... Just the same, before leaving the building, Vincenti swung by his office and put in a call to the victim. Maria Fuentes was at home, still evidently unable to deal with returning to her job, or the world at large.

"I did what I could with this man we picked up," he explained with as much empathy as he could muster, "but he wasn't giving up anything, if he was involved. So far as I can tell, he's not our guy. Course we'll keep an eye on him, but I think it's best right now if we move on to other leads."

The problem – he didn't say it aloud – was that there *were* no other leads.

Maria's responses were foggy, even half-comatose. He promised to do everything in his power to bring her assailant to justice, but when she changed the subject and began complaining of depression, Vincenti felt impotent. Maria Fuentes was going to have to endure a roller coaster of emotions, from disbelief, to anger, to grief, and so on, before she got it out of her system – if she ever did. The emotional ride she was on wasn't about to end anytime soon, and everything depended on how tightly wrapped she'd been in the first place. Vincenti wasn't a shrink, so he had no idea where she was on that ride, or how snugly she was buckled in.

"Did you make an appointment to see anyone?" he ventured.

She had an appointment with a counselor at the hospital for next Thursday, but she didn't know if she'd be able to last that long, as despondent as she felt right now. What was more, she hated what the anti-anxiety agents she'd been prescribed did to her: they sucked the life out of her, made her feel as listless as a zombie.

"And just the thought that he's still out there roaming free – that the son of a bitch might've given me some disease. I won't even know about all that for a couple more days. Why does it have to take so long to get test results?"

"I understand," Vincenti assured her.

"Do you? *And what if he decides to do this to me again?*"

"It's not likely."

"How can you be sure?"

"Well ..."

He couldn't be sure, of course. He advised her to try and hang on; he'd do what he could to get the offender off the street. In the meantime, she had to make an effort to keep herself together. Did she have any friends she could talk to? There was a women's crisis center in town – had she tried them? Sometimes, unfortunately, the apprehension process could be a drawn-out affair – and that was only the first step in bringing a criminal to justice. He was blowing smoke, but smoke was all he had.

"One more thing," he said. "Ever hear of someone by the name of Mohammed Phillips?"

"No, should I?"

Next, he dialed the number Phillips had given him for Elisha Wilkins. After a few rings he got the phone company's canned message that the number was no longer in service. He shook his head and laughed.

He would have preferred to head straight over to 209 Hudson Street after leaving headquarters to resume talking to Gail Kenmore's neighbors, but instead he turned west on Second Street. He wasn't out for exercise – he owed someone a visit.

Angelina Vincenti lived down on Addams Street, north of the high school, in a chunk of Hoboken that used to be a gritty jumble of sweatshops, stables, shot-and-beer joints and mom-and-pop corner stores. Most of the decay had been converted into chi-chi lofts and condos during the ongoing gentrification of Hoboken, except for the occasional blight, like the worn brick-row house that Vincenti's mother refused to abdicate. It was there he was born and raised, and he knew for a fact that the sharks would love nothing more than to roust the elderly woman out of that potentially lucrative property. He also knew for a fact that his mother was going nowhere until the hearse came for her.

The windows of 1217 Addams were dark. It didn't mean anything. Angelina had simply never given up conserving electricity, one of the old-fashioned customs she'd been fanatical about since before Vincenti and his brother were born. While at one time it nettled him, he now chalked the quirk up to her 'Depression mentality' – an affliction that was impossible to cure.

Rather than barging in (he had a key, but would only use it in case of emergency), he opened the storm door and rapped. Within seconds he heard the familiar creak of the floorboards. With a suck of air the inner door opened.

"Oh – it's you, Brian."

"Hi, Ma ..."

That Angelina looked no worse than the last time he saw her was a relief. Her hair was still a ball of white steel wool, her jowls still sagged nearly to her collarbone, and she still walked stiffly as a result of the war she was losing with arthritis, but the fact that she recognized her son, that her faculties remained solidly intact, counted for more than anything. Before his life had gone down the toilet, he liked to think that he'd inherit her genes and make it beyond the age of eighty with all of his marbles. Now he wasn't sure about anything.

Without a word, she backed away to let him in, the same protocol she observed every time her son came to visit. Did she realize she was doing it?

Even though it had been weeks, maybe even a couple

of months, since he'd been 'home,' there was no need to
check whether anything had changed. Because nothing
here would ever change until Angelina was gone: the carpet
was decades old, the arrangement of the ancient but still-
serviceable furniture was exactly the same, the faded paper
from his boyhood still adorned the walls. On the mantel
stood pictures of his father in his prime, himself in street
patrolman's uniform, his brother in his cleric's collar.

He followed his mother into the parlor.

"Coffee?"

"Is it fresh?"

"I brewed it only fifteen minutes ago."

"Then I'll have a cup."

Angelina, in her Coat Factory sweater and pants, moved
laboriously around the kitchen while her son sat at the
antique mahogany table a few feet away. If he felt anything,
it was a nebulous sense of guilt. He'd been largely avoiding
this house since shortly after his troubles with Reggie began.
Angelina knew about them, because he'd told her a little,
but she wasn't privy to the fine details, naturally. Nowadays
he didn't feel like talking about the situation at all.

If only his old man were still alive ... It had been a long
time, twenty years, since Gennaro had passed on, after a
lifetime spent in his cobbler's shop around the corner
near the bottom of Eleventh Street (it was gone now, the
building transformed into a gourmet grocery). Gennaro
was the victim, his son had always surmised, of the deadly
chemical fumes that pervaded his daily tasks. How else does
a strapping man with no family history develop inoperable
brain cancer at the age of fifty-eight? Even though they

never quite saw eye to eye on most things, in times of crisis Gennaro demanded nothing whatsoever of him. He might even understand what it was eating at Vincenti now. With his mother it was different.

"So how's my little grandson?" she asked after carrying two steaming coffees to the table. Vincenti remembered the yellow porcelain cups from long ago. Remarkable, that they'd survived all this time.

"Pretty good, considering. Have to get you two together soon," he offered half-heartedly.

"You know where to find me," said Angelina with defiant self-pity.

Vincenti felt chastised. Why on earth hadn't he made more of an effort to keep his mother content? What the hell was wrong with him?

He and Angelina sat listening to the loud tick-tock of the tall grandfather clock standing a few feet away, near the plastered-over fireplace.

"If you want to know what I think ... I think you should be ashamed of yourself for keeping that child away from his grandmother for so long."

He grunted. It was like a dagger in the heart. He could feel the blood rising to his face. What was he supposed to say now? Was he supposed to come out with the truth – that he couldn't find the strength to try any longer? That he'd been defeated? That nothing mattered to him, not even the relationship between his mother and his little boy?

"What did I tell you before, Ma? Didn't I tell you it wasn't my fault?"

The worst part of something like this was that it made

him sound like a crybaby. Angelina didn't know the first thing about her son's life – it would be all the worse if she did – the real reasons behind certain difficult circumstances, and he wasn't about to enlighten her. All his mother knew was that her son was a cop – a good cop, she was convinced – and there was absolutely no reason on earth his life shouldn't be successful in the personal realm too.

Vincenti scooped up his cup and went to stand at the kitchen window that looked out on the two-by-four backyard, the postage stamp of crabgrass and eroded bricks that had been his childhood playground. It had been a mistake to come here today. And it wasn't just the current disaster that tainted the atmosphere, it was also the failures of the past that hung over him like a miasma.

For instance, there was his first marriage, the one that ended after only two years, the casualty of his obsession with the job, back in the early days, when being a Hoboken cop still meant something to him ...

Sandy. Sandy had split one night when he was working the graveyard, staking out drug deals down in the projects. When he got back to the apartment on Washington Street in the morning, the place looked as nude as if it had never been inhabited by human beings at all. She'd made off with everything but the kitchen table and the dust balls sitting forlornly in the corners. Why, she hadn't even left him a chair to sit on, which to this day he still found grimly amusing.

The saddest thing was that he and Sandy really were cut out for each other, he saw that in retrospect, and he saw it very clearly, though he'd been blind to it at the time. Life was always such a goddamned devious proposition. You never knew what you had until it was too late. There was an edge to that girl, a razor-sharp daring that complemented him, an untamed streak that drove her to do things like jump out of planes, or scuba-dive with sharks, or pose naked for his instamatic camera.

Sandy was Jewish to boot (he thought of her whenever he happened to see a photo of the young actress Natalie Portman), but not your typical Westchester princess, not at all. They'd met in a bar on the Upper West Side, and he liked that she was different, that she hadn't married a doctor or a Wall Street suit, that she was open to dating someone like him – a goy, a guy from the streets. That, of course, was part of the allure for someone like her. But her headstrong attitude was the very thing that ultimately drove them apart. When the bad times arrived, as they inevitably do in any marriage, she was about as easy to deal with as a trapped wolverine. And when she was finished with Vincenti, she was finished for good. There was no talking her out of anything once her mind was made up. Come to think of it, maybe most women were that way, especially the new, updated, liberated models.

"I can do better than this," were the last words she ever spoke to him in anger. He knew what had done them in – his endless hours on the street, the nights when after being assigned a fresh homicide he never came home at all and stayed away for two or three days running. There was also this: Sandy had quickly grown bored being a cop's wife, and that part was only going to get worse the longer they went on together. And at her age – twenty-six – what was the point? She had her own job, as an account exec for a hip clothing manufacturer in the city, she could take care of herself, so what was the point?

"Go ahead and try! Be my guest! And I hope he's a very nice mama's boy!" he'd challenge her whenever she threatened him like that, though he should have known better, should have realized she would take him up on the dare. On the other hand, maybe he'd known what was going to happen all along, that one day Sandy would wake up to the chasms between them and say to hell with it, and him. Still, her decampment had come as a rude shock; it always does, even when you half-expect it. It's the quiet, the stillness, where once there was life, that comes as such a jolt – that brings a man into confrontation with his own pathetic self. Walking into their unlocked apartment that morning was something he'd never forget as long as he lived. It was like finding himself in a cemetery.

Those are the moments you remember, Vincenti reflected now. For a long, long time – almost two years – he'd been unable to have sex with another woman. He'd never let on to anybody, not even his friends: that's how good he and Sandy had been together. "I'll kill you, you ever walk on me," he'd warned her more than once, and he didn't know himself whether or not he'd been serious about the threat. But he knew that she'd believed him. When it happened, he'd done nothing except make some intimidating phone calls when he finally tracked her to her sister's house up in Nyack, but after a little while it seemed absurd, and he got embarrassed and gave up. It was nothing that hordes of other dumped men hadn't done, he had to sometimes remind himself. He'd just been human.

In the present, though, Vincenti never felt sorry for himself whenever he thought of Sandy, wherever his ex was these days. To go on in life, to survive, you had to carve out pieces of your heart.

"You look tired, sonny boy."

It was Angelina, cracking into his reverie.

"Maybe because I am."

"You should take it easier. Take some time off, go down to Florida and see your brother. Little Nicky would like that. You could take him on his first trip to Disney World."

The detective's younger brother was one more component of the family portrait that had gone very awry. There was something different about Salvatore even as a child, everyone could see that. It wasn't just the unearthly blue eyes or his fair hair – recessive genes from his ancestors in the north of Italy – that set him apart, but, as he grew, his fierce devotion to the Catholic Church. Most kids in the neighborhood were altar boys briefly, but for Salvatore it was more than a Sunday duty, more, even, than a garden-variety vocation – it was an unearthly preoccupation. And in those days, no one thought for a second that it was unhealthy. And that was all right with Angelina and Gennaro, since for them Rome's Church was the *alpha* and the *omega*, and sacrificing one of their sons on its altar was viewed as a privilege that would pretty much assure their places in Heaven. And so Sal went straight into a seminary in Maryland after parochial school in Hoboken, the nuns and priests there having agreed unanimously that this was one boy who had heard the call early, loudly, and clearly, and that there could be no better destiny for one of God's own than the priesthood. Sal made it all the way, becoming Father Dominic Vincenti, but in the process he also tumbled into a dark cave that his brother, mother and father had not suspected the existence of.

Father Dominic had thrived even during the years he'd spent behind monastic walls, but once he got out into the real world, his seams began to show. After all the perfection, something had to give. But it wasn't until he was accused of raping one of his altar boys in the sacristy of a working-class parish church in southeastern Pennsylvania that the seams turned into earthquake-wide cracks. He confided to his detective sibling a few years after the fact that he and Holy Mother Church, in the person of the bishop, struck an unholy deal behind closed doors: if Father Dominic agreed to reassignment elsewhere in the country, the Church would do everything in its power to parry any legal reverberations from the incident, and in fact was prepared to make a substantial payment for damages (on the condition that it not be made public) to the family of the alleged victim. He went for the deal, but with one drastic revision – he'd defrock himself as well in the process. He knew who he was now, he'd accepted himself as a gay man – if not a pedophile – and he needed to escape the yoke of the collar. He held that stiff white straitjacket responsible for what had happened with the underage boy – once he was able to live openly with his own kind, nothing of the sort was going to happen again. If he could just be himself, if he could breathe, he wouldn't have to take advantage of kids. Whether or not that conviction had played out in his lay life, Vincenti didn't have a clue, and he found himself not wanting to look too closely.

And Father Dominic decided that one other place he wasn't coming back to was Hoboken. After a trip to Florida to regain his bearings, Sal slipped quietly into Miami's alternative life, supporting himself by teaching courses in basic philosophy and world theology at southern Florida community colleges. On rare occasions he'd fly north for one of the holidays, still looking for all the world like a cleric, but as time went on, it happened less and less. After a trip to South Beach some years ago to check out his brother's new life, Brian decided that Salvatore had been quite lucky, all things considered. If he got caught as a priest with his hand down a minor's underwear today, he'd be facing serious jail time.

No, he wasn't taking his son anywhere, especially not to South Beach to visit his brother. Nevertheless, he said "Yeah, Ma, maybe I will."

Angelina never found out the real truth of what had happened to her precious baby. All she knew was that "Sal decided the priesthood wasn't for him after all," and that he'd found his true calling as a teacher in the semi-tropical sun. While she was brokenhearted by his defection from the church, and that he hardly ever came home anymore, she was able to live with that excuse for her crushed dream. Maybe she sensed the real truth. Her older son, in his desire not to inflict more pain, opted not to enlighten her on the more unsavory reasons for Salvatore's flight into the night.

And that qualified Angelina as lucky, too, Vincenti often thought. Because discovering that your closest blood relative was at best a misfit, at worst a deviant or pervert, had the effect of a tick under a person's skin, sucking the blood out of him slowly but stealthily and lethally. And he wasn't perfect either. Far from it.

The funereal atmosphere of his childhood home and the onrush of unsavory memories it generated was beginning to suffocate him.

"All right, Ma, gotta go," he announced after checking his watch. He said the same thing at the end of every visit, didn't he?

Angelina pushed her chair out from the table. "Go if you have to. I know how busy you are. Don't be a stranger. Stay longer next time."

She trailed him like a lame old dog to the front door. "You don't look so good, Brian. You taking care of yourself?"

"Sure, Ma."

"You can't let this thing with Regina get the best of you."

"Ma –"

He shook his head. He wasn't going there, not now. He just couldn't deal with it.

"Bye, Ma."

"Goodbye, my *bambino*."

The street was deserted. There was a lump in Vincenti's throat. He sucked in a deep breath of the clammy Hoboken air and began to walk. What was the point of putting himself through that? To assuage his guilt, that's what. Sometimes it seemed that his life was determined by nothing but the devious machinations of guilt.

Angelina was old. Her eyesight was failing, and despite his pleas she refused cataract surgery. Her blood pressure was a problem, too, and she was having more and more trouble walking. One of these little visits was going to be Vincenti's last. Despite the horror of death, it would be a relief.

Friday evenings always made the detective feel out of sorts. Whenever the premier party night of the week descended on Hoboken, he was tugged back in his mind to his days as a single man on the prowl, to that period of several wild years after he finally snapped out of his funk over the loss of Sandy, and spent his off-duty hours in the bars and clubs of Manhattan and North Jersey, picking up all kinds of women and finishing up the night at either their place or his. For some reason his luck had always been best on Friday night, and before the AIDS plague threw a wet blanket over the scene, it was one of the best times of his life.

But that was all in the past, a distant dream. Now that his marriage to Reggie had curdled, he was faced with the prospect of having to do the singles scene all over again, but the prospect disheartened him. For one thing, he was a lot older now, not nearly as good-looking as he was fifteen, twenty years ago. For another, the idea of having to hear himself lay down a line to a babe was enough to make him puke.

Instead of turning up Eighth Street, he kept walking. He wasn't up to going back home yet. Hell, why go home at all? He didn't want his son rubbing shoulders with his demons, and he was convinced it was possible, by osmosis. Besides, Vonda was on duty – it was the one night of the week she least minded staying late since her husband usually went out after work to drink with his cronies. As for Reggie, she wouldn't be pulling in until late, no doubt ...

It was still early, a sinking, mist-shrouded sun spilling gassy light over the world, but the twentysomethings were already making their way east on the numbered streets toward the center of town or Manhattan. Without thinking, Vincenti swerved and went the other way, in the opposite direction of the river. At Ninth Street he hooked a right and continued west. One by one the names and faces of the people he'd collided with over the past few days coursed through his brain in a higgledy-piggledy parade: Freddie Opallo ... Alex Danko and the other residents of 209 Hudson ... the doormen Johnny and Lenny ... the battered, pitiful Maria Fuentes ... Mohammed Phillips ... and, of course, on the center float, the mysterious Gail Kenmore. They all seemed somehow linked, even though not one of them really had anything solid to do with the next. This sort of multiple-car mind-crash happened to him when he was wiped out, and Angelina had been right on the money about that – he *was* tired.

At Madison he made a left. This was as far west as you could go in Hoboken without running smack into the projects, which was where Vincenti – and most cops – reluctantly had to spend a significant amount of their time. During the stretches when he worked the graveyard shift the projects were Vincenti's first and last stop; while the rest of Hoboken was sleeping, the projects were a seething quagmire of domestic disturbance, gang warfare, drug-dealing, rape, assault and battery, and, on occasion, murder. More than one of his colleagues had lost his life back there in that maze of triangular, fourteen-story, rat-brown tower blocks where you could never quite make out what was going on at any given minute.

That was where Daisy had come from, the projects.

At the beginning, unlike lots of his compadres on the police force, Vincenti made it a hard and fast rule never to get his dick stuck inside a wench from the projects. Too messy. And way too dangerous. And in fact for the longest time he held fast to his code – it wasn't until he ran into Daisy Salamanca up on Washington Street, out of her natural habitat, that he deviated from it. Certain women from the wrong side of the tracks had a thing for cops, it was undeniable. As it was for lots of people, forbidden fruit was the eternal enticement. By the time they crossed paths, Daisy had moved out of the projects to her own railroad flat on Madison Street, and was working as a receptionist for a dermatologist across the river in Tribeca. At that point Vincenti's troubles with Reggie were an established fact, and he was a sitting duck for the right temptation.

Across the street a bunch of Hispanic delinquents were fighting a war with toy Uzis against the backdrop of a rubble-strewn lot, where in the next few months another condo was scheduled to rise into the sky. Right now they could all have been in a Third World country, but it was only a matter of time before the yups encroached on the projects themselves and the final siege for control of Hoboken would be on. There was no doubt in Vincenti's mind who was going to win that battle.

As soon as they set eyes on him, the punks' game immediately sputtered out. As if, like chickens in a henhouse sensing a weasel, they could feel the presence of a predator.

The word "fuck" was hissed, and he knew it was directed at him. On another day he might have growled back at them, but tonight he couldn't muster the effort.

Vincenti stopped in front of 556, a drab, four-story apartment building girdled with faded yellow siding. He looked at his watch. Just after six. If she wasn't already out for the night, she was probably at home, since her doctor wrapped early on Fridays. He craned his neck at the third-floor corner window – sure enough, there was a light.

Vincenti knew what he was here for. He climbed the three steps and pushed on the buzzer for 3D.

"Who's there?" The voice in the speaker was a skeptical crackle.

"It's me – Brian."

He imagined he could detect Daisy's vacillation through the static.

"Daise –"

Vincenti propped his elbow against the door frame and rested his forehead in his palm. Why was he subjecting himself to the humiliation?

"Daise. I'm still here."

"I was just about to go out." Her voice was tight, on guard.

"Yeah, well ... I won't hold you up. I mean, if you wanted to talk for a few minutes ..."

This was more than tiresome. Just like he'd done with his mother, he and Daisy had played this scene out before. If he had it all on tape he was sure he'd find that they used the same exact words with each other, like actors beating a well-worn script to death.

"All right – but just for a minute. You gotta promise."

He had no choice but to do as she asked. If he had any dignity left, he wouldn't be playing this asinine game at all.

The door release sounded. He turned the handle, let himself in and began his trudge up the dreary wooden steps, past the soot-covered windows, and the bicycles, scooters, and strollers stored on the landings. What the hell was he doing here? Maybe he was beginning to lose his grip altogether.

On the third floor he could hear the evidence of human life as he passed each door: muffled voices, the chatter of kids at play, hyperactive salsa music. He knocked softly on D and shortly heard footsteps. The door cracked open. The black iris of Daisy's eye appeared in the aperture above the chain.

Without a word she let him in. Vincenti hadn't seen her for a while now, several weeks or so, since just after the holidays. As usual, she looked fine. Goddamned fine. Tonight she was poured into a skin-tight black suit cinched at the waist by a silver chain that emphasized the sweep of her flanks. And Christ, did she have flanks. Daisy was put together the way Vincenti liked women put together – out of succulent flesh and wicked curves, with something to grab and hold onto. Her black hair was swept straight back – he dug that, too – highlighting the prominent bones of her face, which was a blend, like the best coffee, of her African, Spanish, and East Indian forbears.

From a purely physical standpoint, Vincenti was drawn to Daisy like a magnet. Which, according to some fucked-up law of life, spelled doom for the rest of the relationship.

When their fling first kicked off, they would go at one another like a pair of starving animals the minute they were in each other's presence. He wanted to take Daisy like that right now, but things had changed between them – it wasn't so simple anymore. That fact – complexity – was what always ruined the physical side of an affair.

"Hey, baby."

Daisy shook her head at him as if he were a disobedient child. "Goddamn it, Brian. I thought you weren't going to come around anymore. I thought you were going to leave me in peace once and for all."

Having to hear something like that, even when it was true, was painful. Vincenti didn't know how to respond, except to mumble something about how they'd agreed to be friends, hadn't they?

"Friends – yeah, right. We were *never* friends, Brian."

"I tried, baby. Really, I did."

That was a lie. Not that he hadn't tried, but that he'd had to see her. It was something else he wanted from Daisy now, something he couldn't even put into words. Without doubt he missed having sex with her, but that wasn't the whole of it. But whatever he told her wouldn't matter – she was all of a piece, unlike him, and she would take his words at face value.

"I don't know if I can deal with this shit, Brian."

"Okay, you don't have to – I just stopped by to say hello." Another bold-faced lie.

Daisy turned away with a toss of her hair. "Like I said, I gotta go out, and I don't want you or anybody else interfering."

She was seeing another man. He expected that. A firecracker like Daisy was always seeing someone. Which was okay; he had no desire to be responsible in any way for her emotional well-being. Hell, he couldn't care for his own.

"You can do whatever you want, Daise."

"I *know* I can do whatever I want. You're not telling me anything I don't already know."

He let it pass. Nevertheless, she seemed appeased, at least slightly.

"You want something to drink?"

That proved it. He nodded, and followed her into the cramped kitchen at the rear of the unit, looking in en route at the bedroom where they'd spent many good hours together, and where she was now presumably spending time with someone else.

Daisy stood at the counter filling a pair of tall glasses with water from a plastic jug. A halved lemon sat on the slicing board, a serrated knife beside it. Vincenti came up behind her, moved in as close as he could without touching her. He could smell the soap and perfume on her skin. And he wanted to touch it, but he didn't try.

He watched her run the knife through the yellow sphere of fruit and drop slices of it into each glass.

"I can feel you breathing on me, you bastard."

Just as he hoped, she was already weakening.

"Hey – it's not my fault."

"It never is, is it?"

He tried to edge even closer without making contact.

"I guess it's still lousy at home, right? You poor, misunderstood husband."

This had been at the root of their impasse, or so Daisy thought; it had been chewed over ad nauseam before negotiations fatally broke down. The last thing she needed was to be doing a married man – and a cop, no less, that's what she always told him. There'd been more than a few gruesome tales in the papers over the years about how those relationships ended. But as Vincenti explained to her at least a hundred times already, he was in no position to change his life in any way until his bond to Reggie was completely – meaning legally – sundered. Sure, he was dodging a commitment to her, Daisy, but he had his son to think about, don't forget. There were other things, too – things he couldn't talk about. Secrets that maybe he should have told her instead of divulging to his wife. But he hadn't, and it was too late now to fix that. And it was too late for second thoughts.

And of course it always went straight back to that fateful evening down on the pier ...

"Here I am, Brian," Tommy had called out that evening. He'd been sitting on a bench not five feet away, getting a perverse kick out of watching his partner scan the crowd in frustration.

Vincenti had looked over both shoulders. *Where was that voice coming from?* It was Tommy's, but Tommy was nowhere to be seen.

"Here, Brian. Here."

It was some kind of joke, that's what he thought at first. Why the hell would Tommy be dressed up like that – in *drag*, for Christ's fucking sake? For some ungodly reason Tommy was playing with his head, though practical jokes had never been his thing, unlike some guys on the force.

He and Tommy sat on the bench two feet apart. Vincenti didn't want anyone, even in passing, to think they were lovers. They talked in the gathering dusk of the summer night. He kept waiting for Tommy to let him in on the joke, but he never did.

"I was gonna tell you sooner or later," Tommy confided. "It's been eating me up inside for a long, long time now. I mean, you can't even begin to imagine, Brian."

Everything came gushing out in an eruption, complete with tears, all of Tommy's torment, the heavy years of it, the insanity that would cause a human being to take a step so drastic as having his balls clipped and his penis converted into a fake woman's organ.

Vincenti was dumbstruck. Was he dreaming? He had to be ...

"You're wrong about that," he said in answer to Daisy's question. "It's worse. A lot worse."

"So why don't you get out already?"

This was the problem with people who didn't have kids – they didn't get it. "It ain't so easy, baby. It just ain't so easy."

When she turned with the glasses, she bumped him for the first time. He refused to give ground. Their lips, their bodies, were within centimeters of each other.

"How's the boy holding up?"

"He's just a baby. He'll hold up for a long time, years maybe, then it'll come down on him. Or maybe it won't, and he won't even know what's driving him crazy."

"Like you?"

When he didn't answer, Daisy pushed her pelvis up against his.

"Like you?" she repeated in a whisper.

"No. I know what's driving me crazy."

He took the glasses out of her hands, placed them on the counter, and nudged her back against the sink.

"I don't know about this, Brian. Brian –"

What he really wanted was to see his naked white skin next to Daisy's brown skin – for some reason this was a fantasy that swirled through his head ever since he'd had her the first time. Sometimes when he was at home by himself, he would pop in a porn video that he picked up at a discount outlet on Fourteenth Street, and watch a series of Caucasian men having sex with a succession of African-American women or Latinas so that he could vicariously relive his busted fling with Daisy. But it could never top the real thing.

He undid her jacket, then her blouse, and sucked in the tawny nipple of her left breast. With Daisy there had never been much in the way of foreplay, and today there was even less. It was as if desperation was built into their lovemaking. Like a dog, he chased her into the bedroom. Once they were completely undressed and he was inside her, he pulled up like a guy in mid-pushup, turned toward the mirror over the bureau, and watched his stocky white thighs parting her dark legs, and for a few seconds he felt the satisfaction that his fantasies had been realized.

The best thing about Daisy was that her physique, which was exquisite, had the power to obliterate the whole world. And Vincenti needed to have that oblivion for at least a few minutes or he would go mad. That was why he'd come today.

He didn't doubt that Daisy knew it too, and that's what made her feel abused and hostile.

But even for her, once swallowed up in the sex act, it was impossible to stop. Like mating rattlesnakes, they curled and twisted into a medley of positions. When it was over, Vincenti lay staring at the ceiling. Within a few heartbeats his satisfaction succumbed to the yawning pain he'd arrived with.

Checking the digital clock on the night stand, Daisy mumbled "Shit – now I'm gonna be late."

She reached over the side of the bed for her thong. "I gotta get out of here. Hurry up, Vincenti, I need you out of here, too. Come on – move."

She actually kicked at him, grazing his calf with her toe. But his mind was already elsewhere – on the funeral tomorrow.

Like a sleepwalker he rolled off the bed and got into his clothes, and on quivering knees staggered into the bathroom, pulled out his still-throbbing organ and pissed. The reflection coming back at him from the mirror wasn't reassuring. He looked like a man who'd been deprived of sleep for days: strung-out, wasted, the eyes hollow and staring. He was seriously ill and didn't know it – that's how he looked.

Maybe he was. He had a creepy vision: he was hurtling out of that eleventh-floor window on Hudson Street just like Gail Kenmore, flailing his arms in the doomed attempt to fly, then to grab onto something, and, just before the end, trying desperately to break his fall.

"Vincenti –"

Daisy's metallic voice cut through his hallucination. "All right, all right – I'm out of here."

He turned his back on the mirror. Daisy was standing in the bedroom door, doing something to her hair. He brushed past her and started down the hall.

Would this be the last time?

From behind him he heard her say, "I'm not doing this anymore, Vincenti. Never, okay? Get that through your thick fucking dago head."

He turned to see her kneading the diamond stud in her left earlobe. Her obsidian eyes were focused, unwavering.

"I got somebody else now, and I don't want this – *this* – fucking it up, you hear me? You fucked me up enough already, cop!"

"Whatever you say." He nodded, and kept walking.

————————

Vincenti felt lost. There was no question whatsoever that going up to Daisy's tonight had been a blunder, but there was nothing he could do about it now. It was only just after seven – he still had a night to kill. He wandered south on Madison, then up Third. Lorenzo's Grill was one of his hangs. He ducked in and grabbed a stool at the end of the bar. It was dead – the thick dinner crowds hadn't arrived yet.

"Paulie. How's it going, man?"

"Detective Vincenti. Long time no see. What can I get you tonight?"

"A beer out of the tap does it, Paulie."

Paulie Frascella had been pouring drinks at Lorenzo's

for an eternity, since long before Hoboken had been lost to the yuppies and Gen X-ers and punks, when instead of just another downtown bar it was the best stop in town for its specialty – fried calamari. Now everything had changed: establishments like Lorenzo's were giving way to high-end Indian, exotic South American, homemade Thai, dainty sushi bars, and weird Mongolian barbecues. Vincenti enjoyed them, but what he really missed were the dinosaurs like Lorenzo's, with their scuffed floorboards, their black and white autographed celebrity photos on the walls, their odors of sweaty bodies and stale perfume, rancid tobacco and pissy beer. If the fare no longer cut it, that was okay.

At a dark moment like this, Vincenti truly appreciated the lived-in feeling of Lorenzo's, the young Sinatra (the favorite son of Hoboken and its greatest hero) warbling in the background, and not least because trying to squeeze a word out of Paulie was like trying to draw the proverbial blood from a stone. The barkeep was one of those rare souls who understood at a glance when you wanted to be left alone. He was the sort who never even asked a guy about his wife.

Which was good. Because Vincenti was still preoccupied with the needles piercing his brain. Now add Daisy Salamanca to that bunch. All on account of Gail Kenmore, who'd done her chilling swan-dive out of a high-rise window and was bound to be hovering over the service tomorrow out on Long Island.

Which reminded him – he'd had another dream last night. About those nightmarish paintings this time. One of them actually, the one hanging over the dead woman's bed. In the dream, he was in the bedroom staring at it. Frozen, almost. The head in the painting looked nothing like the mountebank, though. It was a horrible gargoyle now, the kind of Beelzebub you see on some landmark New York buildings. Dead, but alive. He'd been afraid, but he didn't know why. The sight of that grotesque mishmash of color and hideousness had made him want to run. But he couldn't, for some reason. For some reason he had to stand there and keep looking at it, until his heart exploded. Or until –

Again he couldn't shake the nagging sensation that there was a connection somewhere.

Vincenti ordered another beer from Paulie, who managed to keep endlessly busy counting bottles, swabbing glasses, and holding curt, mysterious conversations on the phone. The detective envied the old dog's Zen-like absorption in the most mundane activities. He drained the second beer and asked for a third. By the time he was ready for a fourth, he was feeling the stuff, especially since he'd forgotten all about dinner and had no food in his belly to absorb it. These days, whenever he knocked a few back something a little vile, what he referred to in his own mind as a 'negative chemical reaction,' would result. Any quantity of booze seemed to cast a pall over the world, and the numb emptiness inside him deepened, like an expanding black hole in some remote corner of the universe. Sometimes his throat tightened and tears welled in his eyes, and it was all he could do to keep from breaking down. 'Bacharach' moments, he called them, like when he heard that song in his head the other night.

He had to get out of Lorenzo's. Rather than ask for a fifth beer, he got up, left a five-spot tip for Paulie, and walked out.

In the meantime, darkness had come down over the streets. Vincenti hiked toward the center of town. A vague idea had been clunking around in the back of his mind for a few hours now like an unmoored crate in the flooded hull of a boat. It had to do with Reggie. When he reached headquarters, he decided to duck inside.

The night patrols were already out, leaving the building pretty much a ghost town. Hampton liked to say that Hoboken needed bodies on the streets, not behind desks, especially after dark. Calderon was at the front desk, tapping on the computer. The telephones in the dispatcher's booth behind him jangled incessantly, but the desk officer kept at his task like an automaton. Some of the calls were being directed to other extensions. The phones that rang more than six times were going to have to be picked up and answered personally by the dispatcher or Calderon. Vincenti never could figure out how the guys on the desk could stand all the racket.

Calderon greeted him in a tired voice. He petted his coppertoned mustache and reached out for the insistent desk phone.

"Hoboken Police. Calderon."

Vincenti circled the desk and reached underneath to the key rack.

"I'm taking number 8."

Calderon cupped the mouthpiece. "You on something?"

"Just going for a little ride."

The cars were docked behind the back wall of the building. Number 8 was a black, unmarked Chevrolet Impala sedan.

Vincenti pulled out onto Hudson Street, past the moviegoers queued up for the latest runaway hit, a crappy-looking thriller starring Bruce Willis. It didn't entice him in the least – the Hollywood pap never had. He swung a left onto First Street, then another onto River, where the cold lights of Manhattan unfurled. The crest of the Empire State Building was still illuminated in shafts of emerald green, paying belated homage to the Irish holiday, and from a party boat on the river, raucous music, mostly blaring horns, floated into shore.

At Tenth Street, across from the demolished Maxwell House Coffee factory where the foundations for a spate of new townhouses were being dug, he hung a third left. Easing into a 'No Parking' zone at the intersection of Washington, he cut the engine and headlamps.

The lights inside the wide front window of the Uptown Real Estate Agency were still burning. Frank Gallagher, in jacket and tie, was as usual jawing on the phone. Gallagher was one of the agency's hot-shots. No, that wasn't quite right. He was its hottest shot. When they were first married, Vincenti had the hunch that Gallagher was after his wife. He'd suggested a motel (he was married too) once when he and Reggie were having lunch, but Reggie had been so taken aback that she'd said nothing, and nothing had come of it; in fact, she'd rushed home that night and told her husband all about it. Vincenti had laughed. He didn't feel he had to confront Gallagher, but things were different then. He and his wife were still tight, and they trusted one another implicitly; it was just before she got pregnant with Nicky. Nevertheless, he'd always thought it was a ballsy gambit on

Gallagher's part, making a blatant play for his wife, but the hotshot was nothing if not ballsy. After all, that was how he'd set records selling overpriced properties in Hoboken – by going straight for it. And he knew that he was covered, too: if things ever got hairy where Brian Vincenti was concerned, Gallagher's old man was a former mayor of Hoboken whose best friend just happened to be Chief Hampton. It was a small, sordid, incestuous world when you got right down to it. A further distasteful reality was that had Gallagher scored with Reggie, there would have been little Vincenti could have done about it, given the hot-shot agent's pedigree and connections ...

In the background bodies scurried between and around the other desks – one of them was Reggie, who was rummaging in her oversized handbag at the same time.

Vincenti checked his watch – she was due out at any second.

Somewhere – and he wouldn't be able to pinpoint where, exactly, if he were ever forced to testify to it – between Daisy's apartment, and Lorenzo's, and his brief stop at headquarters, he'd hatched a plan. It was something he'd always sworn he would never do, but everything that had happened in the past seventy-two hours – the suicide, the rape of Maria Fuentes, the interrogation of Mohammed Phillips – had played on him. His numbness had morphed into a wounded surliness. He was feeling mean, and the thought of his wife – and what she was about to do – was enough to push him right to the edge.

"Come on, baby," he whispered, "come on out ..." He pulled the plastic comb out of his left pants pocket and ran it through his hair. It was a meaningless gesture, a release for his nervous energy. Now Reggie was sitting at the desk behind Gallagher, and she was on the phone herself, animatedly yakking with someone, her thick listings directory open in front of her. At intervals she would stop talking and turn the pages of the book before opening her pretty mouth again.

"Come on, Reggie, you bitch ..."

Hearing the boozy echo of his words, he could hardly believe he was saying them about the mother of his only child. He was about to give up waiting when Reggie suddenly put the phone down, slammed her book shut, and stood up. He could almost read her lips when she addressed Gallagher – "I'm finished for the night" – before pulling her coat on and hoisting her handbag.

Once out the door she started north at a rapid pace on Washington. Vincenti hit the ignition. A fine, late-winter rain was misting his windshield. A gang of delinquents in baggy shorts and hooded windbreakers darted in front of him just as he was about to swing onto the main boulevard. The detective was furious, against the entire world. He had the wild, momentary urge to mow the kids down like so many weeds.

He could have flipped on the siren, but it would have screwed everything up, set Reggie immediately on the defensive. Tonight he wanted to follow her all the way to where she was going, that was his plan. What he'd do when he got there, he'd figure out then. By the time he turned onto Washington, she was already in her gold Audi and in the process of backing out of her space in front of Silvano's hair salon. He kept at a distance from her bumper as they moved toward the city limit. At Thirteenth, he let an SUV slip between them for camouflage ...

Vincenti didn't really have to tail his wife. He knew where she was headed – if not exactly, then generally. He'd tried following her once or twice before, just far enough to confirm who she was going to see when she claimed to be showing homes in the evenings. Sure enough, the gold roof climbed the old viaduct that marked the limits of Hoboken and was headed in the direction of the Lincoln Tunnel ...

His heart was pumping furiously. Tracking your spouse had to be the low point in any marriage, even when it was gasping its last. He wondered how Tommy Flaherty's wife must have felt when she discovered at that fateful point in their long union that she couldn't even be sure of the *sex* of the person she was married to, that she was battling a phantom rather than another human being. When your husband or wife was cheating, you had a legitimate chance of winning them back, or at least learning to live with it.

Sure enough, the Audi slipped beneath the double helix that siphoned cars in and out of the maw of the big tube into the city.

"You lousy whore," hissed Vincenti. He patted the weapon strapped to his torso. Maybe he'd end up using the damned thing tonight.

The Audi's right blinker began to flash, and it sheared off from the stream of traffic heading onto Boulevard East, with its glitzy, overwhelming view of the heart of Manhattan. Vincenti glanced into his rearview mirror. Reggie's car and his were the only vehicles on the residential street. He hit the gas, ran straight at the Audi, then swerved with a scream of tires, running it into the curb.

He took his time getting out.

"Just what the hell do you think you're doing?" demanded Reggie after lowering the window.

"I thought you were showing a condo tonight," he said casually, leaning on the roof. "Aren't you a little out of your territory?"

Even with his wife's perfect features distorted by disgust and fury, her comeliness stabbed at Vincenti.

"Fuck you, Brian. Fuck you."

"Nice words for a mom to be using."

"All right then – I hope you burn in hell, you bastard! Is that better? Now just leave me alone! I don't snoop around after you like some two-bit gumshoe, do I? Don't I have the right to a little privacy? What happened to our agreement – you go your way and I go mine? What happened to it, you louse? This is pathetic! You're pathetic!"

Reggie's vehemence had escalated into an outright scream. This was dangerous – the last thing he needed was someone siccing the Weehawken fuzz on him. Though he was on a first-name basis with nearly every one of them, a confrontation like this was always best kept in your own backyard – especially when a beautiful woman, even if it was your wife, was involved. You could never tell when some asshole would try and make a hero of himself in order to impress a damsel in distress. He'd seen it happen.

"Wanna know what I ought to –"

"Get out of my way, Brian!"

Reggie tried to pop the transmission into drive. Vincenti

reached in and shackled her arm with his fist.

"Let go of me! Let *go*, goddamn it!"

She struggled free of his grip and succeeded in jerking the stick. The vehicle lurched, forcing the right front wheel to hop the curb. Across the street a door opened and a yellow mutt bounded onto the front lawn. The animal immediately launched into a volley of growls and barks.

Vincenti slipped his palm onto the butt of his service weapon. "I ought to blow his fucking brains out, then I ought to do the same thing to you – what do you say to that, Reg?"

He detected the first sign of genuine fear in his wife's eyes.

"I know what you're capable of, Brian. You don't have to remind me."

Just then a porch light flashed into life.

"Let me go, please, before – *Jesus*. Think about your son."

Nicky's image immediately invaded his father's head. Nick, his own innocent flesh and blood, and how the kid's young life would be irredeemably messed up by the loss of his mother. Even the armor manufactured by the alcohol he'd drained couldn't keep Nicky out.

He released the grooved grip of the pistol and walked back to his car. Reggie bounced the Audi off the curb and peeled out with a squeal of smoking rubber.

Vincenti was drenched in his own sweat. He watched the gold sedan disappear into the blackness beyond the stop sign on the next corner.

He snapped the stick into drive and followed. Beneath the porch light of a miniature Tudor on the east side of the street a man in a light-colored parka ogled him like a hawk. He ignored the guy and made a left at the stop sign.

More homes nestled cozily in the March darkness. Near the end of the block, the Audi was parked deep in the driveway of a free-standing, three-story gingerbread box. Vincenti hit the brakes, cut his lights and engine. A shadow – the shadow of a darkly dressed, six-foot-plus man – burst out of the front door and jogged down the steps. Evidently he'd been waiting for Reggie. He extended an arm to her, but after jumping out of her car she pushed past him, ran up the front steps and disappeared inside the house. The man didn't follow at first, but instead peered in the direction of where Vincenti was hiding. Did he see the detective's vehicle there beneath the nude branches of the horse chestnut tree?

After a second or two, the man scurried back into the house. There wasn't a live thought in Vincenti's brain. If he wasn't going to force his way into the house, pull out his Glock and blow the guy's head off, then what the hell was he doing sitting here in the dark?

He started the car and made a k-turn. Why the hell had he followed his wife tonight? Of course he knew that she was seeing – fucking was the more accurate word – Carl Bartano, the way she knew that he'd been doing Daisy Salamanca, but it was no excuse for totally losing it.

Reggie had met Bartano at the fitness center above the Sam Goody's in Hoboken where she did aerobics and Pilates, she'd been seeing the jerk for a few months now, but Vincenti had never gotten into his face, had never planned to. Bartano was one of those super-handsome, body-beautiful, Latin-lover types, nothing like himself at all. Maybe he was the kind of guy Reggie should have been with in the first place. He was majority owner and manager of a high-end restaurant called Milano Tulipano on Fourteenth Street that his old man – who was rumored to have been "connected" when the Genovese crime family still wielded influence around town – had bankrolled for him. Ironically, Vincenti had gotten the lowdown on Bartano from none other than Tommy Flaherty, who knew pretty much everything there was to know about every capo to wannabe who'd ever had anything to do with the mob in Hoboken.

By now it was a bitter joke in his mind: there she was, his squeaky-clean, gorgeous wife, whom he used to meet so innocently on Sunday mornings in the first months of their relationship at the Portuguese bakery up on Washington Street when he was buying pastries for his elderly mother, the good Catholic girl who, unlike him, had never been married, consorting with the offspring of the devil himself. The single time Bartano's name had come up during an argument, Reggie had defended him, calling him a "nice guy." Which made the joke all the more bitter.

In a blind rage, Vincenti lurched the unmarked car through the constricted arteries of Weehawken before beating a retreat to Hoboken, where the mindless Friday night craziness was in full swing.

It was late, and he had to get up early in the morning for Gail Kenmore's funeral. On a whim he decided to swing by Biggies Clam Bar for a bite and one last pop before letting Vonda go. Maybe he needed more to drink after all.

As he cruised along Madison, he caught a glimpse of something – someone – leaning on the link fence of a messy construction site at Tenth Street. There were two of them when he looked closer, shadows, talking and laughing. Slowing to a crawl, he recognized Mohammed Phillips in the stray ray of a street lamp.

Tenth and Madison wasn't all that far, only a few blocks north, from where Maria Fuentes had been attacked. At that moment, Vincenti didn't want to consider the reality that in a mile-square city, everything was in relatively close proximity. He double-parked beside an SUV and cut the engine. When he climbed out of the car, the surprise of recognition registered on Phillips' face. He swung his right arm behind his back like a child trying to hide a forbidden piece of candy.

"So whatcha up to, Mohammed?" Vincenti mustered an effort to sound innocuous, despite the fact that he was lugging around a deadly cocktail of hatred, jealousy, regret and shame.

Phillips' companion bolted off into the darkness.

"Later, dog ..."

"Stay right where you are," hissed Vincenti when Phillips began to follow his friend.

The ex-jock stopped. He stared sullenly at the cop. Then he brought a paper bag up to his face from behind his back and took a long pull from the bottle inside.

"I asked you a question."

"You gotta be wearin' me, man ..." There was a slide in Phillips' words from whatever he was drinking. "You jumpin' into my shit right here on the street?"

Vincenti moved closer. He searched Phillips' face.

"I figured maybe you remembered something by now

about what you did to Maria Fuentes, since you had a little time to think about it."

Phillips' eyes were on fire. "Take that shit outta here! You gonna be ridin' my ass forever over some shit I dunno nothin' 'bout? You fuckin' crazy or somethin'?"

"Give you a piece of advice, Phillips. You better be careful the way you talk to me."

"Why? The fuck you gonna do to me, faggot?"

Later, it would occur to Vincenti that he never entertained even a single thought at that instant, that he couldn't, because his mind was still preoccupied with his encounter with Reggie on a Weehawken side street. Everything that happened next was the product of instinct – starting with his overhand right, which intentionally landed high on the bridge of Phillips' nose, a particularly tender point of the human anatomy. It was launched with such blinding speed that he was sure Phillips never even saw it coming. Vincenti was confident in his skills as a fighter – he'd boxed the Golden Gloves as a teenager, even won a few bouts by knockout. The fact that his physique was going to seed didn't altogether negate his physical gifts, especially in a confrontation that didn't call for endurance.

"Mothafucka –"

When Phillips head snapped back into place, he stared into his blood-filled palm with disbelief. He lunged at the detective, but found himself looking down the barrel of the Glock.

"Dumb-ass crazy mothafucka! You busted my nose!"

Vincenti knew that he should have been careful, but he was caught up in a frenzy, a madness that was almost frightening, and he was powerless to stop himself. Mohammed Phillips seemed to sense it, too. His eyeballs bulged with fear. He was standing in the dark with an angry white cop and no witnesses in sight – this was how very bad things happened. Maybe he was about to lose his life at the hands of this maniac.

A narrow passageway separated the fence from the adjoining building, a vacant factory that was being made over into artists' studios. Vincenti waved his gun.

"Move," he ordered Phillips, "in there."

"What the –?"

"Now! Before I spill your fucking brains all over this sidewalk."

He undid the safety. Hearing the click, Phillips hesitated, then, pressing his hand to his rearranged face, obeyed.

The cop trailed the moaning man into the lightless nave. For some reason this sign of vulnerability from Phillips infuriated him even more.

A few feet in, Phillips tripped and stumbled into a bank of trash cans lined up against a wall. He couldn't go any further.

He was turning to face Vincenti when the detective smashed the heavy sidearm against the side of his skull, driving him to his knees.

"The fuck you want from me, man?" cried the ex-football player. His voice broke like an adolescent's.

Vincenti was in a trance. He was aware of nothing except for Phillips' bleating, which was exactly what he wanted. But he believed he knew the truth: Mohammed Phillips was most likely *not* the person who'd raped Maria Fuentes. He didn't *ever* think that Phillips had something to do with it, and yet here he was rattling the poor bugger's brains. He didn't know why he was doing what he was doing; he was simply acting out some blind, primitive impulse.

Spying on his wife, and now this ... He'd lost it altogether a couple of times tonight, worse this time than the first. If he included what happened with Daisy, maybe he'd lost it three times. He suddenly saw himself standing over a bleeding man in a cul-de-sac for no good reason – for no reason at all. Crazy – he was out of his mind.

His loud, erratic breathing brought him back to the here and now.

"All right, Phillips. Beat it ... Just get the fuck out of here ..."

"You mean you dragged me down this alley just to beat on me ...?"

Even when Phillips spat out "You racist mothafucka, I'm gonna get yo cracker ass for this!" he refused to rise to the bait.

"Go. Get the fuck outta here." Vincenti jerked his head over his shoulder. "Now – before I change my mind, and I cut your heart out and stuff it in one of those trash cans."

Gingerly clutching his battered skull, Phillips staggered to his feet and reeled past the cop toward the powdery light of Madison Street.

Vincenti's chest was so tight he could hardly breathe. Maybe he was about to suffer a coronary. When he no longer heard Phillips' erratic footfalls, he whipped out his handkerchief, wiped down his weapon, and slipped it back into its holster. Then he retraced his own steps up the passageway.

The avenue was deserted and Phillips was nowhere to be seen. In the light from the street lamp Vincenti could make out that the stems of his trousers were spattered with the suspect's blood. He cursed.

Before starting the car he sat there and tried to collect his thoughts. What had he come down here for? That's right – Biggies Clam Bar. But he was exhausted now, had no trace of an appetite. The residue of something foul rose into his mouth. The best thing was to forget all about it and go home, try and get some rest before the funeral tomorrow. It had been a long day. And an even longer night.

Saturday, March 20

He is in a consulting room somewhere, waiting. There are scientific charts, and x-rays, and illustrations of the human anatomy on the walls, so it must mean this is a doctor's office. A middle-aged woman in a medical smock is behind him – how he knows that she's there, wearing the smock, is unclear. She reaches out and takes hold of his skull like a cantaloupe, squeezes it, manipulates it, as if she's in a supermarket trying to decide whether or not to buy.

"Hm..."

"What? What is it?" he demands.

She seems to be agonizing over something. "Your head – it's not the head of a normal man."

"But ... what does it mean?"

"A head of this size usually indicates some sort of psychotic pathology."

At this he spirals into a blind panic and bolts.

By now Vincenti was thoroughly lost, not being all that familiar with Long Island, and despite the road atlas spread out on the seat beside him.

It was an unpleasant morning, charcoal clouds from the Atlantic drifting low in the sky, a freezing, bitter chill in the air. Strangely enough, it wasn't the hangover from the night before, nor the incidents involving Daisy, his wife and Mohammed Phillips that were getting him down this morning, but rather chunks of that creepy dream that smacked him in sneaky volleys as he drove. When he woke up a couple of hours ago, he had trouble figuring out whether the walls and ceiling of his makeshift bedroom were reality, or belonged to the consulting room in that bizarre night vision. It was only when he forced himself off the futon and looked in on Reggie and Nicky fast asleep in the master bedroom that he finally regained his senses.

But that wasn't all of the dream – or, more accurately, the dream with the ghoulish lady doctor was just one of the dreams. It seemed like he was in the grip of yet another wild hallucination every time his brain broke through to waking consciousness during the night. Or maybe it was that each new nightmare woke him up.

... He is wading through the dense crowd of a street festival in New York, somewhere downtown, in the Village, or Little Italy, and it's hot, very, very hot, and he's sweating profusely. He's tailing someone, but he can't say, maybe doesn't even know, who it is. All he knows is that he has to bring the subject down no matter what – in order to stop him? Save him? The strangest thing is that when he does, he might or might not arrest him – he may beg forgiveness, throw himself at the subject's mercy. Why? He doesn't have an answer for that question. It's a dream, after all. Despite the chintzy merchandise stands, the greasy, stomach-turning stench of frying meat and other junk food, the warped song of the organ grinder, something's wrong with the scene, a sinister pall hangs in the suffocating atmosphere. But as he pushes against the sticky, stinking bodies, he can't make

out what it is that's not quite right, all he knows for sure is that
what's at stake is a matter of life and death ...

After doubling back to Levittown on the Expressway,
Vincenti finally located the turnoff for Seaford with the
help of a gas station attendant who barely spoke English. At
first the fellow, an Indian or Pakistani with a wispy, uneven
mustache, was totally uninterested in giving him the time of
day, dodging between cars and pumps as he was, but when
Vincenti showed his badge, the guy motioned him into
the office and pointed at a large map tacked up on the wall
behind the counter. "You find there, okay? Okay?"

Normally he didn't like having to pull it out, but that
shiny ID almost always got them moving, and fast.

By the time he'd made it home last night, Vonda was
gone, and a light was burning in Nicky's room. He popped
his head in. Reggie was curled up on the bed reading to the
boy, a yarn about twin field mice who'd left home to break
into their neighbors' houses in search of cheese that he'd
read to the kid himself.

"Way past his bedtime, isn't it?"

If her run-in with him on a dark side street up on
the Weehawken bluff had ruined Reggie's date with Carl
Bartano, she wasn't saying.

"Mm-hm," was all he got out of her. She went back to
reading.

"Hi, Daddy," said the boy, in a tiny voice that was still
very much like a baby's, especially when he was tired.

"Hey, big guy ..."

Reggie waved him off. It was the signal for Vincenti to

beat it because the child was just about to fall asleep. Just as well – he didn't want his wife getting a look at his trousers, especially down low, around the cuffs. He undressed in his room and then stuffed his clothes into the washing machine that was set next to the tub in his bathroom.

This morning, after his restless night of deranged dreams, he'd wanted to wake the kid up and say goodbye, but decided against it just before leaving. Let him sleep; no doubt he needed it.

Then it comes to him what's cockeyed about the street scene. The men, the women – are really neither. They started out as one sex and then turned into the opposite. Wherever he looks he isn't really seeing what he thinks he's seeing because by some frighteningly insane process, reality has been turned on its head.

By now of course he'd puzzled out the obvious connection between what went on in his nightmare and Tommy Flaherty. But there was another component to it – that a guy could never really know for sure what was going on in life, whether he was doing the right thing or the wrong thing. No, he was always in the dark, and things weren't ever exactly as they seemed.

Just like that night down on Christopher Street ...

Vincenti had sat on that bench on the river in a state of utter shock. It was downright pathetic, witnessing Tommy, this rock of a man, this good father, this dependable husband, this toughest of cops, reduce himself to – to nothing, to some creature he couldn't even put a name to.

He'd felt like a man ambushed in a blind alley – what he'd

done to Mohammed Phillips. None of it made the least sense.

Tommy proceeded to explain to his partner that he was in the process of becoming a female, that indeed two surgeries had already taken place during his vacation weeks, and more were scheduled. Of course no one knew about all this except for his wife, and now ... him, Vincenti. Not even his kids had been let in on it at that point.

He and Tommy had gotten up from the bench and begun walking. After night fell the game changed – the more dangerous trade came out, the hard-core druggies and the hustlers, the freaks like Tommy and the sex-crazed cruisers desperate to find someone to take home before it got too late and, here and there, the predators out prowling for victims. By this time Tommy had his emotions a little more under control, and the partners were actually talking over one of the cases they were working in Hoboken – the execution-style murders of six prominent members of various "social clubs," traditionally a front for mob activity. The cops were at wits' end, and nobody was talking. It was a nut they were most likely never going to crack, but being long-timers, it wasn't in their blood to give up. For the moment, Tommy was a detective on the job, and not a female in the making ...

Saint Elizabeth's Cemetery was splayed over a serpentine chain of undulating hillocks adjacent to a weather-beaten suburban housing tract full of cookie-cutter Cape Cods dating from just after the Second World War. Vincenti maneuvered the car beneath the wrought-iron arch and rolled past the tight columns of gray headstones. Between flaps of the windshield wipers a dove-colored tent came into focus.

He's running at full speed now, slamming into bodies, overturning tables, trying to keep his quarry in sight. The subject is swathed in a kind of hood or burnoose, so he can't get a clean look at him, still can't tell who it is. There's nothing else in the world now, no city, no other people, but himself and whoever it is he's chasing down. The thing veers around a corner and hurtles down an alley. He scrambles furiously to keep pace, but his legs are cramping – he doesn't have a chance in hell of catching up.

Well, there aren't any alleys in Manhattan, Vincenti remembered reading that somewhere, but a dream is a dream, with a logic all of its own. He cut the engine at the tail end of a row of glistening vehicles that coiled out from the path leading to the steam-shrouded canopy. The last thing in the world he felt up to this morning was interviewing Gail Kenmore's family, but it had to be done. He'd come this far; he might as well see his investigation through to wherever it would take him – if it took him anywhere.

He got out of the car and made his way over the sodden grass. The interment ceremony was already underway. A silver-haired clergyman in a black cloak was reading aloud from a missal. Feeling like an intruder, Vincenti squeezed himself in against the other raincoats. No one even turned to look at him.

As he listened to the smooth tenor reciting prayers, Vincenti wondered how Gail Kenmore had managed to merit a proper Catholic burial. Suicides, according to church law, are condemned to Hell and thus not deserving. Maybe somebody had pulled a string or two.

Or maybe the Catholic Church, reeling in the wake of thousands of accusations of sexual abuse, had decided to loosen up the rules. *Right.* The priest went on mumbling, but Vincenti didn't pay attention. He was still caught in the web of his nightmare.

The alley is a cul-de-sac. There's nowhere for his target to go — he's trapped. Vincenti's managed to slice the distance between them in half. The subject loses his footing and slams into a bank of trash cans that magically turn into paint cans as they fly through the noisome air, a transformation that fills Vincenti with dread. Completely winded now and with a fiery ache burning every muscle and sinew of his body, he finally catches up. He fumbles for the pistol hanging under his armpit, draws, and flicks off the safety. Then he points it at whatever is on the inside of that hood.

The priest shut his book. Vincenti found himself studying the living bodies all around him. Standing near the casket was a burly man with salt and pepper hair combed straight back and a neatly-trimmed beard. He was wearing an olive-green trenchcoat, and he might be interesting, Vincenti decided, because he was standing so close to the dead woman. He would talk to that person later.

An older, balding man stood close by the bearded mourner, and there was a woman with peroxided hair next to him. Maybe the bald guy bore a faint resemblance to the girl in the picture frame back in Gail Kenmore's apartment. Maybe not.

None of the others under the tent meant a thing to him.

Whatever's inside that hood, he doesn't want to see it. He'd rather kill whoever – whatever – is in there, but now, when the opportunity presents itself, he's frozen with panic. No – he can't do it after all, he can't pull the trigger. What he really wants is to rescue the poor hunted soul, but he's afraid he won't be able to, that something far more powerful than himself holds sway over what's going on here.

When that thing inside the hood realizes that Vincenti is not about to murder him, he leaps to his feet and makes another run for it.

"Wait! Wait!" shouts Vincenti as the thing leaps onto a nearby fire escape like a speed-jacked monkey.

It's too late to save anyone – too late.

The priest reached for a trowel and tossed a rocky lump of clay onto the casket lid. Shaking off his nightmare again, Vincenti listened to those always ominous words about how we must all return to dust, including "our dear daughter Gail." Shoulders sagged. Heads bowed. Vincenti heard a sniffle or two. The priest stepped forward and whispered something to the balding man, who approached the oblong copper box and dropped a long-stemmed flower onto the lid. Then he moved to his left and took up another position at the end of the casket, clasped his hands in front of his groin, and stood there motionlessly, lost in thought, or prayer. His companion, the woman, followed suit. The bulky bearded fellow then did the same thing. The rest of the mourners formed a ragged queue, made their way to the casket, and said their final goodbyes.

The priest fitted his Fairbanks hat on his head and

made his way out of the tent and toward the cars. Vincenti scurried after him.

"Say – padre," he called when he caught up. He noticed a shiny black Mercedes waiting at the lip of dead grass.

The priest stopped. "Do I know you?"

He was strikingly handsome, Vincenti saw now, the kind of man who when he was young should probably have tried his hand in Hollywood.

"Don't think so. The name's Vincenti. Hoboken Police."

"What can I do for you?"

"Not sure, exactly. I'm looking into the death of Gail Kenmore."

The cleric's eyebrows twitched. "And what have you found?"

The question was curious. It wasn't meant to be a challenge, but it wasn't intended to be a straightforward inquiry either.

"I don't know that I've found anything."

The priest's chin jutted out. "So let me ask you again – what can I do for you?"

"You can tell me who it is I need to talk to up there," said the detective, indicating the tent. He explained that he'd never actually talked to Gail's father personally, that Hugh Kenmore had left a phone message where to come for the funeral, and when – that had been the extent of their contact. "It's been a rough few days for him, I'd have to think. Problem for me is, I wouldn't know Kenmore from Adam."

A flock of geese in V-formation flew screaming over their heads. The priest's body tightened.

"What exactly are you after here?"

"I'm not after anything, Father. I'm just doing what I'm paid to do: determine the true cause of Gail Kenmore's death."

The priest smiled, showing his perfectly polished white teeth.

"Now that *implies* something," he said, his eyes darting over Vincenti's shoulder.

The detective's brain was still stuck in first gear, still entangled in the skeins of the dream he'd not finished reliving. The words "that implies something" were like a mathematical problem he was too stupid to crack.

"I don't follow."

The priest smiled again. This time it seemed practiced, unctuous. "What it implies is that you think there *is* something to find."

"Not necessarily ... Are you saying you know different?"

Vincenti was doing his best to keep the exchange from becoming contentious, but something about the clergyman – an underlying arrogance, a whiff of defensiveness – threatened to undermine him. The image of his brother Salvatore skidded across his brain. What was it about men of the cloth that made them so smug?

The priest shrugged. "I'm not saying anything of the sort. But it's not likely you're going to find anything other than what we all think." He opened his hands in a gesture that included the people under the canopy.

"Which is?"

"That the poor young lady ... fell. Do you have any evidence whatsoever of anything to the contrary? I know what the official reports said, but –"

"I'm not interrogating you, Father. I was just asking for a little information."

He smiled suddenly, a one-hundred-watt smile. "So you were."

He took Vincenti by the elbow, turned him toward the tent, and nodded discreetly. "That man, the one standing near the head of the casket, is Gail's father, Hugh. The woman next to him is her stepmother, Renee. The rest are old friends, parishioners, acquaintances and the like. I'm sure they wouldn't be of any use to you."

"How about that guy there, the big fellow with the beard?"

"That fellow – that's Doctor Keane."

Vincenti detected sudden indecisiveness in the priest's voice.

"Keane," he repeated. "Would you happen to know his connection to the deceased?"

"Friend, I believe."

"Anything else I should know?"

The priest shrugged again. "I don't think so."

"By the way – what's your name?"

"Me? I'm Father Raymond." The vacillation hadn't completely disappeared.

"Thanks for the information." Vincenti was about to extend his hand for Father Raymond to shake, but decided not to.

"I hope you don't mind my saying this," the priest said just as Vincenti was about to head back to the tent, "but ..."

"Go on."

"You seem like – and forgive me for saying it because

it's none of my business – a man under a great deal of stress. Please – don't take it the wrong way."

What a goddamned strange thing to come out with, thought Vincenti. And how else was he supposed to take it? Of course hearing something like this wasn't quite a surprise to him. But he was tired, another headache was brewing behind his eyeballs, his mouth was parched, and he wasn't about to launch into explanations – especially not to a man wearing a collar. What was more, he had the impression that the unrequested observation was Father Raymond's attempt to gain the upper hand or blow smoke at him.

But why?

"The strains of the job," he offered. But he was thinking something else: *You, too, Padre. Something stinks on you, too. Maybe it takes one to know one.*

"Good luck, Detective."

Vincenti half-expected to hear the cliched, smart-assed caboose "because you're going to need it," but it didn't come. Before reaching the top of the slope, he did a one-eighty.

"By the way, Father –"

"Yes?"

"What's the Church's official stance these days on the sacraments for suicides?"

"The same as it's always been. If that girl had taken her own life, this service wouldn't have been allowed."

Vincenti nodded once.

"Are you a Catholic, Detective?"

"Used to be. But that was a long time ago." With that he set his sights on the tent, its roof running with gray rainwater, and marched up the hill.

Damn it to hell. While he was talking to Father Raymond, everyone but for the people closest to the casket – Gail Kenmore's parents and Doctor Keane – had scattered.

He had no choice but to follow the hood. The cast iron ladder was flimsy; it shook violently with every step he took. He never quite realized how much the sensation of height petrified him. Sheer, dizzying terror wracked his limbs as the city receded below. There was something about the lengthening distance between himself and what was down there on terra firma that added to his horror. Cars, humans, buildings, were as puny as germs without the benefit of a microscope. But he couldn't help looking down, just as he couldn't stop himself from climbing. And when the hood disappeared over the top, it ratcheted up the intensity of his dread: he was left alone, dangling by his sweating fingers, like a luckless animal trapped between two forms of torture. But somehow, against all odds, he pulled his carcass up to the final rung of the ladder, swaying from side to side like the crown of a buoy on an ocean swell. There was no railing, nothing whatsoever to prevent him from tumbling headlong into the abyss. The slightest breeze would have done the trick. He held his breath, leaped through space and grasped for the edge of the roof. With an inhuman effort he winched himself up to his waist and rolled onto the tarpaper. Jesus fucking Christ. The hood was scaling the pediment now – to where?

The same trio was standing near the casket. In the fog a short distance away was a pit of reddish clay, like the open mouth of a vulture. Vincenti waited in the background until Hugh Kenmore turned up his coat collar.

"Mister Kenmore –"

Kenmore and the woman jumped as if they'd touched a live wire.

"Brian Vincenti. Didn't mean to scare you. And sorry to have to meet you under these circumstances."

He stuck out his hand, and Kenmore reached for it. "My condolences for your loss."

"Thank you. My wife, Renee."

Renee Kenmore was one of those well-into-late-middle-age matrons who did certain things to herself in a futile attempt to subtract years. In her case, the too-obvious dye job on her hair, which was cut into an out-of-fashion pageboy, made her look sadly ridiculous. Vincenti hardly had time to wonder why she allowed herself to go out looking that way when there was movement in the periphery of his vision.

The bearded guy made a see-you-later motion with his hand to the Kenmores, and went lumbering down the incline toward the remaining parked cars.

"Guess I said the wrong thing," joked Vincenti.

"Oh, he's usually very busy," chirped Renee Kenmore obliviously, "and always running late."

"Ah-ha. *Doctor* Keane, isn't it?"

Renee Kenmore's severely plucked eyebrows went into an arch. "That's right, Doctor Keane. A friend of Gail's from the hospital. How did you know?"

"I had just enough time to nose around a little ... Would you happen to know where he lives?"

"In Manhattan – somewhere downtown," answered

Hugh Kenmore. "What do you want with him?"

"I'd be interested in talking to any friend of your daughter – just to make sure that when I'm finished I've covered all the bases."

"Well, I appreciate that, Detective – I do," said Hugh Kenmore, his eyes welling with tears, his large head suddenly giving way to gravity. "If there was something – anything that could ..."

His voice trailed off into a crack. *Bring her back*, he was going to say. His limbs appeared to quiver beneath the black wool overcoat. Vincenti felt sorry for the man. He could only imagine what it would be like to lose his own son. No, he couldn't – it was unimaginable. Renee moved her hand from her husband's forearm to the biceps and gave it a squeeze. The gesture seemed pathetically inadequate.

"If you want to talk, Detective, why don't we go somewhere ... Being here" – he stole a glance at the container where his dead daughter lay – "is too – too –"

"I understand."

The Kenmores moved with excruciating deliberateness, as if each step had to be painfully thought out first. It was Vincenti's impression that the tragedy had come close to destroying both of them.

"Where you parked?" asked Kenmore when they were halfway down to the road.

Vincenti pointed.

"This is me, over here," said Kenmore, indicating a maroon Mercury Sable. "Why don't you just follow me – there's a diner around the corner."

Vincenti would have liked to talk right then and there,

but if the old guy would be morbidly distracted near Gail's corpse, he'd have to go along for the ride, wouldn't he?

He grabs for the hood, clenches it in his fist, gets dragged upwards to the pediment. Whatever's inside has the strength of a rampaging elephant, enough to annihilate his pursuer ten times over with laughable ease. And yet Vincenti knows that he has to finish this, he has to see it through to the end. His shirt gets snagged on the apex of the roof, then rips on the ragged angle – it's here that Vincenti realizes, when looking down, that he's climbed out of the reach of anyone who can help him. And it's here that he realizes that he's being suckered – that it's him who's really the prey.

The Empress Diner was out on the highway that had brought Vincenti to the cemetery. The lot was crammed with cars, and he wished now that he'd suggested somewhere else. Why the hell would Kenmore want to be surrounded by a horde after losing his child?

Well, maybe he needed a little distraction, maybe that was it. They took seats at the table, Kenmore and Renee on one side, Vincenti on the other, while the waitress passed out menus. He would have preferred the privacy of a booth, but there wasn't one available. To his surprise, the couple ordered generous breakfasts.

"Coffee for me – that's all," said Vincenti to the waitress, a dour forty-something wearing an overload of mascara and outsized false eyelashes.

She scurried off with a grunt, leaving the table in tense silence.

"So what is it, exactly, you came out here for this morning, Detective?" Hugh Kenmore asked without looking up from his interlaced fingers, which were thick, like overcooked hot dogs. "What's the point?"

Vincenti didn't expect the salvo of questions. Inches away, Renee stared at him as if he were a creature from another planet.

He decided to counter with a question of his own. "What do *you* think happened to your daughter?" He wasn't about to say that there was something familiar to him about Gail Kenmore, it would have only confounded matters.

"What do I think happened to my daughter ...?" Kenmore seemed mystified. "She went out an eleventh-floor window." His words were spoken as if the detective were an idiot. Renee looked down. At that moment the blowsy waitress returned, carrying a tray crowded with steaming coffee mugs and a silver cruet full of half-and-half. She dealt the mugs first, starting with Kenmore.

"But *how*? How did she go?"

If it was Kenmore's voice on that answering machine, then he was most likely – but not definitely – the last person to talk to the victim.

Kenmore's head twitched.

"It's my opinion she lost her balance and fell ..."

He fixed Vincenti with a hard stare.

"What, Detective? You're not convinced."

"Well, as a matter of –"

"There's no way it was the other – suicide. Her roommates didn't want her smoking up in the apartment, and unfortunately Gail had the habit. She'd open the window and perch there in the frame when she was in the apartment by herself. It was a whole lot easier than trekking all the way down to the courtyard when she had the craving."

"How do you know this?"

"Saw her do it myself when I went to Hoboken to visit."

"I see ..."

So – Hugh Kenmore was the older guy Alex Danko had seen at the door of 1108. Well, most likely he was.

"I was always giving her hell about it. I flat-out ordered her to stay out of that window frame. But she wouldn't listen. You know – kids. Think they know everything. Think nothing can ever happen to them ... But I thought it was dangerous – especially under the circumstances."

"What circumstances?"

A spasm yanked on the tendons of Hugh Kenmore's neck. "Gail was having medical problems. Don't know if you were aware of that – probably you weren't. How could you be?"

"What kind of medical problems?"

"Episodes of vertigo, for lack of a better word."

"Vertigo?" The image seemed to activate the febrile energy of Vincenti's nightmare. His brain even regurgitated that old Hitchcock film, with all the leaping from rooftop to rooftop.

"Spells – whatever you'd want to call them. She felt like she was losing her balance sometimes. She'd had thorough medical examinations, MRIs, went the whole route. That's why I wanted her to stay away from that goddamned window."

Just as the detective was about to pose another question,

the waitress breezed in with a second tray. She laid out plates of greasy eggs, home fries, toast. The sight and smell of the food nearly tilted Vincenti's queasy stomach.

She dropped her hand onto her thick hip and stared at Vincenti. "Change your mind?"

"Just more coffee."

Again she disappeared without speaking. Vincenti knew she was a little ticked off. Here she was, shlepping out coffee after coffee to this deadbeat, and her tip would end up pennies.

"And what did they find, the doctors?"

Kenmore speared a pyramid of golden-brown potatoes with his fork. Vincenti watched as he swirled it in a dollop of glistening ketchup.

"They were looking for a growth – a brain tumor. But the tests were negative."

"A brain tumor ..."

"It's anybody's guess what the problem really was. But something was wrong with my daughter, no doubt about it. The question is, what?"

Out of his long experience with damned near every species of human, from the sleazy to the saintly, Vincenti felt this guy was on the level, hardcore salt of the earth, that he wasn't holding back. What possible reason would he have for holding back?

"That *was* your voice on her answering machine Tuesday morning, then?"

Kenmore laid his fork down and let out a shaky stream of tired air. The memory of his last conversation with his daughter was evidently still raw to the touch.

"It was."

"What was going on in that apartment Tuesday morning, Mister Kenmore?"

"Gail was upset about something. I could hear her smoking a cigarette through the wire – I could always tell when she was smoking. I figured she must have been sitting in that cursed window."

"Did she say what it was that had her upset?"

"Not that day she didn't. But I knew her. I could tell. Some days she just called and wanted to hear my voice."

"How about other days?"

"We never got too particular about things – you know how it is between parents and their kids. She didn't want me too taken up with her problems. But – there were ... things."

"What 'things?'"

Kenmore looked into some unfathomable distance.

"Mind if I ask you a question, Detective?"

"Shoot."

"What is it you're after? What are you trying to find out here? Does it really matter if she fell or –"

"Or committed suicide?"

Kenmore refused to react. Maybe Vincenti *was* wrong – maybe the guy was hiding something after all. His wife's eyelids fluttered, and she took another nibble of her toast.

"Is that what you think? That she might have committed suicide?" prodded Vincenti.

Kenmore's tired blue eyes were pools of pain. "Like I said – does it matter? She's dead. Dead. No matter how she died, nothing's going to change that. Nothing's going to bring her back."

"That's true ..."

"But the answer is no. No way she committed suicide."

There it was again. *She couldn't have done it. She wouldn't have committed suicide.*

Vincenti thought of his son. Despite the tangle of complications the kid had unwittingly injected into his life – and that the cop had injected into his – the idea of Nicky dying before Vincenti himself was like a knife in the solar plexus, a wound he'd never recover from. This was the hurt Hugh Kenmore was suffering. And he refused to believe anything uglier had happened to his daughter.

"I'm not one of these people who's going to bring suit against the management of the building, or chase this thing down to the ends of the earth, Detective. She's gone. Why don't we just let her rest in peace."

Vincenti chewed on it. He really did sympathize with Kenmore, and had it not been for that elusive, tantalizing something in the portrait in the bedroom, he would have let it all go right then and there. Even so, if Gail Kenmore's own father wanted to let go, what was he doing chasing his own tail?

"You don't seem satisfied," said Kenmore, searching Vincenti's face. "Something's still eating at you."

"Because I still have a question or two. Was there a disgruntled man in the picture somewhere?"

"A disgruntled man?"

"Yeah. You know. Somebody who thought Gail was making his life miserable."

Kenmore's brow knotted. "You think that –"

"What I'm saying is, d'you think there's any chance she was pushed out of that window?"

"No. Nah." The notion seemed to have occurred to Hugh Kenmore for the first time. "Why would any –"

"Just asking," Vincenti apologized. "Believe me, I'm not trying to manufacture something that's not there. But I'm supposed to ask questions. I know it's something you'd rather not consider, but ..."

He was getting a little tired of having to justify himself, even to the victim's father.

There was dead silence at the table. Renee's head had drooped even further, practically into her plate. Vincenti felt like he'd forced Hugh Kenmore into a confrontation with a surprise intruder – him.

Finally he shook his head. "Ah, hell, Detective. I don't know what to tell you. In my opinion you're barking up the wrong tree. I –"

"Don't get me wrong. I've got no evidence in that direction whatsoever. And I know that some of these questions might be painful, but before I let go of the case once and for all, I have to exhaust all possibilities. I hope you understand."

Kenmore nodded dubiously.

"So, how 'bout it – was your daughter having trouble with any man – or men?"

Kenmore dropped the thin triangle of toast in his fingers. "Don't they all, at that age? But again, Gail wasn't the type to go into detail."

"Did you know any of them?"

"Only her ex-husband. After that, she stopped bringing them around."

"She was married ... I didn't know that."

"You wouldn't. It was only for a short time, not even a year. This was back in, oh – when was it, dear?"

Kenmore's wife dabbed at her mouth preciously. The motion looked absurd to Vincenti.

"Ninety-seven, wasn't it?"

"I think so, yeah. A long time ago."

"What happened?"

"Agh – they were kids. And they were on different pages, as they like to say nowadays, which didn't help. He wanted to get out of New York, move out to California and try his hand at something or other in the movie business. That wasn't for Gail. She was committed to what she was doing. She had the nurse's mentality from the get-go."

"Where did that come from?"

"I sent her to Catholic school. I think maybe it set in there."

That was true for Vincenti and his brother, too. Inculcation with a heavy dose of Catholic guilt made you feel like you had to serve your fellow man.

"So whatever happened to this guy?"

"Not a clue."

"His name?"

"Bruce Clancy."

Vincenti pulled out his pen and wrote the name on a napkin. In his stupor on leaving the house this morning, he'd forgotten to bring along his notebook.

"So, presumably, he doesn't know what happened."

"Well, I didn't tell him. I wouldn't know how."

"Last known address?"

"West Twelfth Street in the Village. When he was still

living with Gail. Don't recall the number now."

None of it was likely to help, but Vincenti took it down anyway. "Wouldn't happen to know whether or not Bruce Clancy ever did go out to L.A., would you?"

"He did, now that I think about it. At least as far as Gail knew."

Vincenti was growing restless. Kenmore and his wife were through eating, and they were looking around for the waitress. They seemed restless, too, but where were they going? What was their life going to be without their daughter?

If he was going to get anything solid here, he'd have to think and act fast.

"What about her mother?"

With those words the atmosphere immediately clouded over – as if it could be any blacker, given the day. It was like he'd just dropped a fantastically tasteless joke. The sea-change made him sit up.

"What about her?" grunted Kenmore.

"Still alive? Did Gail see her often?"

"If she did, she wouldn't say anything to me."

"Excuse me," said Renee, getting up from her chair. "I have to visit the ladies' room."

"Problem there – with her mother?" inquired Vincenti gingerly after she'd gone.

"Old stuff," sniffed Kenmore evasively.

"Meaning?"

"Meaning I don't care to hash over my ancient history with Gail's mother. We've been divorced a long time. Divorced yourself, Detective?"

"As a matter of fact, I am."

"Then you should know something about wanting to bury the past."

"Any idea where I might be able to find her – Gail's mother?"

"You could have found her this morning."

"You mean –"

"Yeah. She was at the cemetery."

Damn it to hell – somehow he'd missed the woman. No thanks to Father Raymond. He said there was no one else to talk to, didn't he?

Renee returned and started putting on her coat. Her husband took the cue and stood up to do the same. Before they could make a dash for the register, Vincenti asked for Gail's mother's name and address.

"Lydia."

"No last name?"

"Detective, I try not to pay attention to anything having to do with Gail's mother."

"That bad, huh?"

Hugh Kenmore didn't answer.

Vincenti followed him and his wife out to the parking lot, where they parted ways near Kenmore's car. Just like a date that went sour, thought the detective as he stood in the drizzle and watched them disappear into the highway traffic.

The dream is almost over. It can't go on much longer. If it does, the dreamer himself will implode. Vincenti makes one last desperate lunge for the hood, crushes the hem in his fist, wills the figure towards him, and they grapple like a pair of wrestlers.

This time the struggle is meant to end in death, and so the dreamer fights with all that's left in him, for all he's worth ...

Before he dies, he has to see with his own eyes once and for all who's inside the shroud, and as they somersault over each other toward the edge of the roof the hood falls back, and there – at long last – is the object of Vincenti's delirious pursuit: Gail Kenmore – but not really – she's a male now, a boy who looks like the suicide, then like Tommy Flaherty – or Ellen Smith ... then, as if by magic, she's nobody, nothing, a skull, most definitely dead, the features contorted into the ghastly, mocking smile of the unliving. With superhuman strength, the skeleton-corpse pushes him over the side into freefall, and then it's truly over: the chase, the struggle, the nightmare – everything.

Instead of the pain of death, Vincenti feels nothing but stark, abject horror at the sight below. Like an albatross, he soars into eternity.

End of dream.

Sunday, March 21

"Daddy! Daddy! It's time to wake up!"

Nicky did a boisterous, bang-and-crash running tour of his father's cave, knocking yesterday's sports page off the coffee table and nearly toppling the lamp.

"I want my breakfast! I want my breakfast!"

Even though Vincenti was wasted, he reached out and snared the exuberant kid as he ran laps around the futon, pulled him onto the mattress and tickled his ribs, which made Nicky erupt into squalls of laughter. The boy's raw bumptiousness could still coax a smile onto his face, and obliterate, at least for the moment, every unsavory circumstance in his life.

"Mommy says it's gonna be hot like summer outside today, and she says we can go to the park and get ice cream! And I want you to go *wif* us, Daddy, because you never come *wif* us anymore! Will you, Daddy – will you?"

Being forced into Reggie's presence wasn't exactly an enticing prospect.

"We'll see, my man, we'll see."

"Daddy, please? Please, Daddy?"

Any expression of disappointment from Nicky tore at him.

"Okay, big guy, let's do it."

Nicky was in seventh heaven. Vincenti hauled himself off the mattress, and hand in hand they walked down the hall to the kitchen. The feel of Nicky's cool, tiny fingers in his never failed to bring back his own childhood in flashes, like the shadows of fish in a deep, murky stream, and the weird fact that he could summon up no recollection whatsoever of his own father ever giving him even a single physical sign of affection. Come to think of it, the same went for his mother. So maybe he'd accomplished a little something, by reversing the trend of parent-child distance.

"So what's it gonna be today, big fella – gorilla munch or panda puffs?"

"Koala crisp!"

"Koala crisp? You're throwin' me a curveball here, dude."

"What's a curveball?"

"A curveball, Nicky, is a baseball that comes straight at you and then breaks away." He made a snake-like motion with his hand.

"A baseball? I din't throw a baseball at you, Daddy."

"Well, that's not *exactly* what I meant ..."

Vincenti thought it over as he poured the brown cocoa-flavored pellets that looked like dog chow or worse into a plastic bowl festooned with blue chickens and green ducks.

"What is it, Daddy? What's a curveball?"

He was about to try again to make a stab at the metaphor when Reggie walked in, wrapped in a silk dressing gown he'd bought for her from a chichi department store like Bloomingdale's or Nordstrom's, just after Nicky was born. The thought that another man – Carl Bartano – was getting his hands on the flesh beneath that pink garment was enough to boil his blood all over again. But he was determined to keep a lid on his emotions today, if for no other reason than to make sure that his son was shielded for at least one day from the poison that oscillated between his parents as if they were a pair of mismatched magnets.

Reggie kissed Nicky on the top of his head, but said nothing to her husband. He could tell by a glance at her frosty eyes that she was still fuming over what had happened on Friday night, when he'd followed her like a cheap snoop all the way to Bartano's doorstep.

"Good morning, Mommy," he exclaimed with phony brightness. Might as well put on a good show for the kid, right?

Reggie's brows rose languidly over those beautiful eyes that still had the power to destroy him.

"Good morning ..."

"So – we're all going to the park today," he announced evenly, insinuating an unspoken message to his wife.

"Looks that way ..."

Reggie turned to the coffee-maker, filled it with water, and went to the freezer for the sack of Starbucks Breakfast Blend.

"Okay, then – we got a plan." He winked at Nicky. When Vincenti passed his wife en route to the bathroom a few minutes later, he whispered, "Let's be civil to each other, at least for today – for him, okay?"

They must have looked like any contented American family as they strolled along the river promenade. Nicky smiled proudly to himself and clung tightly to the hands of both his parents, but the fact that Mom never addressed Dad directly must have seemed odd, even to a little kid. Vincenti took solace in the realization that the present impasse couldn't go on forever, that the dam would one day have to burst, that something would have to give.

But – who could tell? – maybe things would be even worse then. A man could never predict anything in life, could he? He might get up one morning and be washed away by a tidal wave. Or report to his job and never come back. Like damned near three thousand did on a certain September morning, when the sky was blue, the temperature perfect, the world a relatively peaceful place, the kind of day a man or woman would never *think* ...

Vincenti winced at the sight of lower Manhattan. The eerie fissure in the skyline would forever remind him of one long, incomprehensible late summer day, first spent watching the World Trade Center towers collapse into a heap of smoldering rubble from this very waterfront – a surreal scene he still hadn't completely processed – and later escorting hordes of shaken commuters off overcrowded ferries in Jersey City. On that day, Vincenti was at his best as a human being, the antithesis of the beast who laid a hurting on Mohammed Phillips night before last. It was shortly afterwards that his relations with his wife went south. Whether there was any connection between the events, he still couldn't say ...

The fishermen from the projects, fixtures all summer long, already had their lines in. Nicky scampered from one filthy plastic bucket to the next, inspecting for the day's catch.

"Daddy! Look!"

"That's squid, Nicky. They use it for bait."

The anglers hadn't had any luck so far today, but maybe they didn't care. This was a day for soaking up the premature warmth, for kicking back and inhaling the fresh air, for taking it a little easier than usual. If you could. The apartment block that Gail Kenmore had fallen out was directly across the street, and Vincenti calculated that he'd already lived nearly twice as many years as she had. Just like that, the dark clouds began to gather.

"What's wrong, Daddy?"

"Nothing, Nicko, nothing at all."

His lie drew a pregnant glance from Reggie. After doing a leisurely turn of the huge pier and watching the frisbee-throwers, touch-football players and dog-walkers, the Vincentis strolled over to Sinatra Park, which was swarming with throngs desperate to get out of doors on a tantalizingly temperate day in March. The refreshment stand inside the atrium was open year-round, and that's where they headed.

Ice cream cones in hand, they watched a barge laden with construction materials, girders and cement containers, laboring its way slowly north against the river current from their window table. Nicky insisted that the vessel was one of the Theodore the Tugboat characters. Vincenti was just about to pass a pleasant remark to Reggie about the beauty of the day, the kind of thing that might in a far-fetched fantasy rekindle a flicker between them, when his cell phone went off. He fumbled in the pocket of his windbreaker.

"Vincenti."

"It's Hampton."

The chief's voice was a little flintier than usual. Vincenti didn't have to ask why.

"So, Vincenti – what's your beef with Mohammed Phillips? I got word this morning you roughed him up a little. I think you know the kid. He was brought in for the Fuentes rape."

Of course Hampton knew that he knew who Phillips was. What the hell was this?

"Phillips has himself a two-bit Johnnie Cochrane from Newark doing his talking for him. I don't know if you're familiar with him, Vincenti – Karim Smokely's the name. He's glued himself onto a few other cases like this, made lotsa noise, especially against the police. He said – and I quote – 'We ain't gonna take this shit anymore.'"

The name Smokely didn't ring a bell. There were so many Kubys and Maddoxes out there on the prowl for some kind of action, it was impossible to remember them all. No doubt Smokely got vomited out of some podunk law school and was looking to make a name for himself however he could.

"Uh-huh," grunted Vincenti, scanning the faces of his wife and son. "Hang on a second, will you ..." He lowered the phone. "Back in a second."

He got up and walked out of doors, where he found a spot facing the soccer field that was being swarmed over by a pair of frantic, muddy teams out to get a jump on the season.

"Right – I'm back."

"Smokely was about to blow a fucking gasket, tell you the God's honest truth. What the fuck did you do to this guy, Vincenti? And why?"

A soccer ball came flying over the fence and nearly clocked the detective in the face. He swerved in the nick of time, and it bounced off the wall behind him.

Vincenti considered his boss's question, but he couldn't come up with an answer.

———————

That phone call marked the end of the Vincenti family outing. But instead of immediately trying to get hold of one of the department's on-call attorneys as per Hampton's advice, Vincenti kissed his son on the top of his head – a "noggin kiss," as he liked to call it – and dialled Ellen Smith instead.

"It's me, Tommy. Come on – pick the damned thing up." His old partner's habit of screening incoming calls was irksome, but Vincenti understood it.

"Hello there, Detective."

"Why the hell are you sitting inside on a gorgeous afternoon?" rumbled Vincenti. The temptation to slip into the patter of male camaraderie was still there, but nowadays he felt awkward whenever he gave into it. He was talking to a woman now, wasn't he? Tommy Flaherty even sounded a little like the genuine article today.

"What the hell d'you think I'm doing? I can tell you this much – I ain't sitting here waiting for a date."

"Very funny."

"My dear, you need a hell of a sense of humor to lead the life I'm leading. Take my word for it, a laugh here and a laugh there goes a long way."

The purpose of the call, explained Vincenti, was that he needed to talk. They agreed to meet at a shot-and-beer joint down on Fulton Street in what used to be the shadow of the World Trade Center. That neighborhood was a ghost town on weekends except for the ghouls who ventured down there to look at the big crater in the ground left by 9/11 and purchase memorabilia of the slaughter.

"Two o'clock, say?"

"There's not a thing on my calendar, darling."

The old Tommy Flaherty would never use flowery words like "darling" and "dear," and Vincenti felt strange whenever Ellen Smith trotted one out now. He thought he knew Tommy, but it was a long time since he could say it safely.

Fortunately, Nicky was ready to go home and play with his toy trains. Vincenti jumped the PATH and was in town in a matter of minutes. The canyons of lower Broadway were fairly deserted. The kitten-sized Norway rat that appeared out of nowhere, scampered across the sidewalk, and disappeared down the steps of the subway entrance for the Brooklyn-bound train, was the most animated character Vincenti encountered as he made his way along Fulton Street. Something vital had been ripped out of the city on that horrific September morning, and it seemed to him that it hadn't been replaced. Maybe it never would be.

If Vincenti's life wasn't in such a mire – in other words, if he needed to give a damn – he would have been flat-out embarrassed at being seen, even in a dead-end joint like the Blarney Stone, with its stench of urine, sour cabbage, and singed hamburger, with a wreck of a human being like the former Tommy Flaherty. The chipping polish on

Ellen Smith's fingernails and the tawdry phoniness of her wig didn't help. The same could be said for her body, which seemed to be breaking down by the minute and going to the seedy fat usually seen in hardcore juicers and heavily medicated mental patients.

Maybe one of us is crazy, Vincenti decided. He and Ellen sat with their mugs of flat Budweiser in the window alcove and contemplated the erratic flow of humanity on the narrow lane. Seeing the men in turbans and the women in saris made Vincenti wish he was on the other side of the world.

"You're not gonna believe what I'm up against now ..." He proceeded to run down his confrontation with Mohammed Phillips. Ellen chewed on the grizzled nail of her ring finger. The erstwhile Tommy Flaherty was not usually one for passing judgment – given his life it would have been impossible. But now she cast her old friend a sidelong look of real concern.

"You can't just – you gotta get hold of yourself. What the hell are you doing, man?"

Vincenti went on staring blankly through the glass, which had been smudged by untold millions of New York fingers. "If I knew, I'd tell you," he said finally, in a barely audible voice.

"The more important question is – why."

"Yeah, well, what can I say?"

Both of them knew what wasn't being put into words, what the other was thinking about.

"Well ... maybe now's the time to –"

"Uh-uh, Tommy. Why talk about it now? The past is the past. It's dead. Nothing we can do about something that's already happened, is there? You know that as well as I do – you more than anybody. Some things have to be lived with, right? I mean, I got a *son*. I think about the consequences for him – as if it's not already too much of a fucking disaster as it is. You, too, you got kids, even if they don't want to know you right now. You don't really want to add to their torment, do you?"

Vincenti hadn't meant to be hard, to throw Ellen's sex-change into her face, but they were both responsible for misdeeds in the past, and the way he saw it, why they'd occurred was beside the point right now, even though he'd lied a little to Tommy – he wanted to talk about that dead kid all the time, it was pretty much all he ever wanted to talk about. That was partly why they were both here right now, and they both knew it.

And that's why he was always being pulled back to that night ...

He remembered now how he checked his watch and exclaimed "Jesus Christ!" when he saw that it was just after three a.m. The gay crush had nearly broken up and the West Village was quickly turning into a desolate landscape irradiated by smog-haloed street lamps. He and Tommy had drifted out onto the crabgrass-and-gravel pier that was undergoing a facelift after having been roped off for years. They found themselves all the way out at the terminus, leaning on the corroded railing looking across the water toward Hoboken. In fact, they could practically make out the lights of headquarters from where they stood. Vincenti could even recall now what they were talking about: where, since they were famished, to grab a middle-of-the-night breakfast, something they did whenever they had the graveyard shift. Tommy had wanted to drive out to the Tick-Tock Diner not far from Giants Stadium because he was a fan of their sausage-and-egg plates, and since he no longer cared if the world knew who he really was. He was going to make a statement, he decided, come clean to the Hoboken Police Department, and it was going to include reporting for duty as Ellen Smith. If it meant repercussions, if it meant lawsuits filed back and forth, then so be it. In fact, that was one of the main reasons he wanted to talk to Vincenti, to get him ready for what was about to come down. He owed him that much before the shit hit the fan. He didn't want him blindsided, didn't want him to have to answer embarrassing questions without being prepared, if he could be prepared.

Normally Vincenti would have gone for Tommy's suggestion in a heartbeat, but he didn't relish the idea – back then even more so – of being seen in one of his regular haunts in the company of someone dressed like a bad circus attraction, especially since that someone was his partner on the police force. And so his vote was for something right in town, on Sixth or Seventh Avenue, where not a single eye would blink at the sight of a rugged guy in a dress. He'd called Reggie earlier and told her he'd be late getting in. As usual, she'd said nothing more than "Be careful – I love you." Even now, remembering her words made him wince with pain.

Then there was the caterwaul of a siren in the distance, he recalled, and how it seemed to provide cover for the shuffle of gravel behind himself and Tommy. They heard a voice; something like the word "cock" hung in the air, though afterwards he would doubt a million times that he actually heard it ...

"Look, I slipped, okay?" Vincenti went on after coming back to the present and trying to explain about Mohammed Phillips. "It was one of those bad, bad days, y'know? It wasn't just the rape investigation ... it was Daisy, it was –"

"*Daisy?* I thought you put that to sleep long ago."

"If I had even half a brain, I would have. But I don't."

"Oh, come on, Brian –"

"Look at me, man – look at me!"

"You're that hard up for –"

"You come on! *You* come the fuck on –"

Their voices were raised. Ellen glanced over her shoulder, then grabbed her ex-partner by the biceps. "You're one of the best cops Hoboken ever had, Vincenti. That's something you can't deny. No way. No fucking way."

"'Had' is the operative word."

Ellen shook her unsightly head. "Brian, Brian, Brian."

"But the icing on the cake was following Reggie to this fucking hump's house up in Weehawken."

"Why the hell'd you do that?"

"Because I'm a moron. A moron who just can't help himself. You'd think after getting my rocks off I'd just fold up my tent and go home, right? *Not.* After I was finished with Daisy I stopped by Lorenzo's, said hello to Paulie and had a few pops. Lately the stuff's been hitting me all wrong. No sooner did I have two or three down the hatch than my mood went black, and I thought to myself, what should I do next, and –"

"The next thing you know, you're tailing your wife."

Vincenti regarded Ellen Smith's sagging profile in the muzzy light of late afternoon. There was a flabby gullet growing out of her throat, and whoever had changed Tommy Flaherty into a woman had neglected or forgotten to completely get rid of his Adam's apple. He'd read somewhere that the aging process went like wildfire once you hit middle age, and it was true. That thought was followed by one about Ellen's sex life. As a newly minted middle-aged woman, what the hell were her prospects? A nice middle-aged man for a cozy relationship? After all, as Ellen told one newspaper reporter when the story broke, she was fully a woman, with a woman's desires. Not gay, not a freak of nature, but – a woman. But Vincenti didn't want to go there. It was worse than imagining your parents in the act.

"Tailing her, shit. I fucking *leaned* on her right there in the middle of the street. I mean, I knew where she was heading and all, and I was – I was gonna *kill* her, I think. That was the scary thing. I was *close*. Real goddamn close, Tommy. But at the last second I didn't. I don't know what stopped me." *Nicky*, he thought. The kid had already saved his mother's life. "So I just let her go on and ... screw pretty boy Bartano."

"And instead you tried to kill Mohammed Phillips."

"Know what's the most tired thing of all? When you kinda figure out why you're doing something and you still can't stop yourself."

In a sort of delayed reaction, his hands had begun aching from pounding on Mohammed Phillips' head thirty-six hours ago.

"I wouldn't know," deadpanned Ellen. "So now you got yourself painted into a corner ... Got anything legit on this Phillips joker?"

"Not really. Ain't that a bitch?"

"Because it would help if you did." Ellen jostled her mug, which caused the silver and amethyst charm on her wrist to tinkle. "Another drink? On second thought, maybe you shouldn't."

"Yes, Mother."

Ellen shrugged the jab off. "Contacted an attorney?"

"Nope."

"What the hell are you waiting for?"

"I don't know. Maybe I'm past giving a fuck."

"That doesn't sound so good."

"I don't figure it does."

"But your boy, Nicky – no matter what, there's still him to think about. You said that yourself. Hell, man, you don't want to end up doing time over some ridiculous bullshit like this. Not with what we –" Ellen Smith came to a screeching halt and shifted gears. "I mean, you know what this is gonna look like: once you introduce race into the equation, you're tossing a lighted match into a lake full of gasoline. An explosion is inevitable, and there'll be no survivors."

Vincenti knew all that, and it still hadn't been enough to keep him from crossing the line with Phillips.

"I'm no fucking racist. Look at Daisy, for Christ's sake. And if anybody ever needs further proof of my tolerance, there's always you."

"So what are you gonna do?"

"Who knows? Maybe nothing. Somebody wants me,

they know where to find me. In the meantime I'll go on with the Kenmore thing."

At this point, Vincenti wasn't sure why he'd wanted to see Ellen Smith in the first place. It was like he was just thinking out loud.

Ellen was incredulous. "The Kenmore thing? You mean that with all this other mayhem going down you're gonna keep chasing some phantom that –"

"I know, I know. You don't have to tell me. I've thought it over every which way there is to think it over. All I know is, there was something about her picture that –"

Silence. Neither of them moved. The dank air was rife with a thousand unspoken thoughts.

"You know what you're doing, don't you?"

Ellen Smith wasn't looking at her friend anymore. She was peering through the window at the ancient street that had been there for centuries before Tommy Flaherty and Brian Vincenti were born. And, thought the ex-cop glumly, it was a byway which had witnessed damned near every kind of evil – including mass murder – that man could perpetrate upon man, somnolent and harmless though it appeared on this dull and empty Sunday afternoon. There was evil on this side of the glass, too. There was evil everywhere.

"What am I doing? What?" said Vincenti.

"You're using this to ... to make up for that kid. For what happened."

"I know what I'm doing. Maybe I need this to keep my mind off everything else. And maybe you're right, maybe it's to make up for ... for something else. Well then, that's the way it is. But I have to keep at it until I'm satisfied."

"You poor, misguided man."

It was the second time today Ellen Smith sounded like a genuine woman. This time a perturbed one.

"What's that old saying about the pot calling the kettle black?"

"I think that's the saying."

"So now what?"

"You got a computer at your place, right?"

"Without a computer, Vincenti, I would be like a man stranded on a desert island." Ellen clucked sadly. "See? Sometimes even I forget."

Pushing his empty mug away, Vincenti got up from his stool. "Mind if I use it?"

The Yahoo "People Finder" showed that Doctor Keane lived on Seventh Avenue at Houston, just a few blocks from Thompson Street, where Ellen Smith was holed up. Vincenti was astonished when Keane himself answered his buzzer. Following the announcement that he was a Hoboken police detective and wanted to talk, there was nothing but the crackle of static for a few seconds in the small speaker set in the door frame.

"Mind if I ask the reason?"

"I'm looking into the death of Gail Kenmore. It's my understanding you worked with her."

"So I did. Um ... uh ... I'm a little busy at the moment, so ..."

"I won't kill your day, Doctor, I promise."

"Well, yes ... I suppose I should talk to you ..."

Fumbling. Bumbling. An odd response. But maybe it was just the preoccupation of a man who held people's lives in his hands on a daily basis.

"I'll be down in a sec ... or – or would you rather come up?" The poor guy couldn't figure out what he wanted to do.

"Think I'll take you up on your invite."

Not only did he want to get a look at Keane's surroundings, but Vincenti's feet hurt, as they often did when he traipsed through the asphalt jungles, and they were throbbing now after a long day spent hiking around Hoboken and downtown Manhattan.

"Number 4D. Guess you know that if you're looking at the directory. Sorry, no elevator, so you'll have to climb."

The building was a five-story square of buffed yellow brick. There were only seven flats listed, which meant that the units had to be quite ample, which in turn meant that their occupants were well-fixed. Hell, you could hardly afford even a studio apartment the size of a cupboard in Manhattan unless you were pulling down six figures. Leave it to Ellen Smith to find one of those in a rent-controlled building.

The buzzer blasted in his ear, loud and whining. Vincenti pushed on the glass and ascended the scuffed staircase. 4D was at the end of a short hall and faced the rear of the building. He pressed the button in the upper center of the glossy black door, just below the peephole. It produced a mellow "ding-dong," the sort of sound you'd expect to hear coming from the inside of a split-level in the suburbs. A pair of slender, bearded young guys in bomber jackets steering a huffing bulldog on a tether squeezed past him. Gay, no doubt. The majority of the residents of this building were probably gay, as they were in most West Village apartments. He wondered about Doctor Keane.

The detective leaned against the jamb while he listened to the chink and chunk of chains and bolts. The man he saw hovering near Gail Kenmore's casket on Long Island was dressed today in khakis, a blue and blackchecked flannel shirt, black track shoes. He looked like an outdoorsman, or a guy who installs cabinets for a living, not a physician.

"Um – yes, come on in, Detective."

Vincenti swiftly took in the layout: a wide, deep living room, a kitchen and a dining area off to the right, three open doors leading to rooms further inside the flat. The place was huge. Amazing. It was even bigger than his apartment in Hoboken.

"So – what can I do for you today, sir? Oh – have a seat, please."

Vincenti moved to a leather-upholstered easy chair beside a floor-to-ceiling bookcase. He stole a look at the titles: *Dorman's*, *Stedman's*, and *Anatomy* on the top shelf, scores of medical journals on the next, bestsellers like Grisham and King below that.

"You by yourself here, Doc?"

"Yes – by myself. Never been married. Uh-uh."

Keane grinned sheepishly and nudged his frameless glasses back up with a crinkle of his nose. Vincenti attributed Keane's unprovoked coughing up of personal information to nervousness around the authorities; lots of people – like the ones whose blood pressure shoots through the ceiling at the sight of a doctor's smock – were like that. The mere hint of a uniform or badge and they turn into simpering blabbermouths.

Strange place for a single guy, all right. It had been decorated with a deft touch, from the thrown carpets to the copper pots and pans hooked onto the fully-appointed faux-country kitchen walls, replicating a model out of the pages of *House & Garden*. Keane – or someone – knew what he was doing, and he had the money to do it.

"Can I get you something – something to drink?"

"No, thanks, Doc. This isn't exactly a social call."

Like a kid, Keane pulled another face. Vincenti tried to figure him out. Not all that old – in his late thirties, maybe, or early forties. And probably not gay, either, if you could determine that from appearances alone. On the whole, women were better with the facility – "gaydar," they called it. But there *was* something unusual about this man. He was gawky like an adolescent – that was it, all arms and legs on an oversized torso. And a little "off" – shut down, repressed – something like that. He couldn't think of better words; it was as if something hadn't quite gelled or matured in the fellow's personality. And here he was a doctor, no less. Vincenti knew that being stunted or compromised didn't prevent a person from excelling at his profession. Look at Ellen Smith for Christ's sake.

He was part of a practice down near Wall Street and a consulting physician at Saint Vincent's, more specifically, where he got to know Gail Kenmore, he explained when Vincenti asked.

"How well did you know her?"

"We were friends. Occasionally we did things outside of the hospital, had coffee, dinner, things like that – you know."

Vincenti didn't know. He was a guy who didn't make friends with women. Maybe it was no mistake that the only woman he was friends with was Ellen Smith. Women were to be slept with, married or divorced – there wasn't much in the way of middle ground. Maybe he didn't believe that being friends with a woman was possible.

Keane was on the edge of his chair, fingers so tightly interlocked that they'd turned white, the blood having drained out of them. They were unusual hands, slender, woman-like, too delicate for the large frame they were attached too. But they were, Vincenti figured, fine appendages for a doctor.

It was curious, that Keane felt the need to strangle his own fingers. His anxiety made Vincenti feel preternaturally calm.

"I'll come right to the point. Were you her boyfriend – her lover?"

The question practically launched Keane out of his seat. He did a little pirouette around the living room, his face reddening, then darted into the kitchen, where he opened the freezer, dropped a few ice cubes into a glass and used the water cooler on the refrigerator door to fill it.

"The answer is no. No sir. Not her boyfriend. Not her lover." He drained the glass in a single gulp. Then he stuck it under the tap for a refill.

"All right, then ... You must have heard her talk about her boyfriend? Boyfriends?"

Keane's bear-like head swiveled back and forth. "No. Though she did mention her ex-husband once or twice."

"Had she seen him lately?"

"No. I don't think she had. At least she didn't say so. Though I wouldn't know for sure."

Vincenti was annoyed. He was convinced Keane was hiding something, or at least holding something back. The question was how to pry it out of him.

"In your opinion, Doc, what happened to her the day she died?" He searched Keane's face. "Assuming of course you've given it any thought? And I have to assume you did since you were friends."

Keane leaned awkwardly against the wide counter, where an open loaf of pumpernickel bread sat next to a serrated knife on a cutting board. "Well, I – I don't think that's for me to say."

"You mean you never even *thought* about it?"

"It's – I –"

"You think it's possible she committed suicide?"

"I don't know."

"You don't have an opinion one way or the other?"

Keane hesitated. "No."

"You think it's *possible*?"

"It's not *im*possible."

"Why do you say that?"

"There were things that were ... troubling her."

"Troubling her. What 'things?'" Vincenti felt like a dentist trying to extract a tooth that wouldn't cooperate. But it was the first hint he'd gotten from someone who knew her that Gail Kenmore might have killed herself.

Keane shifted his weight uneasily. "If I speculated, it would only be that – speculation, and I don't think it's fair or proper for me to –"

"Were you her doctor?"

Another hesitation. "No – but I'd examined her."

"Why?"

"She asked me to. She was having some ... difficulties."

"What kinds of 'difficulties?'"

"Panic attacks."

This was news to Vincenti. "Her father mentioned something about vertigo. Attacks of vertigo. Were they related, or the same thing or something?"

The doctor gave a wry, all-knowing smile.

"Clinically speaking, they're far from the same. With panic attacks you might have a touch of dizziness – vertigo – but nothing more. The problem is that people sometimes mistake the symptoms of an emotional disturbance for vertigo. It's easier for them to deal with it that way. But true vertigo is an affliction with a purely physical basis – most likely of viral causation."

"So – did she have vertigo as well as these panic attacks?"

"No. That was just something ..."

"That she told her father."

"Kids and their parents. Guess she didn't want him to know the real problem, for whatever reason."

"What was the origin of these panic attacks, in your opinion?"

"At first she thought it might have been the symptom of a brain tumor or something like that, but after extensive tests nothing was found. Her father probably told you all about it."

"A little. So what was really going on?"

"Stress. Anxiety. Depression. The typical triggers. Maybe ... something deeper. Well, at least I –"

"Something deeper?"

"Maybe. But that would be for a psychiatrist to determine."

"Did she have one?"

Just then the telephone rang. A cordless receiver sat on the kitchen counter, but instead of picking it up, Keane went into one of the open doors at the rear of the apartment, shut it, and seconds later the ringing stopped.

Vincenti cocked his ear to the muffled one-way conversation, but he couldn't manage to pick up the thread, only a stray word here and there. Two that seemed to hang in the air were "yes" and "now." And they were spoken with intent, with weight.

Instinctively Vincenti knew he was being talked about. What the hell was going on here? When Keane returned, he decided to put an end to the game-playing. He got out of his chair and went straight up to his host.

"Doctor Keane, you're holding out on me."

"What do you mean?" Keane flushed deep crimson. "No, I –"

"I wasn't born yesterday, man. Come clean with me." The nerves in the doctor's face went berserk, Vincenti could see them jiggling beneath his skin. He thought Keane might actually burst into tears.

"You were in love with her but she wanted nothing to do with you – was that it?"

Just as quickly as it had appeared, the color drained out

of Keane's face. Vincenti saw a ridge of sweat beads glistening over his heavy black brows.

He could feel the old, familiar rage, the rage that led to his pummeling of Mohammed Phillips, coiling up in his gut like a rattlesnake about to strike. But he couldn't let it out today, not again.

"Why don't you let me help you?" he suggested to Keane, who was still frozen in an agony of indecision.

Nothing. Time to apply some pressure.

"Who was it just called you? Could you tell me that?"

"Nobody ... just, um ... nobody."

"'Just nobody' ... Doc, you're laying out a line of bullshit here, and you know it. Why don't you just tell me the truth? You'll feel better, I guarantee it."

Keane slowly shook his head. "I won't feel better," he said with strange certitude. "I won't."

Fascinating. The good doctor was trying to protect someone. He'd have to just wait the guy out now.

"So what's it gonna be, Doc?" prodded Vincenti after watching Keane move from the kitchen to a window that looked out on the irregular horizon of the cityscape. "You know, down the line you can get yourself into trouble over something like this. It's called withholding information. Is it worth it?"

"All right, Detective. All right." The air sputtered straight out of Doctor Keane, as if he were a balloon punctured with a needle. "She had an affair. With someone I happen to know. An ... an older man. But if I – I don't want it getting out. I mean, if I tell you something, this is as far as it goes, this room, right here."

I'll be damned, thought Vincenti. But he didn't open his mouth. He wasn't about to strike any deals.

"And that was the person who just called you on the telephone."

Keane clamped his eyes shut. "Look – there were issues in Gail's life that weren't easy for her to cope with. She needed someone to ... to help her, and she made a mistake."

Like me, it occurred to Vincenti. It was this gnawing sensation all along, that he and Gail Kenmore had something in common, that had him sitting here right now.

"Then the affair was over. Which is why I was reluctant to bring it up in the first place. It had no relevance to – to what eventually happened to Gail."

Vincenti knew he was going to get somewhere now, he was convinced of it. And to ensure that the flow would continue, he decided to ride the doctor very gently.

"I get it, Doc – though it might be best if someone other than yourself makes that judgment. All I want is to talk to the people who can bring me one step closer to learning what really happened to your friend."

Throughout their conversation Keane had been looking at least semi-directly at Vincenti. Now he averted his eyes.

"So – who was it you were just talking to?"

Keane groaned.

"How about it, Doc? Help me out here. Come on. You owe it to Gail."

He nodded, almost against his will. He seemed to have come to some decision. "It was ... my father."

"Your father."

Keane smiled, a little remorsefully. Vincenti didn't get it. He didn't get it at all.

"*He* was the one having the affair with Gail Kenmore? Is that what you're telling me?"

"Like I said, it's history. And he was the one who made it history."

"You're saying he ended it?"

"Yes."

"How'd they meet?"

"Through me. He joined us for dinner one night, and then things ... happened."

"I see." But he didn't really. Something wasn't making sense here.

"I always felt a little guilty about it, you know?" qualified the doctor in a near-whisper, as if he were making a confession to himself for the first time. "Not that my father had anything to do with what happened to her – but that it didn't work out. And that it was my – my own *relation* who was involved, no less."

"Guilt can be a destructive force in a person's life," offered Vincenti lamely. It was a dumb, obvious observation, and he realized it at once.

"I don't think you quite understand," said Keane, glancing in Vincenti's direction.

"Then why don't you enlighten me."

"The peculiar complexities of this whole thing – you couldn't possibly understand. And you couldn't be expected to."

Vincenti was bewildered all over again, in addition to feeling stupid. "I'd like to talk to your father," he said.

"You already have," scoffed Keane. In the interstice of a

single second – when Vincenti hadn't had enough time to notice – everything about the meek, vacillating doctor had changed.

"Come again?"

"You already have," he repeated, a hard glint of smoldering anger – hatred – in his previously hangdog eyes. "He was there, at the cemetery this morning."

It still wasn't adding up. Who, aside from Gail's father, had he actually traded words with?

"No, he wouldn't leap immediately to mind. Not many people would think of Father Raymond."

"Father Raymond – the priest?"

"Yes. Father Raymond is my dad."

Vincenti allowed the revelation a few seconds to sink in. Then he asked: "Where were you on Tuesday morning?"

Without hesitating, Doctor Keane answered "Here. I'd slept in because the night before I had the graveyard at Saint Vincent."

Keane's response had been rehearsed, thought Vincenti. Too rehearsed.

"Were you here alone?"

A forlorn expression stole over the doctor's puffy features. "Yes. I was."

"Can anyone vouch for it?"

"Just me, Detective. Just me, I'm afraid."

———————

Only after he left Keane's apartment did Vincenti put the pieces together – some of them, anyway. The doctor had been in love with Gail Kenmore himself, it was that mysterious x-factor that accounted for his suspicion that he hadn't gotten the whole story, that something still wasn't making sense. And maybe Keane didn't exactly feel 'guilty' about the fact that his old man had been sleeping with the dead girl. Maybe it was *anger* – jealousy – that made him eventually spill the beans. Now it made sense – or more sense, at least. Anyway, it was a theory. Another theory.

And it gave him another suspect. Because if Keane had been furious enough over what went on between his father and Gail Kenmore, then the doctor had a motive. And maybe, just maybe, he'd been in unit 1108 last Tuesday morning.

It was late. Darkness had settled over the city, transforming it into a dead sea of stationary lights, yellow, white, red, with here and there a flare of blue or green. Despite the fact that the vernal equinox had been officially traversed, it was still winter. Every last trace of spring that had touched the earth that day had completely vanished. A gelid wind had risen up from the Hudson and was punishing the streets of the West Village with a vengeance. Vincenti was still trying to process Keane's disclosure that the handsome cleric he'd spoken to at the cemetery had been banging Gail Kenmore when his cell phone went off.

It was Reggie. Reggie in a voice as cold as that screaming hawk off the river. He covered one half-numb ear with his palm and tried to listen with the other.

"You were supposed to be back here hours ago. What happened? *Where are you?*"

In the city, working on a case, he answered as patiently as he could.

"You knew damned well Vonda wasn't available tonight. I had a house to show at six, and you left me hanging. I need to get out of here, Brian! Now!"

It had completely slipped Vincenti's mind, and he'd just now remembered to turn his phone on. Reggie had filled him in on her plans that morning before they headed out for their stroll in the park, but the extraordinary events of the day had wiped out the detective's memory of his more prosaic responsibilities. He would have suggested that she take Nicky along on the appointment, but he knew that for his wife, mixing babysitting with business was a no-no.

"Sorry, Reg."

"Sorry?" repeated his wife bitterly. "Sorry isn't good enough."

The last thing Vincenti needed was a hissy fit. There was no way to smooth over the situation, no way to mollify Reggie. He was on his way to another place, and it was too late to change his agenda.

"There's nothing I can say, Reg. Guess I fucked up again. I'll try and make it up to you later in the week – okay?"

"Thanks a lot, Brian. Thanks a lot. God, how I hate you."

By the time he'd crossed Fourteenth Street into Chelsea the razor-sharp wind had transformed the city into a churning vortex, squalling all the detritus – food wrappers, plastic bags, pigeon shit – from the gutters and sidewalks into chaotic flux. It was fitting, decided Vincenti, that he was in the eye of a hurricane.

As he marched he chewed over his last moments in Doctor Keane's apartment. There was a lot to digest. If he hadn't picked up enough information, it wasn't all a matter of intent on Keane's part. There was also what he himself had forgotten to go after, caught off guard as he was, and even now he wasn't sure just where he should have leaned on Keane. Beyond a thumbnail sketch, the doctor hadn't given up much of anything.

What he did get was this: Father Raymond's name prior to ordination was Clayton Keane. He'd been an executive – achieving the rank of vice-president overseeing all business operations at the apex of his career – with a utilities company before taking the collar. He'd also had an attractive wife and a son – Barry, the doctor – and a beautiful home in Fairfield County, Connecticut, before giving it all up to pursue the way of the Lord. It wasn't all that simple, of course: Father Raymond had come from a devout Irish-Catholic family whose extensions were full of nuns and priests and brothers, and he'd done two years in his late teens in a seminary in Washington, D.C. before abruptly switching directions and opting for the secular life. But when his marriage broke up and his career proved ultimately unfulfilling, leaving him in a "spiritual void," there was nowhere else for him to go but back to the desire of his innocent youth. (All of which proved, Vincenti was thinking now, that truth was stranger than fiction.) The problem was, according to his son the doctor, that Clayton had had enough of the real world to know its temptations – basically, women and sex. That's where Gail Kenmore had come in.

The address Keane had given him was on the northwest corner of Tenth Avenue and West Twenty-first. The Church of the Guardian Spirit was one of those smaller, inconspicuous houses of worship Vincenti had never noticed before. New York was that kind of place: you could pass by the skeleton of a dinosaur every day for years but not see it until you were actually looking for it.

A glass-encased sign announced the times for masses and confessions. Vincenti walked back and forth until he spotted a gate adjacent to the north wall. The word "Rectory" was written in wrought iron beneath the spires. He leaned close to the black box and pressed the button.

Several seconds later it screeched.

"Yes? Can I help you?"

"Detective Brian Vincenti here. I'd like to speak to Father Raymond."

"I'm him."

"You and I talked yesterday at the cemetery, remember?"

A pause. "I remember. What brings you out on such an inclement night, Detective? And aren't you a little lost? Don't you belong on the other side of the river?"

"I'm still trying to find out what happened to Gail Kenmore."

"So why do you want to talk to me?"

Vincenti measured his words carefully. "Because I got a tip you might know a little bit more about her than you let on yesterday."

"I didn't let on anything yesterday, Detective."

"Exactly my point."

Another pause. A goddamned Mexican standoff.

"A tip, you say ... and who might this font of information be, Vincenti?"

The detective laughed. The priest was arrogant, all right.

"That's confidential, and I'd rather not say. You never know – I might have to consult my source again."

"I've only got a few minutes – so you'd better make it snappy."

Vincenti was buzzed in. At the end of the walk was a small bungalow-like edifice that was nearly invisible from the street. A triangle of light emanated from an upstairs aperture. Yellow slivers shot out of the windows on the ground floor. The detective balled his fist, which was still swollen and throbbing, and knocked on the door.

Father Raymond opened up. Vincenti found himself in a tiny office complete with cherrywood desk, chairs, floor and desk lamps. Very cozy. Against the rear wall was a credenza crammed with stacks of bound documents and religious volumes. The gold embossed words "Holy Bible" flashed across his line of vision.

"I'm going to be blunt with you, Detective."

"Shoot."

"I don't have all night for this. I'm due at the VA hospital in little over a half hour. Which means I have to be out of here in fifteen minutes – sharp." He swung his wristwatch up for emphasis.

"Then I'll make it fast."

The priest's arms were folded tightly over his chest. His unearthly blue eyes bore fierce holes into Vincenti's. Suddenly he had a feel for how a woman could be seduced by Raymond's charisma. But it was ironic that the personification of the Spirit, the representative of God on earth, could be so downright stonyhearted and unfeeling. Something about the priest, a carryover from their brief encounter at the cemetery, repulsed him, and that something had grown stronger.

"The tip I got was that you had an affair with Gail Kenmore. I'm not going to ask you whether it's true or false because –"

"Of the impeccability of your source?" taunted Raymond. "That could only be one person, Detective. I'm a little surprised you got him to blab so quickly."

"Really? You didn't look all that surprised to see me a minute ago."

"So – what's driving you, Vincenti?"

"Gail Kenmore is dead. I owe it to her to find out why before the world forgets her altogether. Which is likely to happen within a matter of days, except for what's left of her family. What I'm picking up from the people who knew her is nothing but smoke. It's no way a clear picture of who she was and what happened to her last week. So, when I hear something like this, that a priest old enough to be her father – or grandfather – was sleeping with the victim, it immediately catches my attention. You might say it begs to be followed up, know what I mean? And to be honest, Padre, there's a lot about you that piques my interest."

"It seems to me that you'd be better served by tending your own garden, Detective."

Vincenti caught the sly inference like a hook to the kidneys. Or was it his own guilty conscience acting up?

"What do you mean by that, Father?"

"You don't think that *your* life is a closed book, do you, Vincenti?"

Vincenti was sweating now, clammy streams of water running down his carcass beneath the layers of clothing, and it wasn't just the coughing steam from the radiators that was causing him to overheat.

"Let me put it this way – it seems to me that you should be cleaning up your own messes instead of sticking your nose into what doesn't concern you. The way I understand it, you've got enough of them. Would you like me to enumerate?" The priest raised his right fist and extended his thumb. "Brutality charges pending. Marriage on the rocks, complete with such pretty ingredients as terroristic threats. A steamy liaison with a girl from the 'hood, which will not aid your cause when it comes time to reach an agreement on custody of your son. Oh, and not to be forgotten – maintains 'questionable' relationship with ex-partner, who was at the center of the ugliest scandal in Hoboken PD history, and who just happens to have turned himself into a woman. Want me to go on?"

Like a flash-fire, a crazed ire roared through Vincenti. "Who'd you talk to?"

A sly grin bloomed on Father Raymond's lips. "Like you, I never reveal my sources. What I can tell you is this – it didn't take all that much to find out about you, Vincenti. A single phone call was all. Not that there's much about *you* that interests *me*."

Defiance animated the priest's winsome features. From the way his eyes were pulsing out of his skull, Vincenti sensed that the contempt masked cold fear.

Outside, there was the angry blast of a car horn, followed by a siren, and the howl of the March wind as it flogged the rectory walls. The tentacles of the Catholic Church reached everywhere, and didn't Vincenti know it. Hell, for all he knew, Hampton, a good Catholic himself, had spilled on him – he was just angry enough over the Mohammed Phillips mess to do it.

Vincenti and Father Raymond were practically chest to chest, with barely an inch between them.

"I don't give a damn what you know about me, Your Reverence. What I want to know is whether or not you had anything to do with Gail Kenmore's death. I already know you were screwing her." Because he realized now that maybe he'd been mistaken – the priest, not Hugh Kenmore, was probably the silver-haired gent Alex Danko had seen hanging around her door.

"What are you getting –"

"Did you want her out of the way for some reason? Was she pregnant? You told her to abort it, and she wanted to have the kid, was that it? Was she getting to be just too much of a pain to deal with, especially since you were wearing a nice, clean collar?"

He was firing buckshot, hoping to hit something. The priest's jaw tightened, and the nerves and muscles in his face bulged with emotion. "The answer is no to all of the above, and if it wasn't, it would still be none of your goddamned business, you grubby, two-bit piece of –"

Vincenti body-slammed the slighter man. Father Raymond staggered backward clumsily, his feet catching on the carpet, and caromed into the credenza, jarring loose several volumes that flopped noisily to the floor.

"Don't you dare touch me again, you –"

Vincenti rammed the priest a second time.

"How dare you, you son of a bitch? What do you think you're doing?"

A hysterical edge had wormed its way into Raymond's voice. His haughty exterior was beginning to disintegrate. Vincenti could see the outline of his Adam's apple bobbing like the float at the end of a fishing line.

Nothing but a pussy, as they say in the street. *That's all this boy is.*

Vincenti knew that he was edging close to the precipice all over again, but what would one more lapse of self-control mean? Wasn't he finished already?

The near-panic on the face of the pompous figure of Father Raymond was almost comical. Vincenti wondered where the housekeeper was – the clergy always had housekeepers on hand, he knew that from his time as an altar boy and from visiting his brother. Or had things changed now, was there no money left for perks after having to pay out damages to hundreds of molested kids?

The detective moved his bulk into the door frame, shutting off Father Raymond's means of escape.

"Let me pass – I'm through playing this stupid game with you," hissed the priest through clenched teeth, those perfectly even, snow-white caps Vincenti had taken note of at the cemetery.

"What are you going to do, Padre, call the cops? I'll let you go as soon as you answer me."

Father Raymond stared at his interrogator. He shook his head.

"You already have your answer, don't you? I can vouch for my son, Detective. He'd never lie. If he hedged with you, it was only to protect his old man – even if I let him down. I know I wasn't the perfect father, but who is?"

This was the second fissure to appear in the priest's composure. It was almost as if he were a flesh-and-blood human being now.

"Let me hear it again."

"Yes, we had an affair, Gail and me – I prefer to use that word instead of – of the other," admitted Raymond, melting down a little further. "It was a failing on my part. You pursue a secular life for long enough, and there are certain things that are hard to give up. Memories – of what it's like to have a woman, for one thing – they tend to linger. You take the collar, even at my age, and the doubts creep in. You think maybe you did the wrong thing, made a terrible mistake, you know? Maybe you just had the wrong wife, the wrong kids. Maybe this, maybe that. Maybe you'll just see what it's like to be with a woman again ... Do you understand what I'm getting at?"

The tumult in the priest's eyes was nothing if not genuine now. Vincenti thought of the disaster his own brother's life had been. Every priest he knew was a walking tragedy.

He kept listening.

"So that's why there was Gail. It wasn't planned, of course – how could it be? It was just something that happened. I know how damned weak that sounds, that every last miserable sinner in creation uses it, but in my case it's true. Not that I didn't agonize over it once it started, but by then it was too late to stop. Barry and Gail were acquaintances at the hospital, which is how we happened to cross paths. Maybe he was interested in her himself – don't think it hasn't occurred to me. Maybe that's why he decided to let the cat out of the bag, after putting on a show of reluctance for you, which is what he did, I'm sure – to get back at me. My son never had it with the girls. He was always frustrated – not like his old man ... Anyway, I suppose I sniffed out the need there, with Gail. And I'm sure she must have detected something in me."

With these admissions set free into the atmosphere, some of the strain of the last few days drained out of Vincenti's body, leaving him vacant, spent. He could have collapsed right there onto the rectory floor and fallen fast asleep. But Father Raymond wasn't through talking. Maybe he'd needed to confess all along.

"And when I use that word – 'affair' – I don't mean in any way to cheapen what it was for Gail. Because it was something else altogether for her. A lifeline. She was ... she was going under, Vincenti."

"*Why?* Why was she going under?"

The priest frowned. He seemed to waver. "There were – there were things she couldn't cope with. And she thought that by – by being with me –"

"Yes?"

"The one thing you have to believe is that I would never have hurt that girl. *Never.* You see, I actually –"

"What about your son? Would he have –"

Just then Father Raymond's beeper went off. He reached for his belt, he squinted at the number, then replaced the instrument.

"I have to go, Detective. Now you've got me late, and there appears to be an emergency. No doubt I'm needed for last rites."

Vincenti shook his head. "I have to know more. What was eating at her?"

The wall shot up all over again. "I answered your questions, didn't I? What more do you want from me?"

"I want to know the truth about what happened to Gail Kenmore when she –"

"The only person who knows is Gail. But you can rest assured I had nothing to do with it. It was over between us before the end of last year, just before Christmas. I'd put it to rest myself, when I realized that my vocation was genuine and that there was no need to test it any longer. And she was okay with that decision, she really was. We were on the best of terms when – when it happened. And when I realized that there was nothing I could do to ... Ah, look – I'm not at all okay with being the mouthpiece for someone who's dead, Vincenti. Now, if you'll let me go –"

"If there's something else, I want it," demanded the cop.

"Then try Lydia."

The expression on the priest's face was a little sardonic, as if he were referring to a peculiar relative.

Hadn't Vincenti heard that name recently? But where?

"Who?"

"Her mother."

Now he remembered. Hugh Kenmore had mentioned Lydia, if not by name. The connotation wasn't positive.

Father Raymond pulled the door open to let in a paralyzing blast of cold. "They were close. Closer than

Gail and I could ever be, despite the fact that we were ... intimate. Sleeping with someone doesn't always guarantee that – though I probably don't have to tell you."

"Where is she? Where can I find her?"

"She's somewhere in town. I don't know where, exactly. So leave me alone, please. I'm trying my best to make something better of my own life before it's too late. I didn't do anything to that girl. Whatever did ... is beyond my comprehension."

Vincenti had the feeling that maybe the priest was finally being honest, even trying to tell him something without coming right out and saying it.

"Now if you'd just step outside, please. I have to lock up. Much as I'd like to leave the doors open, sometimes this isn't the safest neighborhood."

Vincenti complied. The New York night had gone beyond glacial. He turned up the collar of his coat. He could have sworn that Father Raymond was about to reach out for him, in an effort to console him. It was as if one damaged man had recognized a kindred soul.

But he didn't.

"Good luck, Detective. And take care of yourself."

Monday, March 22

In his makeshift bedroom, Vincenti flipped the channels on the portable TV with the remote. The stories were the same ones he'd caught bits and pieces of over the last few weeks: the arrest and arraignment of a washed-up Hollywood star for the murder of his wife (nowadays that seemed to happen at least once a year), the vagaries of the volatile stock market, suicide bombings in the Middle East. On the positive side of the ledger, the mercury was going to shoot all the way up to sixty today. He thought maybe there'd be some mention of the Phillips assault, but no. The story was no doubt too small potatoes for big-time coverage.

He could hear Nicky jabbering to himself out in the living room where he was watching a cartoon on the big set. Reggie was long gone. He never saw her when he finally pulled in last night, and presumably she'd taken off early to make up for some of the obligations he'd caused her to miss yesterday. Just as well – any contact between them would no doubt have resulted in something nasty.

The phone had been bleating all morning, but he didn't want to go near the damned thing. Whatever came in had to be bad news. "Let it go, Nicky," he said again and again to the boy, who'd developed the embarrassing but comical habit of picking up the instrument whenever it rang and immediately hanging up on the caller.

Today Vincenti was off-duty, and he was at a loss for

what to do. Once Vonda arrived and took Nicky off his hands, he'd have the place to himself, at least for an hour or two, and he could use the phone in privacy to try and find Gail Kenmore's mother without his son yammering in the background. Gone were the days – especially given the Mohammed Phillips fiasco – when he could mosey into his office and conduct police business on his day off without being harassed. Today, he wouldn't even dream of making an appearance at headquarters.

He picked up his wristwatch. Eight forty-five. In a matter of minutes the nanny would show up. He willed himself off the futon, went into his tiny bathroom across the hall, and turned on the shower spigots.

In his boxers and tee shirt, Vincenti shuffled into the living room, where Nicky was busy arranging a complicated panorama of his toy animals across the floor.

"Watcha doin' there, my man?"

"Making the Hoboken Zoo, Daddy. Wanna see who's in it?"

The phone jangled again. This time Vincenti went into the kitchen and pushed up the volume on the answering machine.

"Brian, this is Vonda."

Vincenti knew the voice all too well. It was Vonda's "woe-is-me, I'm-sick-and-can't-possibly-come-in" whine. He picked up the receiver just as the babysitter was launching into an explanation that she'd been feeling ill since last night and now "ached all over" (her most standard excuse for not reporting in).

"Don't worry about it, Vonda. You just take care of

yourself, get some rest, and we'll see you tomorrow, okay?"
He'd learned from prickly experience not to quibble with
the nanny. Today, since he was off duty, none of it mattered.
Watching Nicky diligently barricading his beasts behind a
plastic fence gave him an inspiration.

"Hey, big guy – how'd you like to go to the real zoo with
your dad?"

"You mean today?" The kid's eyes were ecstatic beams
of light.

"Yeah, today."

"What about nursery school?"

"I'll call Ms. Rubinstein and tell her you're playing
hooks today."

The boy's brow furrowed. Could it really be done so
easily?

"Don't worry, Nicky. Nursery school isn't real school.
That's not 'til next year."

"What about Mommy?" A cloud passed over the boy's
features, which were more Reggie's than his.

"Mommy? Well, she's at her job today. Maybe we can
get her to come with us another day."

"You don't like Mommy anymore, do you, Daddy?"

The question froze Vincenti. How the hell could he
possibly answer it, make it even remotely comprehensible
to a four-year-old?

He opted for the fairytale response.

"Sure I do, Nicky. It's just that we're so busy with our
work, we don't have much time to spend together."

Lying to a child seemed wrong, but what choice did he
have?

"Does she still like *you?*"

Vincenti laughed. "You'd have to ask her."

"I think she does," Nicky said brightly. The delusion seemed to make him feel better.

"There you go, pal. Tell you what – let's get dressed and go wake up the gorillas."

Breaking away unexpectedly like this gave Vincenti the momentary illusion that his life was normal. What could be more emblematic of an ordinary existence than impulsively whisking your kid off to visit the zoo?

"Are we taking the train, Daddy?" Nicky asked four or five times (he asked every question a half-dozen times, it seemed) as Vincenti pulled his jeans on. And each time he patiently explained that they would be taking the Jeep, a vehicle he loved and that Reggie never cared for, which was fitted out with a child's seat and was docked at a lot on Hudson between Third and Fourth Streets. As they crossed the George Washington Bridge and cruised up the Henry Hudson to the Mosholu Parkway, they gabbed about every beast, from the Gaboon Viper to the polar bear. While driving past the mansions of Riverdale the sun broke through the haze and dappled the world with pools of early spring light. It was almost enough to make a guy feel good after the gloom of a long winter. But not quite.

Before leaving the house Vincenti had switched off his cell. He wanted no intrusions into this little romp with his son – there'd probably be all too few in their lives as it was –

and after forking over the admission, the two of them walked hand in hand through the park, which was pleasantly devoid of the typical crowds.

Most of the animals were still relegated to their inside habitats. Nicky's attention never lingered for long on any one creature before he was antsy to be on his way. Like a skittish butterfly he lighted from exhibit to exhibit, as if whatever he happened on wasn't quite what he was looking for, or failed to measure up to his expectations. And that was a kind of strange parallel to his own fucked-up situation, Vincenti decided. Whenever he thought he might have his hands wrapped around the neck of the Kenmore thing, the answer would vaporize maddeningly into thin air.

By noon it really was spring, complete with chirping birds and the tantalizing scent of nascent grass. Vincenti bought pizza and fries for his son and a grilled chicken sandwich for himself, and they sat at a table in the quadrangle surrounded by the carts selling popcorn, designer coffee and ice cream bars. Out of habit he pulled out the cell phone and peered at its blank face. Switch it on and check for messages? Giving into his curiosity would accomplish nothing except for destroying a few stolen hours of peace. He resisted and returned the device to his coat pocket.

"What do you say, Nicky – wanna ride the camel?"

The boy was beside himself. They tossed their trash and hiked over to "Asia," where Vincenti shelled out eight bucks to mount the dromedary.

"Again! Again!" Nicky begged after they got off the enormous beast.

The ebullient outburst stabbed at Vincenti's heart. The

sight of Nicky's miniature eyes, nose, and mouth brought on a wave of stupid, sentimental longing. Maybe what got him most was the notion that he'd once been a little kid himself.

He reached for his wallet. "Let's do it again, slugger."

"Where's Mama?" the boy asked when he'd had enough.

"You know where she is, Nicko."

"Why is she always working? I miss Mama."

Vincenti had another idea, a completely insane idea: climb into the Jeep with Nicky and drive ... just drive in any direction, north, south, west – until they couldn't go any further, until they arrived at a place where no one knew who they were, until they were free, until it was just the two of them left in the world. A fucking marvelous scenario. But it was fraught with problems, and he knew it: eventually the money would run out, and the boy wouldn't fare all that well without his mom, and once his brothers in law enforcement began searching for a rogue cop who'd kidnapped his own child, it would be damned hard if not impossible to hide, short of completely changing identities – tough to do with a four-year-old.

Another spectacular fantasy down the toilet. It was happening a lot lately.

———

Nicky was gently snoring by the time Vincenti turned over the ignition. The volatile sky had changed from blue to an ominous gray. There was nothing left to do but drive back to Jersey.

As soon as he switched on the cell phone, the "ba-ding

ba-ding" that signaled the presence of messages went off. The first was from Hilario Rodriguez at the Hudson County Coroner's Office.

"Got some preliminary findings on the Kenmore death. You can call me here today at ..."

Vincenti hit the callback button. Rodriguez picked up after a single ring.

"It's Vincenti," the detective announced softly, careful not to wake his sleeping child. "Where's Vic?"

Victor Krishnan was assistant medical examiner. He was the person Vincenti normally dealt with when the subject was dead bodies.

"Vic? On vacation this week and next."

"Nice. Anywhere good?"

"He went back to India to visit family. I'm not sure I'd call that so good."

Vincenti was uncertain which part was the object of judgment here, India or visiting family, but he didn't feel confident quizzing Rodriguez, who was someone he'd never met or even spoken to.

"So – what's the story on Kenmore?"

Just then the cell phone connection broke up. Vincenti cursed. When Rodriguez faded back in, he repeated the question.

"Nothing out of the ordinary."

Rodriguez's voice had the unique cadences of the transplanted westerner. Arizona? California?

"No alcohol or illegal drugs found in the victim's system, for one thing."

"How about something legal?"

"A trace of alprazolam – Xanax. An anti-anxiety medication."

"Right, right," said the detective. He knew what Xanax was. He'd taken enough himself over the past few months. "Which means she was under some kind of stress."

"Well, it could mean lots of things, actually," sniffed Rodriguez with the ill-concealed pedantry of the professional scientist. "It could mean she had trouble sleeping, or she needed it to visit her dentist, or any number of circumstances. What I'm saying is that we shouldn't jump to any conclusions here. No joke intended."

"Mind hanging on for a sec?"

Vincenti quickly tried to recall the questions he had about the condition of Gail Kenmore's body. He decided to pull off the parkway so that he could concentrate on the conversation instead of the traffic. He swerved onto the exit that advertised the home of Edgar Allan Poe, and glided into the curb on a side street in the shadow of a multi-story apartment building.

"All right. So what condition was she in?"

Was that a snort at the other end? He was beginning to dislike this guy Rodriguez.

"There wasn't much left of her, if that's what you mean."

"That's not what I mean. What I want to know is were there any bruises on her that might have indicated a struggle. If you can tell that sort of thing when a body is in such bad condition."

"You mean like was she pushed or forced out? Is that what you're getting at?"

"Something like that."

"To answer your question, you can always tell the difference between types of bruises. It has to do with the age of the wound, what was in the wound, such as particles of concrete, or glass, and so on. And if you're looking for signs of struggle, you go under the fingernails, you look for scratches, and –"

Vincenti knew how to read wounds, from the crime scene seminars he'd attended, he didn't need a crash course. But he hadn't personally seen Gail Kenmore's body after she died.

"And what do you think here, with Gail Kenmore?"

"There was quite a large bruise that wasn't a result of the fall. Left biceps. Fairly recent."

"Does it mean she was –"

"It could mean anything. Maybe she walked into a door. Or maybe she fought with someone."

"Hm ..."

"Other than that, she was clean – that is, there was nothing else to indicate any kind of struggle."

Rodriguez oozed attitude, but so far there was nothing in his responses to indicate that he didn't know what he was talking about.

"Mm-hm ... Was she a donor?"

"There was no ID on her person when she was brought in. By the time it was located, it didn't matter. There was nothing left to donate."

"Was she pregnant?"

"Negative. What was a little strange was that she landed on her feet," Rodriguez went on. "And that suggests to me that maybe she didn't necessarily go out that window voluntarily."

Vincenti remembered Franks' report saying the same thing. "You mean she didn't jump?"

"I'm not saying anything definite here, but *maybe* not. Maybe she just lost her balance and fell. Or maybe she changed her mind at the last minute. Or last second, I should say. Lots of maybes. And when you put all the maybes together, you come up with nothing."

This was bad. Very bad. Because what it meant was –

"Did anything else stand out?" Vincenti knew now there was nothing left for him but to grasp at straws.

"No, not really. Sorry, Detective. If you're looking to build some kind of case here to make this other than an accident or a common suicide, then I can't see it from my end. If that's what you're after, you're going to have to approach it from another angle. Like a witness. A confession. A motive."

Rodriguez told Vincenti when he might expect the final report, and they hung up.

Vincenti sat there contemplating the strangely placid landscape of the Bronx. What the conversation with the assistant medical examiner signified was that there was no way, short of a confession by someone, that he was ever going to know what happened to Gail Kenmore that day up on the eleventh floor of the Hudson Arms. And in the process of trying, he'd come excruciatingly close to destroying himself and everyone around him. Hell, maybe he'd already accomplished that. What was he trying to do, anyway? What was this mad obsession about? He couldn't go on dragging it out ad nauseam just because there was something about Gail Kenmore's face that, for lack of a better word, haunted him. It had to end. That's all there was to it. *It had to end.* Because there was nothing to find. He repeated it, in order to convince himself: *There's nothing. You're after nothing. Get over it.*

He rolled into the driveway of the office of an ophthalmologist by the name of Cohen, then backed out and found his way back to the parkway. His mind was a cipher. He looked at the phone on the seat beside him, picked it up and hit the message button again.

This time the voice belonged to Reggie. She was shaken, if not angry. "Where are you, Brian ... Is Nicky with you? I hope to God he is ..."

Jesus fucking Christ! It had completely slipped his mind to call the school! With all the noise in his brain, it was no wonder. Okay – Reggie had a right to be upset.

The final message was from a growling, sarcastic Hampton.

"Where the hell are you, Vincenti? I hate to be the guy to ruin your day off, but you better call me soon as you get this message. Here's the deal: this Phillips guy you busted up the other night is in a coma. He's over at Saint Mary's, lying there like a cucumber in the supermarket since last night. One of his homies found him face-down in a hallway in the projects. Nobody knows if he smoked or swallowed or injected something to put himself into that vegetative state, or it's because of what you did to him – like a delayed reaction from getting his head bashed in. If he did it to himself, who knows – maybe he had something to do with that rape you were looking into, get what I mean? But if not ... if not, then you got yourself a little problem. More than a little problem. More like a king-sized problem. If Smokely starts hollering and persuades the doctors that Phillips is suffering from blunt force trauma or some crap like that, then we're gonna have to bring you in and charge you, put you on suspended leave and all the rest of it. I don't wanna have to do it, but that's the way it'll have to be. I advised you to talk to a lawyer. I hope you took me up on it. Now you're not gonna have a choice in the matter. One more thing, Vincenti – make sure you get rid of this message."

It was the largest volume of words Vincenti had heard out of Hampton's mouth on a single occasion since he'd been on the force.

The chief signed off with another strongly worded request to contact him ASAP. Vincenti thought it over for a few seconds, then switched the phone off again.

———————

Reggie was waiting on the sidewalk, an unlit cigarette in her hand, when the Jeep pulled up. She seemed lost inside the pepper-colored cashmere overcoat that he recognized as one of the more conservative garments she wore when showing clients around Hoboken properties.

She ran into the street and threw open the back door. "Sweetie! I missed you so much!"

"Guess what, Mama? Daddy took me to the zoo instead of school! Wanna know what we saw?"

"I want to know all about it, honey!"

"We saw the biggest snake in the whole world!"

"You did! Wow!" echoed Reggie, trying to counterfeit

enthusiasm for the idea of a gigantic coiled killer.

The words went on tumbling out of Nicky's mouth as Reggie unbuckled him. He was trying to tell her about everything at once: the cheetah, the camel ride, the rhinoceros. Reggie shot her husband an antagonistic glance.

"Take it easy there, big guy," Vincenti said, mostly to himself, when she slammed the door shut.

He wasn't going straight back to the apartment. He parked the Jeep, then strode up Third Street toward the water and cut down River past the building where Gail Kenmore had met her fate. Then he crossed the street and scuttled between the noisy, upturned construction sites where a pair of fourteen-story monstrosities – a chain hotel and a publishing company relocating from Manhattan – were being erected, and entered the pier park.

A soup-like fog was seeping in from beyond the Hudson, and Vincenti could smell the dense odor of salt water. The scent of the ocean usually braced him, but today he skulked along the promenade feeling like a criminal, passing a gang of skateboarding kids, a homeless woman in a filthy parka pushing an overflowing shopping cart, and a pair of fishermen keeping an eye on their lines. Lingering near the cove adjacent to the copper-domed train station, he watched a brace of mallards paddling through the filthy water, his mind as turbid as the depths below. After a few minutes he pushed himself off the railing and headed toward Newark Street.

Something was bucking at the back of his brain. He

passed the dormant fountain on the cobblestone plaza where the bums and delinquents and sometimes the suburban commuters sat waiting for their trains and ferries, and hooked toward Washington Street. A few doors in, between a nightclub that was a blatant Planet Hollywood knock-off and a discount beauty supplies store, there was a shop that sold children's books and advertised, on a small placard inside the window, "Tarot/Psychic Readings Daily."

He'd been curious ever since he spotted the ad, had even considered going in during the early days of his troubles with Reggie and having his future guessed at, but today was the day he had the motivation to actually do it. Someone – one of Reggie's friends – raved about the experience she'd had with the psychic-in-residence.

What he was after was the key – the key to the death of Gail Kenmore.

A scarecrow of a woman in a pleated paisley skirt was behind the counter sorting through a stack of greeting cards, CDs, books. Vincenti couldn't decide whether she was young or old.

"Can I help you with something?"

"The, uh – the tarot readings."

Suddenly he felt like a fool, an old woman, resorting to magic, superstition.

"You'd like one?"

"I think so …"

Embarrassing. He felt the blood rising to his cheeks.

"Today?"

"Now – I mean, if that's possible. I don't have an appointment or anything like that."

The woman peered through an archway into the rear of the store, where the walls were sparsely lined with books and a few stuffed toys.

"That would be Daniel. Let me see if he's busy at the moment."

She came out from behind the counter and darted into the back room. Vincenti watched her whisper something to a lone figure seated at a round, bistro-style table who obviously wasn't occupied with anything whatsoever.

"Come right in ... He just happens to be free."

Daniel was utterly still, like a waiting vulture, a deck of cards face down on the table.

Vincenti pulled out the empty chair and sat.

The scarecrow tapped Daniel on the shoulder. "Your client is here."

"Ah," muttered Daniel, shifting in his seat.

"He's blind," she explained to Vincenti.

The soothsayer looked up. Vincenti saw the opaque blue films stretched over his eyeballs and flashed back to the man whose cane he had to jump in the Hudson Arms courtyard a few days ago.

A shiver ran up his spine. Not only were those dead eyeballs hideous, but Daniel's greasy gray hair was hacked off in different unruly lengths, his skin was pockmarked, and his fingers and hands were deformed. But if he stuck it out, this could be interesting. If this guy Daniel was the real deal, he'd be able to read Gail Kenmore and Vincenti without benefit of *seeing* them in the flesh – sort of like a controlled experiment. Because one of Vincenti's main problems with these charlatans – and he had no doubt that most of them were charlatans, especially after busting his share over the years, and despite the fact that some cops used them on hard-nut cases – was that they sized you up, read your body language, assessed your level of income and education through your clothing, accessories, haircut, and language, and then tossed out bait like a chumming fisherman. "You're married, are you?" or "You're a professional, am I right?" And depending on the way you answered, the quack already had a head start on where to go and the con was on. If you weren't careful – and lots of people weren't – you could find yourself forking over your life savings to lift a "curse" or some other such bullshit.

Well, he wasn't about to give Daniel anything.

The scarecrow had returned to the counter, where she was dealing with a customer. Daniel groped for his cards and fumbled them into his chest.

"All right, let's see here," he whispered, with no apparent awareness of the irony of his own words, "let's just see here ..."

Daniel's body jerked spastically, like a frightened deer's. He fiddled with the cards, removing one from the deck here and replacing it there, patting the stack, fanning it out on the table finally with his peculiar digits. Then he pushed the cards at Vincenti.

"Now, if you would shuffle, please – shuffle."

Vincenti did as he was told.

The soothsayer nodded. His long teeth were gnarled yellow tendrils. How did a creature like him function in the world? Maybe he couldn't. Maybe that's why he sat in the back room of a ladies' gewgaw shop and told fortunes.

"Now, if you'll cut the deck into three piles ..."

Vincenti shook his head. What ridiculous poppycock. And he was going to have to shell out money for it.

"Put the deck back together however you like ..."

Vincenti reassembled the deck and pushed it across the table. Daniel picked it up and felt it with his palms, as if he were trying to assess the ripeness of a melon.

"You're here about ... about someone else, not yourself, but it's you I feel ..."

Vincenti swallowed.

"Your aura ... You have the aura of someone who's trying to hide something ..."

"No," said Vincenti reflexively.

"No? You're sure?"

Then Daniel removed the top card and turned it over, then the next, and so forth, until he had laid out a single-file pattern that went up one side of the table and traveled down the other in a ragged horseshoe.

Vincenti tried to crack the significance of each card, but they quickly became a dream-like jumble. There was a man sitting on a bed, hands clasped over his eyes, in a gloomy, shuttered room ... a ghastly, leering Satan, with horned, naked figures of either sex chained to a slab beneath his hooves ... a skeleton triumphantly astride a demon-like steed ... an oblivious young man about to step off a sheer cliff into space.

The Fool.

Every one of the likenesses seemed to ping with resonance. But what the hell was he supposed to make of them?

Daniel moved his right hand over the spread like a dowser searching for water. "Ehh ... hmm ... ahhh ..."

The grin on his face disappeared. He cocked his head, as if he were listening to a sound in the distance. A bubbling pool of spit had formed in the crevice of his crooked, blubbery lips.

"Ah-ha." A light went on. "You are ... trapped, aren't you? You're in some kind of cage – yes, that's it."

"No," protested Vincenti, though with less conviction now. Because he knew the opposite was true.

Daniel grew more enthused. "Yes – you're in a blind alley, a cul-de-sac, as they say. And you're desperate to find your way out."

Vincenti denied it again.

"No? Yes, yes, I'm sure of it. It's of your own making – this trap? No, not altogether. It's not all your fault. You were forced into it by someone close to you ..."

Was he being asked a question? Vincenti cleared his throat. Suddenly the psychic shook his head and pulled his hands back from the cards. All the air seemed to go out of him. "There's nothing else ..."

"What do you –"

"I can't pick up anything else. Except what I said – that you're in this terrible trap. And the trap is both your fault and not of your making at the same time." Daniel shrugged helplessly. "I don't know how to explain it ... but *you* know. Yes, you know."

"What about the other person? The woman I came here to find out about?"

Daniel's unseeing eyes wandered around the table. "I'm sorry." The drool had narrowed into a thin rivulet that was making its way into a crack in his chin.

"Could you try?"

"I'm sorry," Daniel apologized again.

The detective got up from the table, reached for his wallet, pulled out a few bills, and pushed them into the blind man's hand.

"No, not today. Keep your money. Please."

———————

The detective wasn't thinking straight. He was shaken by the wacky, slightly uncanny accuracy of Daniel's aborted reading. He began heading home along Hudson Street, within feet of headquarters, and ran smack into Villas, who was on his way in for the evening shift.

Villas was one of the last people he had any desire to see. As a matter of fact, Villas was the guy responsible for at least part of his fix, by dragging that goddamned suspect in off the street.

Villas motioned him around the corner, into the entrance of an employment agency, out of sight of the police station where Hampton was waiting for him like a cobra.

"Understand you got problems with this Mohammed Phillips situation," Villas stated in his staccato, all-business cadence.

Vincenti nodded. "You might say that. I'm doing my best to avoid it. But I won't be able to avoid it forever." Actually, he felt the need to open up to someone aside from Ellen Smith. But Villas was without doubt the wrong person.

"Yeah, well, you probably didn't have to get hard with

him, as it turns out," Villas said without a hint of self-righteousness.

"How do you mean?"

"I collared one of his homies last night after they brought him into the hospital. The knucklehead had some grass on his person, and a few hits of crystal meth. Once I shook the stuff out of him, it was easy to get him to open up about all the shit Phillips and him are into, from ecstasy to smack to weed to speed to coke to substances I don't even know about. Big time heads, both of them."

He was beginning to see, at least dimly, what Villas was getting at. Drag this alleged friend of Phillips into court in the event of an inquest – or trial – and Detective Brian Vincenti was most definitely going to have a leg to stand on, even if it was shaky.

"Phillips deals, too. All over town. Like I said, I kept tabs on his movements whenever I could. He was even selling shit in the Hudson Arms."

"Really," said Vincenti. Had he not been so preoccupied with other things, he could have figured it out himself. He wasn't even doing his job. He'd fucked up.

"Really. One of the doormen over there told me some would-be writer up on the eleventh floor was a regular grass customer."

"I'll be damned ..."

It had to be Danko that Villas was referring to. And now Mohammed Phillips could be placed on the eleventh floor, just two doors from where Gail Kenmore went to her death. One of the undesirables Johnnie Rebecki had talked about.

"But dig this. This punk – Norbert Curtains is his name

– says Phillips was messed up real good about an hour before he collapsed."

"How'd you manage to get that out of him?"

Vincenti was genuinely impressed. He knew how hard it was to pry information out of anybody down there in the red zone. It was no secret that homey protected homey no matter what.

Villas showed his large white teeth. It was as if he just discovered he had a winning lottery ticket in his possession. "I suggested to Curtains that he didn't want to get hauled in for possession with intent to distribute. A good way to avoid that was by talking to me about his friend. What's it gonna matter now, I said to him. Phillips is in a coma. When people are in comas, it's not generally considered to be a good thing. Fifty-fifty he ain't coming out of it. So what do you know? All of a sudden Curtains opens up like a steamed clam. He knows Phillips was using because he was at Phillips' place around that time. So what you got here is witness to an overdose – or an attempted suicide."

"Why do you say th-"

Villas hoisted his forefinger like Sherlock Holmes himself. "Curtains says Phillips was asking lots of questions about the rape investigation. Like how long does it take for DNA tests to come back from the lab. What's that tell you?"

It didn't tell Vincenti anything. Maybe Phillips was hopeful that DNA tests would exonerate him – it happened all the time nowadays.

"Did Phillips leave a suicide note or anything like that?" he asked.

"Good question. Not that I know of. And I don't know

that we got enough for a warrant to go into his apartment, at least not at this point, though we could always drum something up if we had to. I'm gonna check into it, see what's what. My advice to you is to stay clear of him and Curtains. The point is, I think you're gonna beat this thing."

Vincenti thought it over, but Villas's information didn't completely set his mind at ease. In the first place, anything and everything could still go wrong with his implied scenario. In the second, it meant that he, Vincenti, was going to be in Villas's debt for as long as they were both on the force. The Mohammed Phillips imbroglio was a big deal. Big enough to spawn repercussions all over the place. Big enough to cause truly sordid things to happen – like investigations into the tactics of the Hoboken Police Department by the county internal affairs unit, which wouldn't sit well with Hampton, to say the least, and could mean his job, too, in addition to Vincenti's. It went without saying that Vincenti's career would be worth less than dog shit if something like that went down.

"Thanks, Herm."

"Don't mention it," said Villas. "Just make sure you get yourself into headquarters ASAP and have a talk with Hampton. If you don't do the honors, I will." He laughed and banged Vincenti on the shoulder. "Once you let him know what we got on Phillips, everything will be cool – know what I'm saying?"

"I hear you."

Villas stuck out his fist, and Vincenti half-heartedly knocked his knuckles into it. "Take it easy, man. And like I said – thanks."

Vincenti watched Villas's wiry frame disappear. So there it was – Villas had in essence issued him an ultimatum: give him credit for singlehandedly saving the Hoboken Police Department, or he'd go and do it himself. Credit always looked better when you didn't hand it to yourself.

Vincenti resented Villas, but he would probably end up taking his advice. But before he did, there were a few things he had to deal with.

———

Nicky had fallen into another doze, on the sofa in front of the TV this time, his little mouth open, his eyes clamped shut, entertaining visions, no doubt, of elephants and snakes, lions and leopards. Vincenti was engulfed by a wave of envy at the child's naivete. It wasn't the first time. But now he was more jealous than ever.

Before he found his wife, he had to walk through every room of the apartment until he arrived at what would have been called the shed in olden days, and was now a sort of second den or breezeway. The room was rarely used, especially in the cold weather. Reggie was curled up, a multicolored afghan around her shoulders, in a high-backed wicker chair, looking out at the twisted crab apple tree in the small backyard.

He went no further than the door.

"Nicky's exhausted. Must have been the long safari."

He hadn't tried to engage his wife in a real conversation for a long time. She looked over her shoulder at him. There was melancholy in her beautiful green eyes.

"I decided to let him go on napping, though it's bound to throw him off his routine. He won't be able to sleep tonight, which means he'll be cranky in the morning."

For the first time in as long as Vincenti could remember, Reggie wasn't making a veiled or outright accusation. She sounded tired, very tired. Tired, thought Vincenti, of doing battle with him. As if reading his mind, that was exactly where she went.

"You're going to leave, aren't you?"

"Didn't I tell you I would?"

"How soon?"

Vincenti let out a bellyful of air. Reggie turned her gaze out the window again.

"It was you who did this, Brian. No matter what happens, you have to remember that. Even before Carl was in the picture, it was you who ..." She shook her head, choked back an emotion. "I wanted to keep us together, especially for Nicky's sake, but ... well, there's no point in dragging it out anymore, is there?"

Vincenti didn't say anything. His wife was right.

"And I'm not just talking about Daisy. Why didn't you just keep yourself to yourself, Brian? Maybe there were some things I didn't want to know about you, did you ever think of that?"

She searched his face.

"Brian? Did you?"

What was done was done, and couldn't be undone. His mistake was thinking that Reggie was someone other than she was.

"I could tell you I wished that I had, but I don't know that it would have made a difference."

———————

Exchanging a few words with his wife, fraught though they were, gave Vincenti an odd yet precarious sense of calm. At least the iceberg between them had finally begun to melt. Maybe it had to do with the fact that he'd not brought any harm to their son. What would be there between them in the long run was just that – they both cared about their little boy.

With a beer at his side, he settled into the folded-up futon and picked up the phone.

As usual, Ellen Smith screened the call before picking up. First Vincenti updated her on the Mohammed Phillips crisis, then asked his old partner for help in finding Gail Kenmore's mother.

"Why didn't you find out where she is from the good padre?"

"I tried. But I don't know if he would have told me if he knew. The son of a bitch made me work for everything as it was."

Ellen played around for a few minutes with the search engines on her computer, but came up empty.

"So chop off my head if I asked you this question before, Vincenti – why no computer at your place?"

"I told you. Between the high-powered jobbies at Reggie's office and headquarters, I never got around to buying one for the apartment. When things went to hell around here, it hardly seemed worth it if I'm not staying, know what I mean?"

"So ... probably Kenmore's mother doesn't go by the same last name anymore. It's one of the advantages of being a married woman. Ever try and find any of your exes on the web?"

"Not really."

"You should sometime. It's a sobering experience."

Vincenti was a little surprised that Ellen Smith would even think of doing something like that. Then he realized that he shouldn't be surprised by anything in this crazy world.

"And let's face it – 'Lydia' isn't exactly a common name. If a Lydia Kenmore was listed anywhere in the U.S., I would have found her by now. Want me to try overseas?"

"Why the hell not."

It was a ridiculously long shot. Vincenti could hear the rapid clacking of computer keys across the line. For some reason, it was a sound that always grated on him, sort of like fingernails on a chalkboard.

"Nah – nothing."

"Shit."

"I'm going to tell you the same thing I told you last time. Give it a rest. But now I'm going to add something else."

"What's that?"

"See someone. You need some help. And I'm telling you as a friend."

"Mm-hm."

"At this point you can't *not*. This thing's eating you alive."

"Since you seem to have all the answers, tell me – how do *you* do it? How the fuck do *you* deal with everything?"

"What have I told you a thousand times already? *Look at me*. Do I look like I cope well with anything? But who knows? Maybe some of us handle the shit better than others. You know what they say nowadays – we're all wired differently."

Vincenti's next call was to Saint Vincent Hospital.

Doctor Keane wasn't available right now, but a message would be forwarded to him at the first opportunity. He hung up and stared at the classic pro football game being replayed on cable. The Miami Dolphins were leading by two touchdowns. They wouldn't be for long. The phone rang a few seconds later.

"Doctor Keane here ..."

He sounded nervous – about what had transpired between the cop and his father, no doubt. Vincenti didn't open the subject up to discussion.

He thanked the doctor for returning his call, then asked if he had some idea how he might locate Gail Kenmore's mother.

"Hmm ... The thing is –"

"Keane, listen – I did you a good turn. Left your old man out of this thing – up until now. Frankly, I don't know one way or another whether he had anything to do with Gail Kenmore's death. Or whether you did, for that matter. But I'm willing to let it ride for the time being if you'll help me out here."

There was a pause. Vincenti imagined he could hear the doctor's brain churning.

"We never had this conversation, all right, Detective?"

"You got it."

"I'm going to be honest with you here. My father's involvement with Gail Kenmore is not the kind of thing he wants becoming public knowledge. Now if I tell you that her last name is Widlock and that she lives in Chelsea, do you think you could handle the rest on your own? There are more than a few patients who need my attention right now."

"It's a deal, Doc. Before you go, would you mind spelling that name for me?"

Getting what he needed from directory information was easy enough. Now he had a telephone number, and since it was listed, he had an address: 216 West Twenty-first Street. The question was whether or not to call Lydia Widlock or to arrive unannounced. He opted for the latter tactic. The element of surprise is everything.

He got off the PATH at Twenty-third Street. So – Gail Kenmore's mother lived only blocks from her daughter's lover. He wondered if she knew about the priest, and decided that he'd ask only if necessary. But if he had to, he would. Lydia Widlock was his last hope.

Two-sixteen was one of those rare Manhattan addresses that was ensconced behind a gate. A two-by-four cement garden sat between it and the brownstone. Vincenti flipped the latch and let himself through.

Lights were burning on every floor. The scroll of names beside the intercom indicated that Widlock occupied apartment 2A. He gave the buzzer a pair of quick blasts.

His heart throbbed erratically. He was on the verge of complete collapse – he could feel it in his bones. No matter what went down with Lydia Widlock, this was definitely and absolutely the end of the road for the Gail Kenmore suicide investigation.

"What is it?" The noise coming through the speaker was the hoarse growl of a heavy smoker.

"Detective Vincenti, Hoboken Police. I'd like to talk to you about your daughter."

Before he even had all the words out, the buzzer sounded. Vincenti had the feeling that Lydia Widlock had been waiting a long time for this moment.

2A was at the apex of the first flight. The frayed, nervous slip of a woman who opened the door wasn't what he expected. Her wide brown eyes were spooked, if they were alive at all. Her file-gray hair was pulled straight back and gathered into a ponytail. The effect didn't work; maybe Lydia Widlock didn't care. She wore a faded purple blouse, a relic of the hippie era, over baggy jeans. The blouse was stained and had lost its shape long ago. How could this half-wrecked specimen afford to keep up rent on an apartment in one of the most expensive neighborhoods in the city? One of the last things in the world he would figure her for was a conventional job.

"How did you track me down?" she rasped in a voice thick with mucus and nicotine.

"I was at your daughter's funeral service on Saturday. You and I happened to just miss each other. But I got a little help from some other people who were out there."

Lydia Widlock sneered, showing a set of yellow teeth. Vincenti didn't ask why.

The place was tight and small, the ceiling low. A place, Vincenti quickly decided, where a person came to *die*. A smudged porthole window faced the worn-out umber wall of the adjacent building; whatever came in through that aperture was the only light from the outside world that ever penetrated this chamber.

Lydia Widlock was evidently some sort of artist, a would-be painter. Damned near every inch of the walls was covered with crude, lugubriously-hued oil and watercolor (Vincenti wasn't sure he could tell the difference between the mediums) likenesses of someone – a boy or young man, though the features inclined toward the feminine – against a variety of backdrops ranging from the beach at high noon to the midnight sky full of exaggerated, primitive stars. In every canvas it was only the face that had been limned, and it was, for lack of a better term, a death mask. The entire place was a shrine to this subject – whoever it was.

In a corner near the porthole stood an easel, and next to it a worktable smeared with paint and messy with plastic bottles, tin cans, rags and brushes. On the easel was the half-finished portrait of someone else – a woman, a young woman. A sister painting to the one he'd encountered last week in apartment 1108 at the Hudson Arms in Hoboken.

Gail Kenmore.

"Please sit," offered Lydia Widlock. "Can I get you something to drink?"

The thought of putting his lips to a glass that was stored in this mausoleum repelled Vincenti. "No, thanks."

He looked around. An ancient aluminum chair with buckled legs was wedged into the space behind the door he'd entered by. He pulled it out. Lydia Widlock dropped to the floor and crossed her legs in the lotus position. She pulled a glass ashtray and pack of American Spirits to her torso. Then she reached for a squat, half-filled glass. Vincenti caught a strong scent of alcohol.

Sitting there, he found himself mesmerized by the crazy daubs all over the walls. Again he was troubled by the sensation that there was something familiar about the likeness, just as there'd been something familiar about Gail Kenmore's. But why? How? No – it couldn't be. Something in his brain had been short-circuited, that accounted for it. His eyes came to rest on the work in progress.

"That's her – that's my daughter."

"Yeah. I thought so."

"She's ... dead – but you already know that."

Lydia took a cigarette between the arthritic index and middle fingers of her right hand, fitted it into her parched lips and lighted it with one of those cheap plastic contraptions.

"Seven-fifty a pack, you believe it? All that money to kill myself. But that's okay, I don't care. I want to be dead."

Not *die*. Be *dead*.

Lydia chirped a weird little laugh, the kind of inappropriate squeak Vincenti had heard from far-gone schizos. The sound echoed in his ears well after she was through making it. Maybe he was losing his mind, too.

"I've been looking into your daughter's death, trying to figure out why she went out of that window, and so far I've been unable to come up with any satisfactory ex-"

"I know why my daughter died. I know exactly why, Detective. Why do you think I didn't come and ask you – the cops – to help me figure it out?"

Lydia's eyes welled up. Her brown and yellow teeth appeared again, this time in a grotesque smile. It made Vincenti think of a demented clown in a nightmare.

"Why?"

"Because of him." She gave a nod at the wall behind him.

For the hell of it, Vincenti began to count the paintings, one by one. There were ten, fifteen, thirty frames behind Lydia Widlock alone. He made a rapid calculation. There had to be as many as a few hundred in this room.

It was way out there, all right.

"Who is it?"

"My son. Gail's half-brother."

Some ominous presence seemed to be coming closer now, like a monster emerging from its lair. Vincenti tried to push the monster away, but it kept coming.

"I didn't know she had a half-brother."

"You talked to my ex-husband, didn't you?" said Lydia, an oscillating shaft of smoke billowing out of her unsymmetrical mouth.

"As a matter of fact, I did."

Lydia smirked. "Bet you all the coffee in Mexico he didn't breathe a word to you about Eugene."

Vincenti's heart bucked anew. Which it did whenever he heard that name – Eugene. He hadn't heard it in a while.

Now the monster was closing in on him.

"I had Eugene before I met Gail's father. When I was

young, only nineteen, and living in Brooklyn. His natural father and I parted ways before he was born. He was a dancer in the ballet, and I'd come East from the wasteland of northwestern Indiana to New York because I wanted desperately to avoid my fate – which was to turn into a Midwestern *hausfrau*. But my father was a doctor, he'd seen a bit of the world, and he knew there was something more out there for women, and so he sent me to Pratt Institute to study painting and architecture. But when I met Eugene's father – Andre-Paul Musti – my plans were derailed."

The name Andre-Paul Musti meant nothing to Vincenti. "I see," he said. But why was Lydia Widlock regaling him with this pointless history?

Without pausing for a breath of unpolluted air she immediately set fire to another cigarette. Most likely she smoked around the clock in a concerted effort to achieve her goal of self-annihilation.

"You're bored, Detective. But don't be. This seedy little tale is going somewhere, believe me."

"I'll take your word for it."

"Andre-Paul was not the kind of man ..." (she laid, he thought, a peculiar emphasis on the word 'man') "who could take responsibility for a child. In fact, by making me pregnant, I think he was trying to prove something to himself – that he wasn't really what he was. You understand what I'm saying, don't you, Detective?"

Vincenti thought so. Lots of gay men tried to change themselves to fit into the so-called straight world, even today, when conditions weren't so oppressive as they once were. And who could blame them for that? All he had to do was think of Tommy Flaherty to know the lengths a human being would go to in order to exist with himself.

"And you know, after a while, I realized that it would have been worse had he tried to force himself to be something other than he was, even if he didn't know he was doing it at first. The result would have been tragedy – for him as well as us. But he woke up. He went off with another dancer – a boy – and we never heard from him again. But I couldn't escape tragedy anyway, Detective ... I have no idea whatever happened to Andre-Paul. And there really wasn't a way to find out, especially since he didn't end up becoming another Nureyev."

Vincenti nodded. But why, when he didn't get it?

"My guess is that he was a casualty of AIDS, or he came to some other unfortunate end ... though he could just as well be living with his wife and kids in Phoenix right this minute. The world is an insane place, you know?"

"Yeah," agreed Vincenti. "I know."

"And so I struggled with my baby for a couple of years, with the help of my parents of course. They wanted me back in Indiana, even my father, but I said no, I couldn't do it, that was the single thing I couldn't do, even if it meant being cut off financially. I wanted to stay in New York no matter what happened. That's what I did. I was able to take classes here and there, work a little, as a waitress mostly, to make ends meet, make my own way. But then Dad died, and finally I was on my own. And it wasn't so easy anymore, surviving the city with a small child. I was waiting tables at an Italian restaurant in the Village when I met Hugh Kenmore. He was working a construction job in the neighborhood, and every afternoon when he came in for lunch we'd talk. We got to be friends, and he persuaded me to go out with him. Normally I wouldn't go near someone like Hugh Kenmore, though he was handsome enough, but you have to understand what I was going through. I said yes, and then one thing led to another, and he began to talk to me about moving out to Long Island. 'Think about it – it's not so far, you can be in the city in a matter of minutes,' and so on. He'd take care of Eugene, he said, as well as me. Forever. I guess at that moment I really needed to hear that from someone. Not that I didn't want to do it on my own," she added defiantly. "It's just that at that point I was so *tired.*"

Another cigarette. The room was floating away on a huge nimbus of smoke. Vincenti could feel the stuff seeping into his lungs. He stifled a hack.

"Vulnerability makes a woman very, very open to persuasion, Detective. Add that I was at least reasonably attracted to Hugh Kenmore, and it's an easy jump to the wilds of Long Island."

Vincenti coughed. He was jumpy with a growing, irrational anticipation.

"Gail was born shortly after we were married. For a few years we did okay playing the typical American family game out there in the suburbs – I was even able to make my peace with living outside the city limits. But it wasn't long before Eugene – the poor child was only in kindergarten when it started – began showing signs of being his real father's son. It was obvious as soon as his personality started to develop that he was ... different. And that nothing was going to change him, not tossing a football in the yard, not watching boxing matches on television, not camping or fishing, or –"

Vincenti was growing impatient. It was as if someone had promised him a gift, then proceeded to tempt him with endless hints about what it might be without ever actually handing it over.

"Ms. Widlock –"

"Please! I know what I'm doing here. Trust me."

What choice did he have but to wait her out?

"I'd tell you that Hugh's and Eugene's differences grew, but that would be shortchanging both of them. It would be more accurate to say their mutual *hatred* grew. If Hugh came home from work and caught him in one of my dresses, he'd go ballistic. So my son's very first goal in life was to escape his stepfather. He must have run away a dozen times by the time he was just a young teenager, and his destination was always the same – the city. Because he knew that no matter what, he'd find some comfort in being near his own kind. Because even then, unlike his real dad, Eugene was reconciled to being who he was. It goes without saying that I always loved him, and he and his half-sister were as close as two people can be. But Hugh Kenmore was *Gail's* true father, and so her loyalties were divided. That girl was just cut straight in half, and ultimately that was what killed her."

Vincenti was bewildered. This pathetic being's meandering was about to lose him altogether. What did Gail Kenmore's death have to do with her brother?

Lydia Widlock's taped-together composure was breaking apart. Tears rolled out of the meats of her eyes. Instead of reaching for a tissue to wipe them away, she used the sleeve of her blouse.

Vincenti got out of his chair and began to pace, stopping to confront an oil-on-board portrait of Eugene with a darkened left eye.

"I don't get it, Ms. Widlock. You're telling me that your daughter was somehow driven to kill herself by some ... some enmity between her father and her half-brother? If that's what you're trying to say, then it doesn't add up. You're feeding me a line of crap here."

He was furious, out of all proportion to the situation.

Lydia Widlock shook her head. "My daughter was dead before last Tuesday."

"What the fuck – How do you mean, she –"

"I mean she was *dead*, Detective. She died the day her brother was murdered."

"Her brother was –"

"Do you know what it's like to have a relative murdered, Detective?"

Vincenti didn't know what to say. He thought of his brother, as he always did at such odd moments, even though Salvatore was still alive and well.

"He was down in the West Village one hot summer night six years ago, on the old pier where Christopher Street runs into the river ..."

At that moment a mini-earthquake rocked Vincenti. Something warm and fleshy, like a slimy frog, hopped through his throat and into his mouth: his liver? His heart? He knew beyond the shadow of a doubt now what was going to happen. And with the numbing force of a lightning bolt came the recognition suddenly that he'd been in denial – that somewhere in his psyche he'd known all along, ever since he saw the portrait on the wall of Gail Kenmore's apartment back in Hoboken, what had been drawing him on day after day and where he was ultimately going to find himself at the end of this investigation.

"Of course I knew what Eugene was doing down there. The bars and clubs in that neighborhood were where he found his companions. But that night his luck ran out."

Without realizing it, Vincenti had taken a step backwards, bumping into the easel on which sat the unfinished portrait of Gail Kenmore. He wheeled around to stop it from toppling off, but his reflexes were too slow and one corner of the frame stabbed into the floor and was flattened.

"Shit," he mumbled. "Sorry."

"It's okay, I can fix it." She stared at him. "Are you all right, Detective? You look –" Was she about to say 'upset' or 'sick' or something?

He shook his head. "I'm okay."

Did Lydia Widlock know he was lying through his teeth? He clumsily restored the oblong canvas to its place and stood there in a daze, inside the miasma that was the past.

He wasn't in a makeshift Chelsea studio any more: he was down on that strip of shadowy causeway by the river on a blazing-hot summer night ...

"Fine," he repeated to Lydia Widlock. "I'm fine ..."

"The police never gave me a satisfactory explanation for what really happened that night," she went on with scarcely concealed bitterness. "I guess they had more important things to worry about."

The police. The New York City Police were the ones who'd eventually handled it – or tried to. Vincenti didn't really need to listen any longer to what Lydia Widlock had to say, though he knew he would just the same. What was more important to him – vastly more important – was his own recollection of the night in question.

And it was odd, taking in Lydia Widlock's steadily tumbling cascade of words at the same time as he was being plunged into his own past, a past that had defined and dogged him for the past six years, even if it was known to only four people, one of whom was long dead.

Lydia Widlock's voice broke through his daze.

"They – the police – told me Eugene must have been mugged. And then something must have gone wrong. Or maybe it was something else. Maybe it was a bias attack in the first place. Though not one of them could ever explain to me how he ended up" – a sob caught in her throat – "where he did ...

"It was difficult to track Eugene's movements that evening. In summer the clubs down there are crowded to overflowing. It's hard for the bartenders to remember a face, let alone what a certain patron was up to, who he was with, or seemed to be with, or ..."

In a few of "those clubs" was where Tommy Flaherty had been that evening, too, before Vincenti arrived on the scene – that's what Tommy had told him.

When Vincenti glanced at Lydia Widlock, her lips were still moving.

"When the cops did nothing, I had to go down there myself to try and piece together what happened. When

I showed him a picture of Eugene, the bartender at the Hangar seemed to remember that he'd been there that night, with a black companion, but he'd never seen the companion before, and he hadn't gotten a good enough look to contribute to a composite. 'It's always so damned busy in here,' he explained, 'that I only ever really see most people out of the corner of my eye.' I tried every other place in that entire neighborhood. The answers were always 'Maybe I saw him, but I'm not one-hundred-percent sure ...'

"What I just can't for the life of me understand is that nobody *saw* anything," Lydia Widlock was complaining, her tears starting up again. "How can that be? How can it be that a young person is murdered and dumped into the river and no one sees anything?"

Vincenti looked away. "I don't know what to say to you, Ms. Widlock," he lied.

"That's all any of you can ever say, isn't it?" she said bitterly.

Vincenti flinched. Normally he would have been insulted, but not tonight. There was silence except for the humming of the steam heat pulsing up through the baseboard radiators.

"I'm sorry," Lydia apologized in the next breath. "I know you're trying to help."

"Forget it," Vincenti answered, though the words sounded hollow and were one more lie.

"But you know what, Detective, nothing can help now. No matter what you do, nothing can help either of them now."

Vincenti thought again of the fortune teller, and how Daniel had been on target about his predicament after all.

He wouldn't have to wait any longer for a shaft of light to be shone on the riddle of the death of Gail Kenmore, because without saying it in so many words, Lydia Widlock had given him all he would ever need. Again and again she remarked on how close the two half-siblings were, and what it did to Gail Kenmore when the fate of Eugene had finally become known.

"But at least I can tell you what killed my daughter, Detective. If that's what you came here for, I can give you that much."

Vincenti was about to say something, but he didn't. He couldn't. Because the events of that fateful night were rushing straight at him like a runaway train ...

He and Tommy had drifted out onto the pier. They'd heard something behind them. They turned and that *kid* – whose face was plastered all over these walls – was there.

"I want to show you something," announced Lydia Widlock, pushing herself off the floor and disappearing through a door to Vincenti's left.

He stared at the cigarette – he'd lost count of how many she'd smoked – left burning in the tray. The ash had grown long and gnarly, like the charred limb of an incinerated tree, and was just about to topple onto the floor. He kept watching it, concentrating on it, as much to block out the visions flooding his mind as for the sake of watching. At the last possible second, he reached over and with his forefinger pushed the smoldering butt onto the top of the dead pile inside the tray.

By then Lydia was back, reverently extending a glossy photo towards him as if it were a priceless gem.

"My son."

Vincenti accepted it. He turned it so that Eugene was facing him. The cherubic face with its wide-set, limpid eyes and heavy lips was framed by a mass of peroxided spikes. Vincenti recognized the picture, of course, from the newspapers, when it had appeared there after the kid was dead. He hadn't seen it in a long time, six years, and in the first painting the kid hadn't had that hairdo, which was why he'd not connected Eugene with what he'd seen in Gail Kenmore's bedroom.

He didn't give voice to anything, though. Instead, he studied the photo, as if searching for a hidden meaning.

Eugene had said something else out there on the pier that morning. It wasn't exactly an obscenity. It was something worse, something strangely provocative, the kind of ugly bomb that in some neighborhoods would precipitate a brawl. He was hopped on something. His eyes had been as wide as saucers, the veins showing, the pupils dilated, all of which Vincenti had been able to see by the strobe of a passing party boat that was blasting salsa on the placid Hudson.

Poppers, he remembered thinking. Amyl nitrate. A substance that gay men took during sex. But it could have just as well been coke, crystal meth, ecstasy, angel dust, anything. Whatever this kid was using, he was way over the top, frantic, like an electrified kite. And the mania had taken the form of an overbearing, obnoxious come-on, as if anybody he approached was his for the taking.

That was Lydia Widlock's son on his last night alive.

Would she want to know?

Eugene kept edging closer, getting into their faces. He

was still talking too, gibberish, trash, until Vincenti heard him say, leering at Tommy in his dress, "Now don't tell me you two don't want some company ..."

"Beat it, asshole," he'd growled at the kid. He wasn't in the mood. He didn't know about Tommy. He didn't want to know about Tommy. That was the single subject he hadn't gone near since finding out Tommy wasn't who he thought he was.

But the kid kept moving in, and that was when it happened.

"Hey, old queenie – didn't I see you in the Ramrod?"

At first Vincenti didn't know which one of them, Tommy or him, was being addressed.

Across the room Lydia Widlock was saying "He's dead. Somebody murdered him, and whoever did got away with it. And that's what killed my daughter. First it was that Eugene had to die, and second, it was that whoever killed him was never caught and punished. Gail was never the same after that. That's what started all of her troubles – the insomnia, the attacks of nerves, the depression, the not being able to get out of bed on the bad days, the not being able to make it all the way through without help on the good ones. I know she tried to put a good face on it, but in the end it didn't work. Nothing worked. Not treatment, not men, not God. And she tried all of them in different combinations, if you didn't know, from doctors to antidepressants to priests, and if they weren't using her – and some of them were – they couldn't do anything to save her. The truth is, she *jumped* out that window. I know it because she told me she was going to do it, just before she did. We had coffee that morning when she got off duty from the hospital, and she told me she'd come to a decision. She'd dropped hints before, but that day she told me she was sure. I just didn't think she'd act so quickly. My mistake was in thinking I had more time to talk her out of it. So, Detective Vincenti, you don't have to look any further."

Naturally there was no way Lydia Widlock could know the cruelly ironic deeper truth of her words. Vincenti handed the photo back to her.

"I'm sorry," he said.

"I'm a little surprised you found me, Detective. I'm sure there wasn't a person out there at that grave site who'd want you to. Maybe someone's guilt got the best of them."

Now Vincenti understood why the good Father Raymond had no compunction about giving his mistress a church burial. The last thing he wanted to believe was that he was in any way responsible for what happened to her.

It occurred to Vincenti that Lydia Widlock would be the next to go. A human being couldn't live like this, in solitary confinement surrounded by images of the dead. At least he had his son. His son who was alive. This poor wretch had nothing left except for lifeless canvases.

She began spewing again, words oozing with mad grief, which drove Vincenti straight back to the pier.

The kid had started to go for him. Love-struck? Just plain fucked-up and out of his mind? The sequence of events was so extraordinary and senseless that to this very moment it failed to add up to an exact sum. Before Vincenti knew what was happening, a punch had been launched, a lightning-fast overhand right that crashed into the kid's face with the velocity and power of a sledgehammer. Now Vincenti heard the ugly sound all over again, flesh and bone mashing flesh and bone, saw it, too.

He shut his eyes to block it out.

"Tommy – what the fuck are you doing?"

The question he'd yelled out that night rang in his ears. Before he knew it, the back of Eugene's skull had met the rusty third rung of the railing with a sickening crunch. He went down like a sack of potatoes toppling off the back of a truck, his gangly limbs splaying in all directions like a cat thrown out of a high window.

He'd never even cried out. It was Vincenti's opinion that he was dead before he hit the ground – but maybe it was just wishful thinking, that after the blow the victim had felt no pain.

He'd dropped to his knees and looked into the kid's face. There were trickles of blood out of his nostrils, between his lips. The eyes were wide open, unseeing.

The aftermath likewise made no sense. An argument broke out between him and Tommy over what to do. Vincenti grabbed for his cell phone to call 911, but Tommy, trying to snatch the instrument away, wanted no part of it.

"We can't just leave him here! Jesus Christ, Tommy – what the fuck's the matter with you?"

Tommy's mascara-lined eyes were on fire.

"Think of what's gonna go down before you touch that fucking phone, Brian! *Think!*"

"Look ... what if we just call somebody and beat it the hell out of here – what if we just do that?"

It was weak, an anemic compromise, but even now, the

right course of action was unclear to him. Because when he looked down at Eugene it hit him all over again – the kid was in serious trouble. And that meant that no matter what happened now –

It was nothing short of miraculous that no one was close by. Out near the bicycle track that ran parallel to West Street, he could make out passing bodies, but aside from the three of them there was no one else on the long pier.

While Tommy stood helplessly staring, frozen, like a child who'd broken a valuable museum piece and was at a loss for what to do, Vincenti knelt and felt for the artery in the kid's neck.

"He's dead, Tommy ... what the hell ... why the fuck did you have to –"

He never finished the question. He straightened up and backed away from Eugene's body.

"I –" said Tommy.

"Shut up! Looks like somebody's coming!"

Simultaneously they turned and resumed leaning on the railing, an attempt to appear innocent and nonchalant.

"What I'm thinking is that we should dump him over right here, just to make sure."

"Dump him over ...?" repeated Vincenti incredulously. But he's gonna come back up, he's gonna float like a –"

The problem at that moment was that there was no time to think, *really* think.

In the years to come, Vincenti often wondered why they hadn't just left the kid lying there and walked away, but in the end his partner had probably insisted on the right thing.

"Because if we don't – if somebody figures out what

happened here and they somehow track us down, it's gonna be ugly all the way around," hissed Tommy. "They'll nail the both of us – you get that, right? And even if you and me tell the truth about what happened here, there's always gonna be doubts. We'll be finished, both of us. We could be looking at hard jail time – or worse. Shit, we don't even have good alibis for where we were tonight ..."

And the truth was that at that moment Vincenti would never have wanted to force Reggie into the position of having to lie for him, especially in a slimy mess like this.

"Look there, in the corner!"

Vincenti watched Tommy, his stupid dress billowing in the fetid air, dart barefoot (he'd taken off his ridiculous oversized pumps when they came out on the pier) across the clumps of crabgrass and crushed stone to the opposite corner of the promontory, the lights of the George Washington Bridge in the background.

"Check this out!"

Vincenti went and joined his partner, who was turning a paint can in his hands.

"And there's a bunch of them. We could fill them with gravel and slip the handles over his feet, maybe, or tie them or something like that, you know – do it that way. Then he won't come up to the surface – at least not for a while."

The most insane thing of all was that it began making sense to Vincenti. He carted four of the cannisters, two in each hand, over to the body. With keys from their keyrings, both he and Tommy pried them open and frantically scooped handfuls of gravel into the coagulated battleship-gray paint at the bottom. The cans were as heavy as small boulders when they were filled and capped.

"Know what you do," Vincenti suggested, "you loop his belt through the handles ..."

That would assure that the corpse would sink and stay under. There wasn't time to debate the merits of an alternative. They were either going to do it or they weren't, and using the kid's belt was better than trying to force the cannister handles over his extremities. Vincenti thought it might even be better if the body could be transported elsewhere and disposed of, but how were they supposed to pull off something like that without being seen? Tommy's car was parked not far away, about five blocks north on West Street, so it could be done. He brought it up as they worked. Again they argued over it, nearly coming to blows. But the risk was too great; somebody would see something, it was inevitable. No – hauling the body off that location would have been an invitation to disaster.

It was the strangest moment of Vincenti's entire life. Afterwards he thought about it a million times, until his brain was fried and he couldn't think about it anymore. What he was about to do had nothing to do with being weak. Tommy Flaherty had saved his life, he'd introduced him to his wife, he was Nicky's goddamned *godfather*. Even if he would have to burn in hell for what he was about to do, he was bound to act out of loyalty.

Finally he was reduced to thinking that as practiced as he and Tommy were as cops, they were just as inept as the commonest ilk of street criminal when faced with an emergency of their own making.

But they had to work fast. In all, it couldn't have taken more than two minutes to get all those cumbersome cans onto the kid's belt and loop it through three eyelets of his leather pants.

"All right – hoist him up!"

By that time Vincenti had become the *de facto* ringleader of the depraved operation. And it would haunt him until this very moment, when he was face to face with the dead kid's mother.

"On the count of three. One – two –"

Heaving Eugene over the railing, getting those paint cans to clear the rungs, was a bitch, and Vincenti's weak back muscles nearly gave out. A second or two elapsed before they heard a splash below. Puffing and sweating, the two cops leaned into the night and watched for any sign of Eugene's resurgence to the oily surface, but all they could see, dimly, was a few large bubbles rise and pop.

"Wish we had a goddamn flashlight," croaked Tommy glumly.

"Why did you do that?" whispered Vincenti as they stood in the quiet of what now seemed like nothing but a typical summer night. "What in the world would fucking possess you to do something like that?"

"He's not coming back," Tommy said finally, pointedly ignoring the question. "At least not here."

The currents would sweep him away, right? Thank God the Hudson was as humongous and powerful as it was.

There was nothing left to say or do. They started to walk away, a little hesitantly at first, as if they might have forgotten something, as if for some reason they should go back and check, then faster, as if they figured out that they were still in danger.

As it was, years had now passed. If there'd been witnesses to what happened that night, they'd never come forward.

Where was he? He hadn't noticed that Lydia Widlock hadn't said a word for a long time, and that it had grown late. She was sucking on yet another cancer stick and watching him with her watery, spidery eyes. Her manic stare was making him uncomfortable.

She bared her teeth again, in a rueful smile. "Losing interest, Detective?"

If Vincenti was exhausted before, it was nothing compared to the way he felt now. Was he dead or alive?

"No doubt you didn't read about Eugene's body washing up on Staten Island. From time to time the river regurgitates bodies – you probably know all about that."

Vincenti said yes.

"But even as a policeman you can't possibly pay attention every time it happens, I'm sure. It was two years, three hundred twenty-nine days ago that Eugene was found. In April, when the 'floaters' usually surface. The water temperature rises, bacteria builds up in the abdomen, and like so many helium balloons they rise. They asked me to come to the morgue and make an ID, but the corpse was so distended and decomposed that ..."

So that's how many days it had been since it was over between him and Reggie – the beginning of the end, anyhow. He'd never bothered to count. Anyhow, it seemed like forever. It was a rainy spring night when he'd confided to her, as they were crawling into bed, "That kid they pulled out of the Narrows day before yesterday, Reg? That was me – me and Tommy. It's been tearing me apart ever since we did it, and I wasn't going to tell you, ever, but living with something like that is enough to ..."

All it took was one look at her face, and he'd known. She'd wavered at first, tried for a good long time to live with the secret in order to keep them together, pretended that nothing was wrong, but in the long run she couldn't do it either. Eugene, a person neither of them had known, was the wedge that divided and conquered them. Life could be cruel and strange that way.

What was it she'd said to him? "I can't live with a man who could toss a human being into the river like a piece of garbage." When all was said and done, he'd completely misjudged her. All the other stuff – Daisy, Carl Bartano – had come later, but they were merely aftereffects. Maybe Sandy could have hung with him through this, but not Reggie.

She'd said something else, too, again and again, something that made him feel that their destruction was really more his fault than hers, that if only he'd been able to put Eugene behind him she might have held it together and made it through.

"You don't know it, Brian, but you're not the man I married. You've changed. I can't reach you since you – since that thing happened. It's like you're behind a wall or something. Sometimes I think I don't even know you anymore. You don't realize what it's done to you. It's like I'm living with a ghost – or trying to."

And he had to admit that it might be true – he couldn't really see into the mirror.

Lydia Widlock made a gesture of dismissal with her hand. "But it *was* Eugene. They used dental records to make a positive identification. Whoever murdered him tried to weigh him down with something, but he'd come loose. I was told that the currents can be surprisingly strong, they can set anything loose given enough time."

But she was wrong about something else. Vincenti remembered when the corpse was found, all right. A report had crossed his desk, as they invariably did whenever bodies were discovered in the metropolitan area, so that a cop on the lookout for a certain missing person might make a match. There were always articles in the New York papers, too, along with photos. Maybe he'd seen the same photo that Lydia had brought out to him. If he had, he'd tossed it immediately, even if he suspected that it was the kid he and Tommy Flaherty had thrown into the river that night, he'd tried to block it out of his mind. And if Ellen Smith had seen it and made the connection, she'd said nothing to him about it.

Even when someone died in your presence, it was hard to remember a face exactly; the reality was that he'd never had a good look at Eugene the night Tommy Flaherty committed manslaughter.

Now, finally, things made sense. Everything made sense. It was Gail Kenmore's hazy, semi-resemblance to her half-brother that had hooked him, made him dog this case down to a makeshift memorial in a death chamber in Chelsea.

Odd, that Gail Kenmore had found her way to Hoboken, a block from where he worked upholding society's laws; that's what he was thinking now. But on second thought, not really. Manhattan and the Gold Coast were two sides of the same coin, the same way Brooklyn and the Bronx were. Thousands of people flipped the coin every day. Vincenti ran into people he knew all the time on both sides of the river. He'd even bumped into Ellen Smith in Central Park not all that long ago. Like they always said, it was a small world.

Too small.

"Blunt force trauma to the head was listed as the probable cause of death, though the medical examiner wouldn't commit to that one hundred percent, what with the damage the river had done to him ..."

Vincenti stopped at the door. He saw the faces of both Lydia Widlock's children in her sorrow-scarred countenance, a connection you might not ever make unless you looked very closely. At that moment, like a knife in the heart, he experienced the purely human temptation to say something – to *confess* – to his complicity in the crime that rendered her son a forgotten victim and her daughter a suicide. Maybe he would have, had he the opportunity to explain everything, to go into every last detail of what had happened that hot summer night. But the ground this woman was standing on was too unstable. And he wasn't all that sure of himself, either.

"You have my sympathies," he said to her instead, and he meant it. "Strange things can happen down in that neighborhood. And there's not always an easy explanation for them. I know it's small comfort, but maybe it's better you don't know what happened to him."

He knew it was inadequate, but it was the best he could

manage. A light flickered in Lydia Widlock's otherwise dead eyes. She seemed to comprehend, at least distantly, what Vincenti was trying to say to her.

Maybe, on some dim stratum of consciousness, she *knew*.

He pulled the door open.

"Thanks for coming," she said. She was on her feet and heading for the easel before it swung shut.

Tuesday, March 23

It was after midnight when Vincenti hit the street. A sheen of frost had settled over the sidewalks. They glittered like the glaze on a Krispy Kreme donut, and he had trouble holding his footing. But the city was still alive. Only a quarter alive, since it was early in the week, and only alive in a somewhat skewed way – a siren here, the rumble of an underground train there – but still alive nonetheless. That energy both irritated and galvanized Vincenti, tired as he was. The idea of hitting an upscale strip club crossed his mind. Or maybe one of those sleazy triple-X shops that advertised peep shows.

That was the thing about sex – it was like an assassin, capable of striking anywhere at any time, and often when you least expected it. And if he couldn't have it himself, he wanted at least to *see* it. He was after something to make him feel alive again.

He walked a block on Seventh Avenue past the locked-down businesses and the somnolent office buildings. Nothing caught his fancy; that was because he was on the wrong artery, he decided. He needed to move over to Eighth Avenue.

A pair of whores were posted like sentinels on a corner in the Thirties. Even at a distance Vincenti figured them out from their skimpy clothes – mini-skirts, red plastic boots, rhinestone-studded denim jackets.

One stepped right up to him when he came near.

"Lookin' to go out tonight, honey ...?"

He thought it over. He wasn't a man who indulged himself with prostitutes, but tonight the invitation appealed to him.

"How much?"

"Fifty for a blowjob. A hundred for everything." Vincenti made a face. He was short on cash and wasn't about to search for an ATM.

"But we can negotiate, baby, dependin' on what you can afford."

The longer she talked, the less interested Vincenti was. If he had a fleeting urge to follow the whore into a dark corner, it died with the realization that his solicitor was a transvestite.

"Sorry – I'm a little light in the pockets tonight."

"You just tell me what you holdin', and we can work somethin' out, baby."

He shook his head and kept moving. Behind him the streetwalkers sniggered.

There was an open coffee shop on the corner. The lights inside were muted. "Around The Clock" was a place for lost souls who didn't want to be seen, an Edward Hopper painting in brick and glass. It was perfect.

Vincenti slid onto a stool at the counter. Scattered around the tables behind him were a handful of downtown types with their cups, newspapers, and books. They all seemed to be staring straight ahead, no expressions whatsoever on their faces. A parlor of the undead, or something like that.

"Can I get you something?"

She was twenty-two, twenty-three, wearing a black

sweater, skin-tight jeans, sequined cat's eyeglasses. She rubbed the counter lackadaisically with a stained towel. The toothy grin she flashed was of the variety calculated to maximize a late-night tip.

"Got any decaf?"

"Hazelnut okay?"

As he watched her move around behind the counter, laying out a napkin and spoon, fetching a saucer and cup and then filling it from a red-hatted urn, he guessed at where she came from (few people who lived in the Big Apple were natives), what she did, where she lived, who she slept with. The fact that Gail Kenmore and her brother had no future at roughly the same age pierced at him.

The girl moved off. Vincenti pulled out his cell phone. No messages. He punched in Ellen Smith's number. It was late, but if he knew his ex-partner, she was still awake. Even if she was sleeping, she'd have to know about Lydia Widlock.

The telephone rang a half-dozen times before she picked up.

"It's me. Vincenti."

"What the hell time is it?" Ellen sounded groggy. And like a man. A cranky man.

"Going on one."

"Jesus effin' Christ – what's up?"

"You'll never guess in a million years who I talked to tonight, pal." He went on to detail his interview with Gail Kenmore's mother.

"What'd you say to her?" Tommy growled suspiciously, not at all like Ellen Smith, but like his crusty, old tough-cop self.

Vincenti was still angry over what had happened years ago, but right now he wasn't out to cause Ellen Smith any more pain than she'd already endured in her tormented existence. As for Lydia Widlock, she was already beyond help or hope. One of them had to be abandoned, even if he'd ultimately be saving only a husk of a human being in his old partner. And he understood that he might well be making a mistake with that choice, that Ellen Smith had already committed a sin too egregious to ever atone for. Wasn't his first duty some measure of closure and justice for Eugene and Gail's mother?

"I didn't give her anything. Not that I didn't want to. But someday I'm going to do something for her, Tommy. Maybe even tell her the truth, someday when you're gone."

There was a sigh on the other end. There was no one close by; the waitress had disappeared, so he could speak freely. "What I want to know is this, Tommy – what made you hit that kid? What the fuck made you do it?"

They'd never talked about it after it happened, it was an ugly secret between brothers-in-arms. But Vincenti wasn't going to keep his mouth shut any longer.

"Wanna know how I figure it? There are a few different ways I figure it – and I've had a long, long time to come up with them."

"Go ahead, talk. I'm listening."

Vincenti looked out on the quiet avenue.

"Number one. Maybe it was all those new hormones raging around inside your body, Tommy, and they were at war with the old ones. You were out of your mind that night and just couldn't help yourself. Maybe you didn't even *know* what you were doing. You were in a – what do they call it? – a fugue state. The heat of the night, what you'd got off your chest to me, the strain of all the years of having to hide your real self – all of it got to you. And you snapped. *Dog Day Afternoon*, like. *Anybody* in your boat would have flipped. And Eugene Musti was the poor son of a bitch standing in front of you when it happened. It could have been anybody that particular night. If it wasn't him, who knows – maybe it would have been *me*. Wanna hear another one?"

"Since you're on a roll, why not."

"Number two. What happened that night was like – and I'm trying to put this into the right words here, so bear with me – was like the final statement of your manhood. Hey, I'm not trying to be cruel. But even though you wanted to be a female, you thought of yourself as a female, you were *convinced* you were a female – you were born with a cock and balls and you were still a guy, and no matter how hard you tried, you couldn't escape that fact. And what happened that night was like, the last vestige of your unbridled masculinity – the very last gasp of Tommy Flaherty before he was gone forever."

"Interesting. Very interesting. Is that all you got?"

"No."

"Lay the rest on me before I take my pick."

Vincenti remembered his coffee. He lifted the cup to his lips and gulped.

"Last one's the flimsiest."

"Whatever. Let me have it between the eyes."

"Okay. Number three. You were jealous."

"*Jealous?*"

Bullseye, thought Vincenti.

"What the hell are you talking about, pal?"

"Hey, take it easy ... Something happened between you and Eugene Musti in the Ramrod earlier that night. You hit on him. That's why he called you that name out on the pier. But it was me the kid was after out there, right? We were a little younger then. Maybe I looked better than I do now, or maybe he didn't go for the color of your dress, or –"

"Stick to tracking people down, Vincenti. That's what you're good at. Leave the psychoanalysis to the shrinks."

Vincenti chuckled.

"So what was it? What was it lit your fuse?"

Ellen sighed. "Want some more advice, Vincenti? Give it up. It's time. You sound like you could use a good night's sleep. I'm a little worried about you."

"If I could sleep, I would, Tommy. Believe me."

Ellen clammed up. Conversation over. Detective Vincenti was never going to get to the heart of certain things, definitely not to the heart of Ellen Smith herself. You could never really know another human being. Maybe, when you got right down to it, you never even knew your own self.

Just then the waitress happened by and offered him a refill. "It's fresh." She smiled. This time her smile was a little less brittle. Maybe she had a good night in tips. Maybe she was about to go home.

"No, thanks," said Vincenti. "On second thought, why not? Where the hell am I going, right? What's the hurry?"

"Right," she agreed.

As he sat there with his second cup, it occurred to him that he still didn't really know the first thing about Gail Kenmore either.

"So what the hell am I supposed to do with you now, Vincenti?"

Hampton's mug was so pale this morning that Vincenti feared he might keel over at any moment. It was a miracle that any man who looked so unhealthy could even be alive, let alone sit erect in a chair.

Vincenti didn't even want to speculate on how bad he must look himself. He was operating on less than three hours' sleep – if it could even be called that. The minute he rolled out of bed he dressed and reported to headquarters, where he was informed that Mohammed Phillips was dead.

Vincenti was in the visitor's chair. Hampton was leaning back in his ancient wooden swivel, the arc of his protruding belly swelling against his powder-blue uniform shirt.

Vincenti let his superior's insinuating question go unanswered. "Villas told me yesterday that –"

"I know all about that."

Of course, thought Vincenti. Villas was the one cop who was on top of everything, just the way he used to be way back when. No way Villas *wasn't* going to leak *something* about his superior police work. It was just a matter of when.

"And that's all fine and dandy, but you happened to lower my ass into some boiling water here, Vincenti. I don't like sweating. I don't like it when my ass burns. We been in pretty decent shape around here for a few years, as far as community relations go. Last thing I need is a case of alleged police brutality. *What the fuck is wrong with you?* Aren't you thinking out there? What have I always told you guys – you have got to *think*. You can't go off halfcocked, especially on some homeboy who's got an ax to grind. God*damn* it."

Hampton was completely exasperated. His voice was up a few decibels. Vincenti had never seen him like this before.

"And then you don't show your face for a few days running, even when I order you in, and I'm left twisting in the wind. I don't *like* twisting in the wind, Vincenti. It hurts my neck."

The detective's eyebrows twitched. He thought of how much his boss must have loved having to take heat about his actions from internal affairs. According to the chief, those boys had already stopped by.

"I've seen guys go this way before, don't think I haven't," Hampton went on. "And you know who I'm talking about here."

He proceeded to reel off the names of a handful of cops who Vincenti had known and worked with, men whose careers had been shipwrecked by booze, drugs, sex, greed.

"But then you don't have to look any further than your ex-partner, right, Vincenti?"

Vincenti nodded, barely.

"Talk about *embarrassing* – by the time Tommy Flaherty flounced out of here in his gown and heels, he was a complete fucking joke. You remember that, don't you, Vincenti?"

Hell yes, he remembered. How could he not? Hampton was rubbing it in now, and it was uncalled for.

"So what's the point, if you don't mind my asking?" He wanted to get to his desk or turn in his badge.

Hampton made a noise like an angry bull. "The point is, you better get your head on straight or you're gonna find yourself out of a job. As it is you might end up in stir or fighting off lawsuits for the rest of your life."

"Right."

"If I were you, first thing I'd do would be to go home and deal with my *wife*. Whether or not you want to admit it, you got each other all screwed up."

Vincenti blinked.

"What – you think nobody's on to that? Don't be a chump. Everybody knows about Regina's boyfriend. And your little Puerto Rican bombshell is common knowledge, too. Now I don't know what you two did to each other, I don't know whether it's beyond repair or not, and I know you got a little kid involved on top of it all, and frankly it's none of my business – but it's fucking you up, Vincenti. I take that back – it's already *fucked* you up."

Vincenti pushed himself out of his seat.

"Look, Vincenti – I like you. Why the hell do you think I'm talking to you like this? Consider it – what do they call it nowadays? – an *intervention*. I'm trying to help you save yourself."

"Thanks a million."

"Got any vacation days coming, Vincenti?"

"I don't know. Maybe a few. I haven't thought about it lately."

"I suggest you take them starting right now. I'd like to keep you on the force, pal. I'll do what I can to make that happen. Your best hope is that the autopsy on Mohammed Phillips shows that he OD'd – and not that he croaked from getting his head bashed in by some over-eager Caucasian police officer. From what Villas was saying, you got a fifty-fifty chance of that happening. You better hope he's right."

Vincenti reached for the door handle.

"But I'm gonna give this to you straight – the heat on me gets turned up any higher, I'm gonna have to cut you loose. Go to the union, maybe they'll stand behind you. But I won't. I can't afford to. Now beat it. I don't want to see you around here for at least a couple of weeks."

Again, Vincenti didn't argue. He couldn't. He yanked the door open.

"By the way," Hampton added as an afterthought, "what'd you end up finding out about your acrobat over at the Hudson Arms?"

Vincenti shrugged. "Nothing more to it than what meets the eye. She committed suicide. You were right after all."

Chief Hampton nodded. For the first time today, he seemed satisfied.

Having an unplanned vacation would afford Vincenti the opportunity to find another place to live, pack his things, and sit down with Nicky and attempt to explain to him why they wouldn't be living under the same roof anymore. They were chores he didn't look forward to. In the long run it would probably be better for everyone, though in his innermost self he wasn't convinced he really believed that.

But before he went back home and tackled that giant octopus, he decided to pay a visit to the Hudson Arms. This morning the inner door was unlocked and Lenny Jenkins was at the desk, hunched over, studying the business page of the *New York Post*.

The tin of breath mints was right there at his elbow. Vincenti didn't believe that Jenkins was guilty of anything, but if he was still on the department in a few weeks and the Fuentes rape remained unsolved, he'd have a little chat with the guy. He hoped he wouldn't have to.

"Mind if I go up?"

"Be my guest. Matter of fact, you're in luck – one of the roommates is there."

Did it matter now? It didn't. He wasn't going to discover anything that he didn't already know about the Kenmore death. Just the same, he couldn't keep himself away from 1108.

"The other one moved out yesterday. They don't want to be up there anymore. The place spooks them. Can't say I blame them."

The door of 1108 stood wide open. Inside the apartment, which seemed roomier now since it was devoid of most of its contents, bodies were moving to and fro. He stood and watched for a moment before announcing himself.

There was a fresh-faced young brunette sitting cross-legged on the carpet, tossing items from the coffee table into a carton. She got up and started toward him at the same time as two strapping movers with kitchen chairs and stuffed crates on their backs pushed past him. He caught a whiff of their sweat as they maneuvered through the door.

"Hi. I'm Heather Weinstock. Lenny downstairs just called and told me you'd been here before." Her eyes welled up. "Isn't it the most horrible thing?"

Vincenti nodded but said nothing.

"I just can't stay here any longer. Neither could Jennifer. She came last night and took all her things. This place is like – haunted or something." A shiver ran through her slender physique.

"Heather, where do you want these prints – the car or the van?"

"The car – on account of the glass. Can you fit them, do you think?"

"I think so." The fellow who was removing the frame from the wall could be taken for Heather Weinstock's brother – probably was.

He took another piece down and gingerly moved toward the open door with the pair.

"By the way, this is a police detective," Heather said to the young man as he passed.

"Hey ..."

He disappeared down the hall. Vincenti ran through a list of perfunctory questions about Gail Kenmore as they stood in the middle of the room surrounded by the odds and ends of a life that had been abruptly deconstructed. There was no point to it, and Detective Vincenti knew it. Heather Weinstock was completely cooperative and forthcoming, but he sensed the still-raw shock behind her words.

"We never knew Gail all that well, Jennifer and I, to be honest with you, Detective, so I don't know how I can be of help. She moved in when our last roommate went to live with her boyfriend. And since everybody works different schedules, we talked for maybe two minutes here, five there, and that didn't exactly make us friends. I know that she had visitors from time to time, but we never even met them ..."

Vincenti asked to see Gail's bedroom one last time.

"Her father was here too, yesterday, apparently. They took everything away," said Heather.

Vincenti changed his mind. He drifted instead toward the window where it had happened.

Heather didn't follow. "I'm just so – I can't really even sleep at night for thinking about – about what it must have been like for her when she ..."

Vincenti flipped the locks and lifted the pane. Like last Tuesday, he peered down eleven stories to the street.

"What do you think happened to Gail Kenmore, Heather? Do you think she committed suicide?" he mused, turning to face her.

Heather Weinstock slowly shook her head, as if she'd been asked to solve a problem in quantum physics on the spot.

"I have no idea. All I can say is that she seemed troubled. She never wanted to talk about anything, and I never insisted, so we never got into any deep discussions about ourselves or anything like that. There was just something about her that – I don't even know how to say it – seemed sad. Very sad. Not that I ever expected something like this to happen ... I mean, how could I?"

Vincenti looked down again. *The perfect opportunity to follow Gail Kenmore into the beyond.*

Just then he recognized two specks on the pavement

below: Vonda and Nicky walking hand in hand toward Second Street, where one of the boy's friends, little Teddy Mulcahy, lived. He remembered overhearing Reggie mention something about the preschool session starting later than usual today on account of annual spring cleaning. At the sight of Nicky toddling along beside his nanny, Vincenti's heart quivered, like a man fatally and unrequitedly in love.

For a moment, he forgot where he was. The tinkle of Heather Weinstock's voice broke the spell.

"It's freezing in here, Detective. When you're through, would you mind closing that window?"

"Yeah," he said. Then he pushed it down until it was snug and secured the locks.

Also by Honest Publishing

The Vorrh
B. Catling

Greetings, Hero
Aiden O'Reilly

Homegirl!
Ryder Collins

The Killing of a Bank Manager
Paul Kavanagh

Nothing Doing
Willie Smith

The Wooden Tongue Speaks
Bogdan Tiganov

Iceberg
Paul Kavanagh

One Last Cigarette
Mary Stone Dockery

Wedding Underwear for Mermaids
Linda Ann Strang

Also by Mark SaFranko

The Favor

Hopler's Statement

Hating Olivia

Lounge Lizard

Loners

God Bless America

No Strings

Dirty Work

Seedy (Stage play)

CPSIA information can be obtained at www.JCGtesting.com
Printed in the USA
LVOW08s0658200714

395093LV00001B/48/P

9 780957 142770